Nineteen to the Dozen

Judaic Traditions in Literature, Music, and Art
Ken Frieden and Harold Bloom, *Series Editors*

Sholem Aleichem (Rabinovitsh).
Courtesy of the YIVO Institute for Jewish Research.

Nineteen to the Dozen

*Monologues and Bits and Bobs
of Other Things*

Sholem Aleichem

Translated by Ted Gorelick
Edited by Ken Frieden

 Syracuse University Press

First Edition 1998
98 99 00 01 02 03   6 5 4 3 2 1

The paper used in this publication meets the minimum requirements of American National Standard for Information Sciences—Permanence of Paper for
Printed Library Materials, ANSI Z39.48-1984. ∞™

Library of Congress Cataloging-in-Publication Data
Sholem Aleichem, 1859–1916.
    [Monologen. English]
    Nineteen to the dozen : monologues and bits and bobs of other
things / Sholem Aleichem ; translated by Ted Gorelick ; edited by
Ken Frieden. — 1st ed.
        p.   cm. — (Judaic traditions in literature, music, and art)
    Includes bibliographical references.
    ISBN 0-8156-0477-7 (cloth : alk. paper)
    I. Gorelick, Ted.   II. Frieden, Ken, 1955–   .   III. Title.   IV. Series.
PJ5129.R2M613   1997
839'.133—dc21   97-29985

Manufactured in the United States of America

For Jack Rosenthal and Simone Harris

"One friend in a lifetime is much; two are many."
I am blessed with two—Ted Gorelick

Ted Gorelick was born in Israel and educated in the United States. He has made the translation of Eastern European literature his field of specialization. His Englishing from the Yiddish and Hebrew of S. Y. Abramovitsh's classic *Fishke the Lame* has won him critical acclaim.

Ken Frieden is B. G. Rudolph Professor of Judaic Studies and directs the Judaic Studies Program at Syracuse University. His published works include *Genius and Monologue* (1985), *Freud's Dream of Interpretation* (1990), and *Classic Yiddish Fiction: Abramovitsh, Sholem Aleichem, and Peretz* (1995).

Contents

Men's Talk

Introduction

From Sholem Aleichem's collected Yiddish works, which span twenty-eight volumes of novels, stories, plays, and essays, the present translation makes available one of the most important volumes of his prose—the monologues. His greatest achievement was to evoke the voices of Yiddish speakers, and nowhere does he create a more distinctive cast of characters than in his monologues. Sholem Aleichem's monologues tap the essence of Yiddish language, literature, and culture. Since its inception Yiddish has been the Ashkenazic Jews' predominant *spoken* language alongside their *written* language, Hebrew. Sholem Aleichem gives expression to nearly all of Yiddish culture through the voices of his monologists.

The monologues create illusions of face-to-face meetings with individual speakers: in each of the monologues a man or woman comes forward to tell the story. The implied listeners—a rabbi, a doctor, or Sholem Aleichem himself—say almost nothing. According to the literary convention, Sholem Aleichem has transcribed these private performances for the reader's benefit, and the author subordinates plot to the act of narrating.

Between 1901 and 1916 Sholem Aleichem explored a range of human experiences by giving voice to diverse characters. Five women and eight men tell their own tales; all they have in common is their irrepressible will to talk. They range from rich to poor, educated to ignorant, scheming to simple. This sequence of confessional narratives provides a unique portrayal of Eastern European Jewish society, and these portraits go a long way toward demystifying provincial life in the *shtetl,* which has sometimes become the object of undue nostalgia. In his monologues Sholem Aleichem combines sympathy and satire toward his speakers. He shows particular sympathy toward the impoverished women who narrate "The Pot" and "Geese"; talking appears to be their only means to rise above misfortune. In contrast, Sholem Aleichem suggests a more ironic and critical perception of the wealthy speakers in "Three Widows" and "Joseph."

Sholem Aleichem was born Sholem Naumovitsh Rabinovitsh in the small Ukrainian town of Pereyaslav in 1859. The language of his impoverished family was Yiddish, but his father took the unusual step of sending him to a Russian high school. This education gave him a strong background in Russian literature and eventually enabled him to join the growing ranks of Russian-Jewish intellectuals. After high school Sholem Aleichem tutored Olga, the daughter of a wealthy Jewish family; several years later, they married. When his father-in-law died, Sholem Aleichem inherited a fortune and the means to pursue his literary career. Hence, Sholem Aleichem moved into a loftier social circle by education, marriage, and inheritance. With one foot in the shtetl he was able to describe Jewish life as it continued there, and with his other foot in Kiev he produced contemporary stories at a high literary level.

Sholem Aleichem was the most popular Yiddish author, in part, because his sympathies remained with the common people. Although he rose to a higher social class, he continued to write for the Jewish masses. Sholem Aleichem's monologues are folksy examples of what the Russian formalists called *skaz,* oral-style narration. Ideally, they should be performed or, at least, read aloud. During his lifetime Sholem Aleichem traveled far and wide performing his stories to large audiences. Contemporary accounts indicate that his popular humor was heightened by a subtle, deadpan delivery, although archival manuscripts show that he prepared for his readings by revising his texts and marking key words with accents.

Satire and caricature as well as humor and social commentary are hallmarks of Sholem Aleichem's creativity. "The Pot" sets the pattern: it begins with a recognizable social situation, but it takes this situation to such an extreme that it becomes absurd. A woman comes to a rabbi with a question about whether her pot is kosher. The intricate details of her unfortunate life intercede, however, to the point that the rabbi cannot finally come to terms with her request. In "Advice" Sholem Aleichem is the listener who becomes entangled in complex issues a young man presents to him.

Many of the humble monologists seem to free associate as they tell their stories, and their digressions are essential. But Sholem Aleichem also wrote another kind of monologue in which dominant speakers exert greater control. In "Three Widows" and "Joseph" wealthier narrators tell more coherent stories and manipulate the reader's response. In "A Business with a Greenhorn" the overbearing and unscrupulous narrator tells a story that becomes an unwitting critique of his milieu.

No direct link to psychoanalysis has been proved, but Sholem Aleichem was presumably aware of Sigmund Freud's "talking cure" in Vienna. One of Sholem Aleichem's monologists, the gentleman in "Three Widows," refers scornfully to psychology. Another monologist, the young husband in "Advice," comes to Sholem Aleichem for counseling and guidance. The patient in the story "At the Doctor's" is clearly in search of a therapist, not an internist. In no case, however, does the monologue become a true dialogue. Like some parody of a Freudian analyst, the listener remains a blank screen, allowing the monologist to plumb the depths of his or her discomfort.

The volume was originally entitled *Monologues (Monologn* in Yiddish). We have opted for the fresh title *Nineteen to the Dozen,* which is taken from one of the monologists' own expressions. In "Geese" Bassia repeatedly apologizes for her long-windedness: "But there I go again, mixing up one thing with another. Though don't be paying it any mind now, for it's only my nature. Besides which, it's as you says: womenfolks inclines to be talking nineteen to the dozen anyhow." Before anyone jumps to the overhasty conclusion that Sholem Aleichem was a sexist, we should note that Bassia is using a familiar Yiddish expression, which refers back to a lighthearted passage in the Babylonian Talmud (Kiddushin 49b). Ted Gorelick has found an exuberant English expression that conveys something of the Yiddish original, which, more literally, says that women have "nine measures of speech." As a whole, the volume celebrates the loquaciousness of Yiddish speakers.

The collection poses serious challenges for the translator by demanding that he mimic such a wide range of characters. At one extreme is Yenta the Henwife (in "The Pot"). Ted Gorelick conveys her uneducated Yiddish, using a suitable American idiom. At the other extreme are two bourgeois narrators (in "Three Widows" and "Joseph"). Ted Gorelick ascribes to them a wholly different level of speech. And in between is a range of voices that, taken as a whole, creates a symphony of Jewish life from Eastern Europe to New York.

Syracuse, New York   Ken Frieden
February 1997

A Note on the Text

The present translation by Ted Gorelick is based on Sholem Aleichem's collection of stories entitled *Monologues (Monologn)*, which appeared in *Ale verk fun Sholem Aleichem* (New York: Folksfond Edition, 1917–23), volume 21. Our edition omits only two short dialogues that diverge from the literary form of the other selections. The monologues constitute a relatively coherent genre: they are first-person, oral-style narratives by Yiddish speakers who, in most cases, address the fictional persona of Sholem Aleichem.

As early as in 1902 Sholem Aleichem began using the term *monologue* to describe his short first-person narratives in a quasi-oral mode. By then he had already experimented with this literary form in three early stories (printed in 1895 and 1899) by Tevye the Dairyman. But not until three years before his death did Sholem Aleichem employ this key word in the title of a set of works in his collected writings: *Mayses un monologn* (Stories and monologues) (Warsaw: Progress, 1913), volume 13. That volume contains the four seminal monologues "Dos tepl" (The little pot, 1901), "An eytse" (Advice, 1904), "Baym doktor," (At the doctor's, 1904), and "Gitl Purishkevitsh" ("Goody 'Purishkevich,' " 1911). Others were scattered among volumes 1, 2, and 14 of the same 1913 edition. Several years later, when Sholem Aleichem's son-in-law Y. D. Berkovitsh prepared the twenty-eight-volume Folksfond edition in New York, the collection of *Monologues* achieved its canonical status.

Oddly enough, there has never before been an English edition of this volume, which provides resonant voices—to the tune of a baker's dozen —as a counterpoint to the family melodies of Tevye the Dairyman. Suggestions for further reading are provided in the selected bibliography.

Women's Talk

Preceding page: Detail from "The World of Sholem Aleichem" by Boris Luchanski. Courtesy of the artist.

The Pot

Well, now, Rabbi, I got this question, I do, which I'm a mind to be asking you. Well, you mebbe know me nor mebbe you don't, howso-ever, the name is Yenta. Only Yenta the Henwife's the moniker which I genly answers to—'cos eggs is my trade, eggs and po'try. That's to say po'try which they is ducks and geese, mainly. Well, now, I got my steady customers, I do, which they's two mebbe three ladies which I enjoys their custom quite regular and which them and theirs keeps me and mine in meat and drink. And God bless and keep 'em for it, too, 'cos I was to borrow the money wherewith to pu'chase, and pay innerest, I shouldn't have so much as a mouthful of my slim pickens left to bless my bread with. This way I picks up the odd thruppenny from one or t'other; I takes a bird here, gives it there, takes another there, gives it here, juggling wares on the fly (so-called), if you take my meaning. Eh? Why, o'course! My goodness, sir, but what you think? Why, if my poor late husband (Godrest) was only amongst the living yet? Well, well, well! . . . Only mind, now, on second thoughts, I can't say as I licked much honey whilst he was alive, nuther, for begging his pardon for saying so, he weren't much of a breadwinner that man. No, 'cos all he ever done was set and study, set and study, and the one which done the toiling was myself, that's to say, yours truly. Well, now, I been toiling from ever since girlhood, I have; that's to say, from since I was little and was still with my mother yet Godrest, which her name were Bassia. That be Bassia the Tallow Chandleress, as she was call, 'cos she were a tallow chandleress, which she used to first buy up the tallow at the butcher shops to dip candles with; "tallow twists" these was, 'cos there wasn't no gas lamps back then with the gas mantle over 'em, which they's forever getting cracked

3

anyhow; why, the other week, one them mantles crack on me when only the week before another done the same. . . .

Yes, so what brung all this on? Well, now, it's like you says: Dying young. . . . 'Cos when my Moishe Bentzion (Godrest) pass on, he weren't more nor six-'n'-twenny, all toll. Eh? Well, now, lessee. How come six-'n'-twenny? Well, now he were nineteen all toll when we wed, and then eight year on he died, so all toll I reckon nineteen add eight; so it seem there were three-'n'-twenny year, all toll. So why had I reckon on six-'n'-twenny? 'Cos I forgot the seven year which he were poorly. That's to say, he were poorly for much longer, for he were never a well man; it was the cough, you see; that's to say, he were quite well otherwise if it wasn't only for the cough; that's what done him in, the cough! 'Cos he use to— an' God keep yourself, sir, from the same—well, he use to be coughing all the time; that's to say, not all the time but only when the coughing fits come on him and he was set to coughing; which when he was set to coughing he just cough, and cough, and cough. . . . Well, the doctors they all call it a kind of a spasm; that's to say, the kind which if you wants to cough you coughs, and if you don't, you don't. Well fiddle-faddle and folderol! And I only wisht goats had so much notion of getting into other folks's gardens as any them—that's to say, doctors—knowed ears from elbows! . . . 'Cos now you only take Reb Aaron the kosher slaughterer's boy; that's to say, the one's called Yokl, which he had a toothache, don't you know? Well, don't think for a minute they didn't try, oh, just about everything in the way of jabber and palaver and dosings and hocusings, which it never done a bit of good anyhow; till what you think he went and done—that's to say, what Yokl went and done—but went and stuck a garlic up his ear, 'cos there's plenty folks say garlic's the cure for a toothache, and which it only sent him up the wall, Yokl, that is; only he never let on about it, you see—that's to say, Yokl never did—about that garlic up his ear. Well, along come the doctor and he took his pulse, don't you know? Now, why any fool doctor ever waste any bother over taking folk's pulses, I'll never know! . . . and certainly if they hadn't of pack him off to away over Yehupetz ways, which it's only t'other end of the world anyhow, well, you know where that poor chile be by now? Why, only where that poor sister of his Pearly end up; which, the dear thing, she weren't laid low by the Good Eye but she die in childbed, preserve us, and that's where that boy be too. . . .

Yes, so what brung all this on? Well, now, it's like you says: Being left a widder. . . . Well, now, so I were left a widder—an' Lord preserve my sistren from the same—whilst I was young yet, with a infant to look after and only the half a roof over my head to myself, over by the "Rookeries"; that's to say, not Lazar the carpenter's but t'other one opposite, if you know it; one close by the bathhouse? Well, most like you be asking why only the half? 'Cos you see the other half weren't mine but belong to my brother-in-law, which his name's Azareel. Well, now, you must know him, sir, for that's the Azareel which he come original from over to Happy Corner's ways, which it's a small town somewheres, and which his business is fish caught and sold, and, oh yes, he do very nicely by it, too, an' Godpraise; only, of course, that depend on the river, mostly. 'Cos if the weather's fair, fish comes to net, and when fish comes to net, fish is cheap, but if the weather's up, fish don't come to net, and fish is dear. . . . Well, now, that's what he always says, Azareel, that is. So I says to him, I says, "But Where's the sense in it, Azareel?" But he only says to me: "Where's the sense in it? Easy. For if the weather's fair, fish comes to net, and when fish comes to net, fish is cheap; but if the weather's up, fish don't come to net, and fish is dear. Only best is if fish comes to net and they's cheap." . . . So I says to him, I says: "Yes, but where's the sense in it, Azareel?" But he only says to me: "Where's the sense in it? Easy. For if the weather's fair, fish comes to net, and when fish comes to net, fish is cheap, but if the weather's up, fish don't come to net, and fish is dear. Only best is if fish comes to net and they's cheap." . . . "Oh, pooh" say I to him, I says: "Try and reason with sich a iggerant fool as yourself.". . .

Yes, so what brung all this on? Well, now, it's like you says: A place of my own. . . . Well, of course, having your own corner all to yourself alone is better than being saddled with neighbors as shares it. For it's as you says: "Mine's ne'er another's." . . . Mind, though, it's not as if I hadn't a whole half a roof overhead, which it's property anyhow, so I'm not complaining. Though ask yourself, sir, what's a humble widder lady (so-called) with only the one chile want the whole half property to herself for, anyhow? 'Cos so long she got a corner where to lay her head down, then well and good, says I! The more specially now it wants mending; that's to say, the roof does 'cos it been standing oh for years now unattended to; so that is why that reefine brother-in-law of mine Azareel took to pestering me recent about thatching the roof over. . . . Says he, "Time we thatch it!" Says I, "So, why don't we thatch it, Azareel?" Says he, "So less thatch it!" . . . Says I, "So less thatch it, Azareel!" . . . Thatchit-Thatchit, Thatchit-Thatchit! Only that's all it ever come to. 'Cos you wants straw for thatching; nor I won't even menshun shingling, for where I ever get money for shingling? So I lets out two rooms, which the one small room is let to ole man Chaim Choneh, which he's deaf and gone quite vague being old, and his childer they pays me five gilden the week rent on it, and every other day they feeds him; that's to say, he feasts the one day and fasts the next, only his feast days don't amount to much, least to hear old man Chaim Choneh tell it. But mebbe that's only a lie. For old folks likes to grumble 'cos it don't matter how much you gives 'em, for it's never enough; nor where you puts 'em, for they's never satisfied; nor where they lies down, for it's always too hard. . . .

Yes, so what brung all this on? Well, now, it's like you says: Taking lodgers. . . . An' Lord preserve all honest folks from such. Well, you only take that 'un. That's to say, the deaf ole party, which he's deaf and by way of only being your quiet sort of a neighbor, "ne'er heard nor seen," as you says. . . . But it were never a good wind which it blew that there millerwife my ways I let the other room to. Gnessy, that's her name. Got that shop she sell flour in, don't you know? Oh, but she were artful that one! . . . 'Cos you ought of seed how she were tender as honeydew dumplins to first, acting all lovey-dovey the while, with her oh darlin' this and oh sweetheart that, saying as how she do this and that and t'other thing for me and be only too glad to oblige if I asks it. . . . For, after all, what she need? (says she). Why only the bit of the stove to be putting the occasional pot on; oh, and p'raps a corner of that bench I got, too, so's to be salting her meat on it, which it won't only be once in the week anyhow; oh, and just the leetlest part of that there table to mebbe be rolling out a doughleaf and chop noodles on it now and again, which it only be once in a blue moon. . . . "But think about the children, Gnessy," says I, "Where you intend to put all them tikes of yourn (bless 'em) which you got?" . . . "Now I cannot imagine what you may be thinking on, Yenta dearest!" says she, "My little 'uns they is good as gold! Summertime? Why, they be knocking about out-of-doors all the day long, anyhow, and in the winter they be out of the way, up above the stove curled up together there on the mantel shelf quiet as lambs, nor you'll even hear a peep out of 'em the while, nuther. Only they do got the one fault; they is incline to like their vittles a deal too many; regular greedy guts they is, bless 'em." . . . Well now, I needn't only tell you I bought me a clutter of trouble which I druther them as hates me may have. Little 'uns, she says. Well-a-well Big 'uns more like, every one, an' may God forgive me for saying so, nor so much as a crust of bread for them to feed on. And all that hooha the lot of them kick up all hours of the day and night? My gracious! There just weren't any end to their yelling and fighting and screaming. Pandemonical's what it were. Purest hell. D'I say hell? Well, hell weren't only paradise next to it! . . . And don't think for a minute that were the end of it, nuther. Else it be only half a misery; on account a chile's but a chile and may be took in hand, for it don't take only the one cuff or slap to put it right. No, 'cos on top of it all, God give that woman a husband which his name's Ozer; oh, you must know him, sir; the one what's underbeadle in the lower chapel at shul? And as pious and upstanding a gentleman as you ever hope to meet, poor man; though no fool, mind! Well, now, you ought to hear the way she ride that man; Gnessy, that is: Ozer this! Ozer that! Ozer here! Ozer there! Ozer-Ozer! . . . Whereas him? Oh, he'll be either tossing a quip her ways to make an end (for to add to his troubles the man's by way of being a wit, don't you know), or he'll pull his cap down over his eyes and march out the door. . . . Well, what's there to say more, 'cept only things begun to look, oh, mebbe a mite short of being perfect. . . .

Yes, so what brung all this on? Well, now, it's like you says: Bad neighbors. . . . Though bad for bad's ne'er good, and I trust the Almighty may find no blame in me for speaking ill of anyone. For what I got agin the woman, anyhow, to be finding fault with her? 'Cos she's a good soul, she is, which she never turn a beggarman away without he get his charitable crust of her first. And all the best to her for it, I says; only when the melancholies come on her and she get all of a fret? Well, heaven help one and all then! Why, it's crying shameful to be talking of it even, nor I shouldn't never dream of telling it to another soul nuther if I didn't only know confidences was safe in your keeping, sir. . . . Shsh! . . . Beat him, she do . . . the husband, that is. . . . Do it unbeknown whilst nobody's about. . . . "Oh, Gnessy, Gnessy!" I says to her: "Ain't you got no fear afore God even? For how can't you fear God, I'm sure I shall never know!" . . . Says she, "Ain't any your granny's business!" . . . Says I, "Well, damnation and perdition's what I say!" . . . Says she, "Well, damnation to them as sticks their noses in where they oughtn't!" . . . Says I, "Well, dickens strike blind them as ain't seed no better!" . . . Says she, "Well, dickens strike dead them as listens in!" . . . So how you like that for mouth, eh? . . .

Yes, so what brung all this on? Well, now, it's like you says: I likes things to be neat. . . . No, I shan't bother to deny it. Nor why should I? 'Cos it so happen I do like things to be neat and tidy, nor I care much who know it. So mebbe she can't bear it—that's to say, Gnessy can't—seeing as how over my ways I keeps things always spick and span and speckless and sparkling, whilst over her ways? Well, you ought to only see it—the way it's ever dingy and grimy there, ever the rat's nest and shambles which the dirt allow to pile up so a body want to gag, and that there fambly slop pail of hern which it forever let to stand about, full up with stool—phew disgusting's what I calls it. . . . And come morning—well, then the stampede's on! Call that children which she got? Well, try shades and sperrits on a rampage! Yes, just like my own darlin Duddy, saving the difference! 'Cos my Duddy, bless him, why he's away at cheder all day long, and at night when he come home? Now you just see if he don't buckle down straightway and be at his prayers or be larning or bury his nose in a book. Whilst them little 'uns of hern? Well, God forgive me for saying so, but with them it's all only chaw, blubber, or raise the roof. . . . You ever hear the like? So I suppose it's all my fault God hath bless her with that awful lot of atrocious howlers and hellions, whereas me he make a gift of my precious darlin which he's a jewel and which God send I'll never lose, for you never shall know what tears I have shed on his account. And forget for a minute about me being only a poor helpless woman 'cos ain't a man in my place which he could of stood it! For there's menfolks about in this world—only saving your presence, sir—which they is a thousand times worse nor any woman in such matters, for only let menfolks come on hard times and they will lose their bearings nor ever find 'em nuther. And what more proof you want of it but that there Reb Yosi what's Moishe Abraham's Yosi, which as long as Fruma Nehama his missus was alive he bore up just fine, but no sooner she was gone, poor thing, well, preserve us if he didn't go all to pieces on account of it and couldn't no more fend for himself than he was a newborn chile. . . . "Why, bless you, Reb Yosi," I says to him, "but what's become of you! I mean a man's wife die on him, well and good, 'cos it ain't only God's doing anyhow." . . . Yes the Lord taketh away what the Lord giveth. For what's it say in our Holy Scriptures? Only I don't reckon you wants telling of such things by the likes of me, sir, 'cos you knows better nor I, most like. . . .

Yes, so what brung all this on? Well, now, it's like you says: A only son. . . . He's my one and only, apple of his mother's eye, as you says. That's to say, my Duddy is. Only p'raps you ain't had the pleasure of his acquaintance, sir? Well, now, he were named for David Hersh as was my father-in-law, don't you know. And you only ought to see him, sir. Image of his father, an' longer life to the living. As alike as two peas, him and my Moishe Bentzion is. Exact same height as him what's gone, Godrest. Same features, too. Got that same yallory look about him and skinnier nor a stick, same as his poor dad were. And frail, ever so frail, just wore to a nubbin, from going to cheder, poor thing, and all that larning he do of Torah and Gemara and such. . . . "Oh but you must rest up chile," I says to him, I says, " 'Cos only look at yourself, why you're all done in. So whyn't you have yourself a bite to eat," I says to him, "Oh do have a morsel, darling—or mebbe you druther have something warm to drink? Here now, you take this glass of chicory water!" Only he says to me he says, "No, mama, you best have the chicory water for yourself; oh, you work so hard, mama," he says to me, "I ought to be carrying your basket home from market, mama, for it only be right if I do." . . . So I says to him, I says: "Now, that's a notion! Whatever you saying chile? You got any notion what you saying? The very idee, carrying my basket! Well, I should hope none as hates me—and rest assured they's plenty as does— well, I hope they may never live to see it! No, darlin, you set and larn," I says to him, "you just set and larn, son." . . . And all the while I were looking at him so, at my Duddy, that is, I were thinking: image of him what's gone (an' Godrest), alike as two peas, even to the cough. And mercy me what misery it cause me! Oh, it's enough to break a mother's heart, each time I hear him coughing so. And you never shall know the tears I have shed on his account, sir, before I see the day he amount to something. Why, you know, nobody believe the chile would even live? 'Cos weren't a solitary pestilence or a ailment or contagion which it pass him by. Now, you want the measles—well, he got 'em! And you want the chicking pox—well, he got 'em, too, and the diphtherias and the scarlet fevers and the mumps and the teething and the Lord only knows what-all else that boy didn't come down with! . . . And the nights—God remit me the nights I spent watching over him. Though I'll allow as the tears I shed wasn't wasted—nor them intervenings from t'other side of the grave (which I've no doubt there was)—by dint of all which I finally seen him through bar mitzvah. Only don't think for a minute that were an end of it 'cos no it weren't. For here's a nugget for you, if ever there was one: 'cos, of all the things, one night he were on his way home, don't you know—only, mind, it were midwinter then—anyhow, he were on his way home from school when what you suppose happen but he come acrost somebody as were dress all in white and which he was clapping both his hands together? . . . Well, now, what you expect but the chile

were scared half out of his wits by it and fall down in the snow in a dead
faint and were carried home more dead nor alive and scarce brung round
from it, too; when what happen but he took to his bed—and oh! it break
a mother's heart even to be speaking of it—for there the poor boy lay
full six week in a raging fever, if it were a day! . . . Though how I got
through that time—well, it weren't but heaven sent and miraculous. 'Cos
what didn't I only do in the way of the vows I give and of pledging and
redeeming the chile, and I even give him a new name which to add on to
his old one—Chaim it were, which it mean Life, so Duddy be called
Chaim David Hersh stead of only David Hersh as before. And the tears
I shed? Why, tears ain't the word, hardly. "Dear Lord," I implores of the
Almighty, "Dear, dear Lord wert thou thinking on punishing me? Well,
go head and punish me if thou wilt, only don't be taking my chile from
me, oh please, please, don't." . . . And when the Lord grant my prayer,
and the boy get well at last, what he do but say to me: "Know what,
mama? Papa sends his greetings. It's from when he visit me." . . . And
hearing him speak so, my soul were like to give out, and my heart?
Thump-thump-thump! That's how it went. . . . Only I says to him, I says:
"An' God willing your papa keep on working on your behalf, darlin. For
it's a sure omen you got a long life and good health in store. . . . Only
my heart? Thump-thump-thump! That's how it went. . . . Though, after
a spell, I finally larn who it were which he was dress up in white and
clapping his hands. And you know who? Oh, go head, Rabbi, guess, on
account you are a man of larning and know about such things. It were
Reb Lippe! That's right, same what's the water-carrier: 'cos, you see, it
happen he'd gone and pu'chase a new fur coat that day which it was
white, and on account of the frost he were warming himself by clapping
one hand in t'other . . . and I only wisht my troubles was on that man's
head is what I wisht! Lordy, you ever hear such a notion? Imagine, a
grown man taking it into his head to be putting on a white coat like that
and no warning? . . .

Yes, so what brung all this on? Well, now, it's like you says: Good
health. . . . Good health, that's the thing! Which it's what the doctor say
as toll me I must look after the boy, feed him on hot broths, he says, least
a quarter-fowl worth o' hot broth every day he says, if I can only manage
it, he says, make a real effort he says, feed him on milk he says, on butter,
he says, on chocolates he says, if I can only manage it, he says. . . . Well,
I asks you, what he mean if I can manage it? As if there wasn't anything
in this world what I couldn't nor wouldn't do for my Duddy. The notion!

'Cos suppose now I was toll, for instance, now, Yenta, you push that plow, hew that wood, fetch that water, make them bricks, go rob a church, only you do it for Duddy's sake—well, even it were dead of night midwinter in the freezing cold, you wait and see if I wouldn't do it! 'Cos, well, now, only this summer he wanted some books, or Tomes, as he call them, which I ain't got such things to home anyhow, hardly. So on account my business take me round to some mighty fine houses—the boy ask me if mebbe I couldn't get them books, or Tomes, or whatever they is, from the folks as lives there, and he put the name of them down on a slip of paper. Well, I went round and I showed that slip of paper and asks for them books, or Tomes, or whatever they is, oh, once, twice, mebbe three times all toll. Only they was laughing the while, saying: "Now, Yenta, what on earth you be wanting them books for, anyhow? Gonna feed 'em to the po'try? Mebbe use 'em for duck feed?" . . . "Well, you laugh all you want," thinks I, "just so long as my Duddy got some-thing to study on." So that's what he done, study on them. Though later on he ask me to bring more of them books, or Tomes, or whatever they is, and then some more after that. So what you think I gonna do, stint the boy? Why, no, 'cos I only took back such as he were done with and brung him some more them books, or Tomes, or whatever they is. . . . Now, along come that fool doctor, which he got the raw gumption to be asking if I can't only manage a quarter-fowl worth o' broth every day for the boy! And I suppose if all of three-quarter of a fowl was wanted for the boy's broth every day, I'd be too proud to be making it? Well, now, I asks you, where in the mischief all them fool doctors come from anyhow? I mean, what kind of a yeast they use which make 'em grow up so foolish, and what sort of a oven they bake 'em in to finish the job? . . .

Yes, so what brung all this on? Well, now, it's like you says: Hot broth every day. . . . So, anyhow, I see to it he get his quarter-fowl worth every day, and evening, when he come home from school, and he set down to his dinner, don't you know? Well, now, I be setting opposite him then, with like mebbe a chore in hand, and having me just a high ole time from only looking on—and I be praying God I have the makings of another quarter-fowl worth the next day, an' the Lord willing. . . . "But, mama," he be saying to me then, "why aren't you eating, too?" So I says to him, I says: "Now don't you fret, son, 'cos I already ate my dinner. So you eat up hearty, chile, hear?" Only he be saying to me next, "So what have you eaten, mama?" But I only says: "What I've ate? Why, bless you, but I've ate what I have ate! Only never mind about that. 'Cos you only eat up hearty, hear?" . . . And after he done with his books, or Tomes, or whatever they is, that's when I pull out a couple baked potatoes from the stove or mebbe grate me a nice bit of onion over a slice of bread, and I be making a regular feast of it then. And I swear, sir, I really do—by all I ever hope to see come of that boy—that I receive more pleasure out of that bit of onion than I should have done from even the finest roast or broth, on account I know now my Duddy has got his quarter-fowl worth, and God send he shall have it tomorrow as well. . . . Only trouble is the cough. 'Cos the poor boy is always coughing: kuff-kuff! kuff-kuff! Like that, just always coughing. . . . Well, now, I ask the doctor if mebbe he give me something for that cough, don't you know? Only he set to quizzing me about how old my husband was—that's to say how old my Moishe Bentzion was, an' Godrest when he pass on, and about what he die of. "It was the death," I says to him, "that's what he die of—the death. 'Cos his time come, you see, so he die. Anyhow, what's that got to do with anything?" . . . "Oh, just something I needed to know," he says, "though that's a fine boy you got there and clever, too." . . . "Well, I'm obliged to you for saying so," says I, "Only I already know that. So I druther you just give me that cure for the cough he got so he can stop his coughing!" . . . Only he says to me, he says: "Well, I'm afraid that's impossible, I'm sorry to say. Though you might see to it he spend less time at his books." . . . "Well, now," says I, "so what you druther he do?" . . . "Eat," he says, "He must have lots to eat. And go out for walks. The boy must go for walks every day. Though the main thing is not to be poring over his books at night. Because if he is ever to be a doctor, he won't lose any by being a few years late." . . . "Oh, yes, indeed, I dessay!" thinks I, "just the thing I have always dream of!" 'Cos now I couldn't make head nor tail of that man, only I reckon he was raving and took sudden leave of his senses. I mean, what was all this about my Duddy becoming a doctor anyhow? And why not make him a governor whilst we was at it? . . . So I come home and toll my Duddy about it. Well, the boy went as red in the face as a turkeycock and says, "Know what, mama?" he says, "you best keep clear of that doctor and don't ever talk to him again." . . . "Oh, don't you worry, son," says I, "for I got no wish to see that doctor's face ever again. 'Cos don't think for a minute I don't know the man's a fool!" . . . Ever hear of such a thing? Doctors which they likes poking their noses into a sick person's business like that, asking about how he make his living and how he get by on what he make and if he got enough to get by on. So what's it all to you, anyhow, mister, that's what I like to know! 'Cos as long as you collect your tuppenny worth of fee, you may as well let a body have his ha'penny worth of cure for it! . . .

Yes, so what brung all this on? Well, now, it's like you says: Being always in a stew . . . Course you just cannot help being in a stew if you are always head over ears in work and must cart a basket of eggs and ducks and geese around with you all the time, and each of them reefine ladies which you got any business with insisting they must receive first choice and getting into, oh, just the worse fret only thinking any the others may have got aholt of the fatter bird or bigger eggs. So naturly you be asking how do I find the time to cook up them broths if I'm out all day and never home? Well, there's ne'er a wit which he won't find a way, as you says. 'Cos early morning before I'm off to market, first thing I genly nips downstairs for a minute to get that quarter-fowl salted up, and then I whups back upstairs to get all them eggs and po'try ready, and then I nips back downstairs to rinse the flesh clean, and then I whups back upstairs to put the pot on the stove and then I be asking of that neighbor of mine, that's to say, I ask of Gnessy, if she only be so good as to keep a eye on the pot; that's to say, when the pot is set to b'iling up, she must put the cover back on it and rake the ash over it so it cover the pot. Well, now, you may of thought mebbe it were too much to be asking of a body to do a little thing like that? Only I couldn't even begin to count the times which I got up a whole supper plus trimmings for her and her lot. Which, after all, it's not as if we wasn't all Jewish folks, anyhow—and Lord a-mercy but ain't we civilize folks as lives together ruther than alone and in the wilds? . . . Come night though, I'm back, and I get that fire going again so it heat up the pot, and my Duddy get his broth piping hot that day. . . . Well now, you may of thought so far so good, eh? And so it might be, too, if only that neighbor of mine wasn't such a awful . . . well, you'll forgive me for saying so, but if she wasn't such a—but no! I dassn't even say what that woman is. . . . 'Cos wouldn't you know but this morning that woman bestir herself for once and set to making dairy dinner for them childer of hern—fritters, I think it was, or mebbe it were only dough dumplins, boil up in milk of all things! Well now, I asks you, what kind of a dish is fritters boil in milk, anyhow? And what in the mischief possess that woman to be fixing Sat'day night dinner plumb on a midweek Wednesday for? Well, I'm sure I don't know nor I care to nuther! . . . Odd woman that millerwife, though. 'Cos it's always either fast or feast with her. Well, I mean, for three day running she won't even come near the stove, and then, lo and behold, there she be, cooking up a whopping pailful of millet groats, so-call, or it's tater soup, mebbe, which, anyhow, you got to put on a pair of bull's eye specs which they was that thick, so as only to see the occasional millet in it, or mebbe she fry up a mess of mince tatercakes, don't you know, which on account of all the onion she bung into it, you be smelling the reek of it for better nor a mile, and, oh my, but all the pepper she put in? Why she pile on such a monstrous lot of it that afterwards it will set the whole fambly to panting and running about sucking wind for full four-and-twenty hour with their mouth wide open and jaw drop down away to here, going: whoo-whoo! whoo-whoo! . . .

Yes, so what brung all this on? Well, now, it's like you says: Worse luck. . . . 'Cos for once that woman bestir herself, and she set to slopping about, whupping up them buckwheat fritters of hern, don't you know? Which the meanwhile she also set a crock of milk on the stove to be heating it up—and lordy! you never believe the uncommon commotion it raise amongst her young'uns. Why, you of thought they never see such a thing as milk before. Though mind! There weren't only that much of it in the crock nuther, on account I don't know if there was all of, oh, mebbe two spoonfuls and the rest was water—which only a poor lot of penniless paupers such as them would even think to make a fuss over, anyhow. . . . Only who should come busting in next if it weren't that beadle. For it seem Ozer had got wind of the doings back home from all the way over at shul, so he follow his nose and next thing he bust in at a run, quipping as her usual, Happy holiday, so what's cooking?" . . . "Your goose, I only wisht!" says she, "And what in the name of mischief brung you back so early, anyhow?" . . . "Now, I shouldn't want to be missing grace before meal, should I?" says he, "so what you got cooking in the oven, eh?" . . . "Nothing you need to waste any bother over," says she, " 'cos it's a small pot!" . . . "So whyn't you use a big pot," says he, "so they be enough for the two of us?" . . . "Aaa, you and your lip!" says she and she picks up the oven fork to take the crock of milk off of the fire—when plunk! on a sudden the whole thing tip over and the milk spill all over the stove. . . . Well, you ought of heard the ruckus which follow then—and, oh, my gracious the way that Gnessy were set to swearing at that husband of hern in just the worse way! And a good thing, too, the man lit out of there in the nick of time and make himself scarce. And them tikes of hern? Why, the poor things they clumb down from off the mantel shelf, wailing and blubbering so you of thought their mama and papa both been kilt. . . . "Well, confound them fritters and milk of yourn," says I, " 'cos my Duddy's broth been spoilt, and God forfend my pot gone unkosher, too, on account of it!" . . . "Well, confound that pot and your broth both," says she, "on account I don't value the one nor the other; 'cos mebbe I value my fritters and milk more than all them pots and broths you cook up for that precious little mama's boy you got!" . . . "Well, you know what?" says I. "Confound you all! 'Cos I don't value any you next to one hair on my Duddy's head!" . . . "Well, you know what?" says she. "Confound your precious Duddy! 'Cos I don't value any hair he got, next to all of us, on account he ain't only one anyhow!" . . . Well, so how you like that for fresh! And ain't that hussy deserve getting her mouth whacked with a wet dishcloth? . . .

Yes, so what brung all this on? Well, now, it's like you says: There's ne'er good come from meat and dairy in the one stove. . . . So when the crock turn turtle and the milk spill all over the stove, well, it put me in a fright thinking, only God forfend that milk get to my pot which I been using for them broths. 'Cos I be in a proper fix then, wouldn't I. Only, on second thoughts—well, I mean, how could the milk even get near my pot, which it were tuck away over in the corner and cover up in ash? Well, it's the old story, ain't it. For how can I tell for sure? 'Cos who knows? Ah, mercy me! Only what if—? . . . Well, to tell the honest truth, Rabbi. I mean, about that broth? Now, I say let that be as it may. Only whatever shall the poor boy eat? See, that's what really bother me. Well now, I expect I'll think of something. 'Cos just yesterday I brung home them geese which I took to slaughter, and I already pluck them and get them strip clean and gutted for market. So I got some giblets left over from it: couple of heads, gizzards too—suchlike. Well, I just reckon I can do something with that. Only I'm up a stump, Rabbi, on account I got no pot! I mean, it do worry me considerable; 'cos if you judge the pot ain't kosher, then I be without a pot. And without no pot I be more helpless than a newborn babe! 'Cos, you see, I ain't got but the one pot. That's to say, I used to have three pots which they was all meatpots; only that there Gnessy, which I only wisht she was in a bad place, well, she went and borrow one pot off me—which mind! it were a brand-new pot. So what did that woman do but give me a busted pot back. Well, I say to her, I says, "So what's this pot you give me?". . . Says she: "Why, that's your pot!". . . Says I, "So why you give me a busted pot if the pot you got was a whole pot?" . . . Says she: "Oh shush! And I'll thank you to keep your voice down, 'cos it only get on a body's nerves! Now then, in the first place, I give you back the whole pot; in the second place, when you give me that pot it were busted already; and in the third place, I never took your pot 'cos I got my own pot, so leave me be and there's a end!" . . . Now, you talk about shameless! . . .

Yes, so what brung all this on? Well, now, it's like you says: There's ne'er a kitchen with a pot too many. . . . Well, so I were left with two pots which they was whole pots and one pot which was a busted pot, so that was two pots which I were left with, all toll. . . . Only, I suppose, two pots was more than poor folks got a right to, anyhow. 'Cos one time I come back from market with, oh, must of been a couple brace of live po'try don't you know? Which the one bird got loose and the cat come along and put a fright into it. . . . So you naturly be asking how the cat come into it? Well, it were only her doing again, and them fool offspring of hern. Which it weren't enough they went and pick up a stray from off the street somewhere, but they commence aggervating and tormenting the creature so, it were more dead nor alive when they finally done with it. "Oh, how can you be so cruel?" my Duddy say to them. "Why, it is a living thing!" . . . Only you try and reason with such a idle harum-scarum gang of ruffians. . . . So what them hellions go and do but tie something to the cat's tail; only this time the creature were set to jumping and bounding about and genly work itself up into such a rare tantrum the bird got scared, too; 'cos next thing it flew clear up into the shelf overhead—and slam! one of my pots come crashing down to the ground. So you reckon mebbe that were the busted pot? Oh, yes, I dessay! 'Cos no, what went and got busted was a sound pot! But that's only the way of the world since, oh, about forever, I suppose. . . . So what I really like to know is—well, now, say there was two people which they was walking along together, and like the one was walking and the other was walking? And one of that pair was mebbe a only son, which his mother dote on him something dreadful, and the other, well, he . . . Rabbi! Gawdelpus, but what's wrong! You took sick or sumthin'? Ma'am! Ma'am! Quick, come quick! Oh, where you keeping, ma'am? . . . It's your husband . . . Oh, but he's gone awful queer! . . . Look to be fallen in a faint! . . . Water! . . . Water!

Geese

A Monologue of a Woman Called Bassia
Who Slaughters Geese on Chanukah
and Fries Goose Fat and Cracklings
(That's to say, Schmaltz)
for the Passover

Why, you know, it wasn't only Chanukah last when I run up against—
an' the Lord only keep you and me, not to say all decent Jewish folks
from the same—well, as I says, when I run smack up against the worst
and best luck, which they was mixed up together both at once. Story's
worth a listen, too, on account a thing like that, why it don't hardly
happen but once in a thousand year maybe. See, geese is by way of being
my trade, which it include also your goose fat plus cracklings for the
Passover. Which, that's to say, I also be making what's called your kosher-
for-Passover schmaltz for the holiday. Well, now, I only been in the
business for upward of twenty year, and I never knowed such a thing to
come my ways before, not ever.

So, now, geese is by way of being my trade. . . . Well, you maybe
reckon that's all there was to it? Well, no it ain't. On account come
autumntide, which that be just after Feast o' the Tabernacles time, you
must buy the birds first, which next you must keep them cooped till the
winter and be feeding and tending them the while; so it ain't till the Feast
o' Chanukah, anyhow, which you can set to slaughtering the creatures
so's to be making any money out of 'em. Well, you maybe reckon that's
all there was to it. I mean, just buying up geese and keeping them cooped
and then only slaughtering the creatures so's to be making any money
out of 'em? Well, no, it ain't. On account you only take that business of

17

buying them geese first. Well, you must have the wherewithal to pu'chase; that's to say, you must have capital, which I ain't got any put by, anyhow. Which that only mean going to Reb Alter. Well, you know Reb Alter, which he's the kind of a gent will keep the pot boiling till all the water is out. See, it's not like he'll turn you down, for he never do that; only he'll tell you to come back the next day, and next day—the day after that, till you are fit to bust of aggervation. Which it is only then he commence sucking you dry—confounding interest, reckoning up days, suchlike. Fine gent, Reb Alter! No wonder he got such a fat mug on him, and her, too, that there missus of his—now, I only wisht her looks on my nearest and dearest, for you ever get a hold of that hefty pair of cheeks she got on her? Why, they's round and firm enough to be honing your knife on. Though now you take that daughter of hern—what's her name, Pearly? Well, it wasn't only recent they got the girl betrothed, anyhow. But dear God what I wouldn't give for the third part of what them betrothals cost —on account you wait and see if I didn't shuck off the goose business then, like that! . . . Though you ought to see the fine bridegroom they went and stuck her with, and God forgive my sins if I was ever to saddle any my own with such a sad specimen. Why, the feller's bald as a new-laid egg! Well, maybe you call it bald, only I suspicion it to be the mange. Not that it's any of my granny's business anyhow, I'm sure, and God forfend I should speak ill of other folks, never mind abide such talk. . . . But there I go again, mixing up one thing with another. Though don't be paying it any mind now, for it's only my nature. Besides which, it's as you says: womenfolks inclines to be talking nineteen to the dozen anyhow. . . .

About buying geese now. . . . So where you think you go and buy geese, at market maybe? Oh, you bet! For if we was all to go to market for our geese, we all be rolling in money then, wouldn't we. No, if you was pu'chasing geese in only a business way, you must first roust yourself at crack of dawn, when the Almighty himself is abed yet, and betake yourself to the edge of town, away past the other side of the windmills, over to where the countryside first begin. Only like as not there's another biddy, just as sharp as yourself, which she's up and about and took to the road even earlier, and another yet, which she's sharper still, and out even earlier than the last—till what you expect but in the end the place be crawling with such a sight of poulteresses as will put a county fair to shame. And every one of 'em just waiting for the first yokel which durst show his face with a brace of geese in hand; which they proceeds to pounce on the feller from every side, crying out in that yokel's mama's own heathen lingo, "Hey, feller, whatcher askin' fer them thar gooses?" Now, if he's your civil sort of a yokel, which they is incline for business and ready to hear a body out, you can at least try and strike a bargain with the man. But if the merciful Lord only put one of them surly sorts in your way, with a meat-ax disposition, which they won't even listen, well, you can call down all nine plagues of Egypt for all the good it do. "Git away!" he'll be hollering, "Ain't got no gooses!" Well, what you gonna do, sue him? So you commence argying with him, saying: "What you mean, you lamebrain halfwit! An' whatcher call them things you got, pigs with wings? C'mon, feller, so what you asking for the one goose?" But he only dig in his heels, saying, "G'wan git, ain't selling!" . . . Only supposing God send and the same yokel be willing to let go of a goose. Well, you must give the creature a once-over, first; which to do, you must know your way around geese; which there's an art to knowing geese as much as knowing your gems and diamonds, saving the difference. Take yourself. Now I suppose you think geese was pretty much alike; so I reckon you didn't know there was geese and there was ganders, and a goose wasn't a gander but a goose; on account geese is geese and ganders is ganders, and a goose will put on fat, whereas a gander? Forget it! So how you suppose to tell which is the goose and which the gander? Well, you just do. Because first off you know by the crest—a gander come with a bit of feathery tuft back of his head and he got a long neck. Besides which, you can tell from his call—on account a gander will give out with a kind of a low growly honk, like your menfolks will, and when he walks, he always walks ahead of the geese, same as a man amongst human folks, saving the difference. For amongst us, even a man's the sorriest and most useless creature on earth, he will walk in front of you only because he's a man, as if he had in mind to be saying, "Look'ee here, folks, it's me!" And what better proof you want than that sorry husband of mine. I mean, you must search pretty far before you will find a creature as useless as my Nachman Ber is; which from the time I knowed him for a husband, the man ain't seed fit to stir himself sufficient even once to bring home so much as two busted ha'pennies! And why they ever bother to make such a monstrous fuss over him before the marriage, I'll never know. For all he ever brung to the business was only a head for pious larnin' and being a distant relation to rich Reb Yoske. That's to say, his nibs Our Parish Squire. Distant is right. Horsefeathers! Why, you need a spyglass to make it out. Like my granddad's rooster once peck his grandma's hen. And what good ever come of it to me, anyhow? Only such humble pie as you wisht your own worst enemy may eat. I mean, folks seem never to tire throwing up to me that one of my own relations, which she's only rich Reb Yoske's daughter-in-law, goes sashaying about in public in her very own hair, which she ain't pious enough to cut nor decent enough to cover. Which it's all true, by the way —brazen hussy! . . . Not that I ever dream of speaking evil of the woman, anyhow, and God forfend I should speak ill of other folks, never mind abide such talk. . . . But there I go again, mixing up one thing with another. Though don't be paying it any mind now, for it's only my nature. Besides which, it's as you says: womenfolks inclines to be talking nineteen to the dozen, anyhow. . . .

Now, about buying geese. . . . So once you have got your geese bought up, you must keep them cooped for the winter. Well, you maybe reckon that's all there was to it. I mean, just keeping poultry cooped for the winter? Well, no, it ain't. On account cooping the creatures be just dandy, if I had my own place, with a room which to do it in—which, that's to say, if it was only me alone had that market cornered, so to speak. Only what you say, for instance if I was to tell you I was lodging with—an' Lord keep you and me, not to say, all decent Jewish folks from the same again—well, anyhow, that I was living with that there Yenta the Henwife woman, of all people, which I didn't have a place of my own then, never mind a room for keeping poultry cooped up in. And my landlady, what's more, that's to say that Yenta woman, was by way of being a poulteress herself, which it so happen her trade include also your geese plus goose fat and cracklings—that's to say, what's called your Schmaltz, for the Passover? Well, now, you just try and keep geese together with that woman, in the one bitty room she got for it, without you end up trading slaps with her three times any day in the week at the least! So that's one thing. Apart from which, well, how you suppose to tell which geese is your geese and which is hern? On account there was this one time—an' Lord only keep you and me, not to say all decent folks from the same again—well, as I says, there was this one time, which I was still lodging with her then, with Yenta, that is, when it happen her coop bust open, and wouldn't you know but straightaway the whole gaggle of her poultry was at my oats in the feeding trough, which I set it out special in that room for my own birds. So who is the injured party, you reckon? I mean, who ought to of raised the roof by rights? Me, or her? Only wouldn't you know, it be her which commence giving *me* the what for. If she'd only of knowed geese was my trade (says she), why she wouldn't never of let the place to me, never in a million years she wouldn't —not even I was to offer her a hundred million in gold, she wouldn't. Well, I says to her, "So what you think was my line, lady—precious jewels maybe?" Only she says to me then, "Well you are some precious jewel yourself, lady, and so's that there precious husband of yourn, and so's them precious childer of yourn, too, I shouldn't wonder!" . . . Well, you don't suppose I let that go? Not hardly, I reckon. . . . Odd woman that Yenta. I mean, the woman got a heart of gold, mainly. Why, she give up her life for you if you was to ask it. Like, preserve us, say if you was sick maybe? Well, there is nothing she wouldn't do for you then. Only my God, you talk about a short fuse? Why, it won't take nothing to set her off, and there's always the dickens to pay then. Well, now, you only take that one time, which it was exactly eve of Chanukah last—why, your hair like to crinkle if I was to tell about it, only I'm not one to stick my nose in where I oughtn't, and God forfend I should speak ill of other folks anyhow, never mind abide such talk. . . . But there I go again, mixing up one thing with another. Though don't be paying it any mind now, for it's only my nature. Besides which, it's as you says: womenfolks inclines to be talking nineteen to the dozen anyhow. . . .

Well, next you got that business of keeping your geese cooped for the winter. . . . Now, if you want your birds to prosper and plump up, you must make certain to always coop them in the *old* month. And God help them as comes near a goose untimely—that's to say, jump whilst the new moon's aborning. For that is sure to put the kibosh on the business. Why the creatures won't never prosper then! For the poultry be big in the bone then and scant in the flesh, so if you was reckoning on seeing them plumped up proper come winter, you can forget it, on account they just won't do it, not in a million years they won't. So forget it! Nor must you coop geese in the daytime when folks is about. You do it at sunset, by candlelight, or even in the dark. Only doing it, you must give yourself a pinch the while you whispers three times, "As I am in the flesh, so shall you be in the flesh." . . . Now, my husband is always laughing at me about it, saying as how he reckon all of it wasn't only stuff and nonsense, which it ain't worth even the half pu'chase of a poor pinch of snuff anyhow. Though I was to take everything which that man says serious, I'd be in a fine fix then, wouldn't I? Why, you know what the man had the raw gumption to be saying just recent—and him fancying himself to be such a fine scholar, which he only set about all day long with his nose buried in a book, morning, noon, and night, the way he always do—anyhow, you know what the man actually said? That Yom Kippur fowl offerings was a foolish practice! So how you like that for a notion, eh? Well, you don't suppose he didn't come out looking pretty foolish himself by the time I finish with him. Not hardly, I reckon. "Now, you're not meaning to tell me," says I, "that you come up with such a notion all on your clever lonesome, eh?" . . . Says he, "Why, it's writ right here in black and white!" "So what you saying?" says I, "that me and my mother, and my Auntie Deborah, and Nehama Bryna, and Sossia, and Dossia, and Tzvia, we was all us only a bunch of ignorant cows which they didn't know A from a gable end?" . . . Well, the man made no answer to that. Knew what's good for him, that's why. For I tell you I could of whistled that fool up such a good morning as might of set his ears ringing into next week if I wished! Though I wouldn't have you believe I wasn't only one your spiteful scolds, which she won't give her husband a moment's peace. For rest assured, I well enough know the value of a husband which he's a man of larnin' and has give himself up to studying on pious writ, notwithstanding he don't do a hand's turn otherwise. For what you think, the man's only lazy? Why, there isn't anything in the world the poor man wouldn't do to put bread on the table if it but come his way. Only it never do. So he set and larn. . . . Well, let the man larn all he want. And what I need any his toil for, anyhow; seeing as I stands on my own two feet, thank you; and one way or another I manages quite satisfactory with the family expenses on my own hook without I need to throw myself on the charity of strangers, an' touch wood I never shall! Yes, on my own, ever on my own. At market and to home, stooped over that stove, which after the hot spuds been dished out, and the kids all dressed and sent off to cheder . . . well, see now that's the main thing where I'm concern. For when it come to bread, there's days which we do without it, and Sabbath-day feasts, too, we do without our holiday loaf sometimes. Only when it come to paying tuition—now mind! I got four boys which I pays for, which that's not counting my girls—well, anyhow, even it was hailing boulders and the world come to an end, tuition always gets paid in this house! For I don't hold with any your modren sorts, which they are only too glad to dump their children in one them gov'mint free-schools, "tendin' classes" I think they calls it. Like say that young Berl, which he's our cantor's son? Well, now, what you expect but the boy come out of it about as kosher as pork sorsages, dern that boy; only God forfend I be talking in His name nor

speak ill of other folks anyhow, never mind abide such talk. . . . But there
I go again, mixing up one thing with another. Though don't be paying it
any mind now, for it's only my nature. Besides which, it's as you says:
womenfolks inclines to be talking nineteen to the dozen anyhow. . . .

Now, once you have got your poultry put away, you need only to
attend to their provender; which you must see to it they gets their vittles
when they are supposed and they drinks their water when they are supposed. And that's all there's to it, really. See, geese, they ain't your ducks
and they ain't your chickens. Ducks fears pox and chickens fears pole-
cats, but your goose all it needs is to eat. And when it come to grub,
geese will eat most anything. They will eat oats and they will eat millet
and they will eat mash and they will eat—only saving your presence—
they will eat fare which it's considerable too disgusting to even mention.
. . . Your goose ain't overparticular. A goose will gobble up everything.
For geese is always hungry, same as poor folk's children always is, saving
the difference. Now poor folk's kids will gladly eat anything which it's
put in their way, bless their hearts, only they are never full. Which that
is something I know firsthand. Because, now, you take my own kids—
an' Lord bless and keep 'em from all harm—well, like when they have
all come home from cheder? Now, I've scarce to turn my back for a
minute and phut! the whole loaf's perished and won't be a spud left in
the pot, even your life depend on it. And come Sabbath eve, you must
pass out the challah loaf in little bits, like it was honeycakes, and put the
remainder what's left under lock and key; otherwise, there won't be much
as a crumb left of it by the morrow. Not that children aren't a comfort
and a joy, and speaking for myself I shouldn't mind having the keep of a
whole dozen of the dears myself, maybe even two dozen, or all of ten
dozen if it come to it. Only trouble is, they got greedy guts. I mean, your
rich folks they don't appreciate how lucky they are, knowing the children
has gone to bed with their bellies full, and you can sleep easy without
you dreaming on beggarfolks and be woken up in the middle of night by
their wailing: "Mummy, I'm hu-u-u-ngry!" Why, it plumb break a body's
heart to be answering them: "Hush up now! What you raising the roof
about food for in the middle of the night! Shame on you! G'wan git back
to bed!" . . . Which, notwithstanding, you ought to see what a fret your
rich folks will generly get into, if God forbid the missus is only brung to
bed of one more child than they reckoned on. Me-oh-my-oh-my! Why,
just recent, one such missus of quality pass on—Bella was her name—
darling girl she was, too, all peaches and cream, scarce more than only a

child herself, and oh, such an angel, so sweet and pious you wouldn't believe and ever so plump and handsome. So what you think the reason for it was, eh? Only on second thoughts, it ain't a fit subject to talk on as the poor creature has gone on to a better world now—which I only wisht her a joyful Paradise there forever and amen, only God forfend I should speak ill of other folks anyhow, never mind abide such talk. . . . But there I go again, mixing up one thing with another. Though don't be paying it any mind now, for it's only my nature. Besides which, it's as you says: womenfolks inclines to be talking nineteen to the dozen anyhow. . . .

Some business, geese. . . . But lordy, ain't it the truth! Which mind! That's not to say geese is necessary a bad living. Why, no. An' God send, your geese prospers, you can be turning a fair profit by it, too. But that won't generly happen only once in, oh, maybe ten years. Mostly you are glad to break even. Nor I shan't even mention losing by it. And then there's all that drudgery! Why, there's such a power of work needs doing round geese, it don't hardly seem worth the headache of doing it. Though I suppose you be asking why a body be having any truck with the creatures anyway if there's no money in 'em? Only what else a body suppose to do if all they ever knowed by way of a living was geese? . . . Well, now, you figure it for yourself. I mean, you must untie thirty-odd brace of geese and you must carry thirty-odd brace to the slaughterer's and then you must lug thirty-odd brace back home again; which you must next pluck them all, salt them all, soak them all, rinse them all, and gut them all—the while laying by the skins separate, the fat separate, the giblets separate, and the flesh separate; which all the parts brings in money, so you durst not lose even the least bit of that truck whilst preparing it. Only mind! You be doing it all on your own hook and alone. Well, first you wants to be cooking up all your fat plus the skins. That's to say, you be making what's called your schmaltz first. Well, now, I always make Passover schmaltz every year. On account my Passover schmaltz got a name in town for being the best, not to say the most prime kosher-for-Passover schmaltz there is. Now me? When I sets myself to making Passover schmaltz to home? Well, now, though it be plumb middle of Chanukah yet and Passover all of a five month away—why, you of thought for sure Passover already come to my place. For I be koshering the stove up special, then. And my mister? Well, I packs *him* off to shul, as the man can as easy set idle and larn there as here. And the kids, well, they all gets shooed out too, for they can as well play at holiday teetotums outdoors as in. And that's when I get to work, cooking up the schmaltz. Well, now, you see your schmaltz don't take kindly to having unwanted company about, which that only go double for your Passover schmaltz. Now, I larn about that the hard way. On account I recollect this one time, which I was still lodging with Yenta then—an' the Lord only keep you and me, not to say all decent Jewish folks from the same—well, anyway, there was other lodgers there, as well. So this one woman which live there—Gnessy she was call—well, she got a sudden hankering to fix up a mess of buckwheat pancakes. Which that was jump on the day I was slaughtering my own geese. "But Gnessy, dear!" I says to her then, "Can't them pancakes keep till tomorrow? For come tomorrow, an' God send, you welcome to make all the pancakes you want!" Says she: "Well, now, if it was up to me, I be most happy to oblige. Trouble is, my young 'uns will find out. For my children," says she, "they are monstrous partial to their vittles. I mean, you talk about a greedy gut! Now, if they was to find out there be no pancakes today? Why, they'd eat me alive!" . . . Well, sure enough, her kids was listening from up on the mantel over the stove where they lay. So the minute they hear talk of pancake dinner being put off for a day, well, one of them— which he's call Zelig, or something, and got these cross-eye peepers— well, anyway, so he went and kick up the worst squawk, saying, "Mama, if you don't make pancakes, I'm gonna throw myself down off the stove!" . . . Well, we both look up and preserve us if the child wasn't actually hanging head down from over the stove, and any second now it be smashed to bits! Well, I set to hollering myself, then: "Oh, Gnessy darling, please!" I says. "You best be making them pancakes, sweetheart, for I can wait!" . . . Now, they say a poor man's gut has got no bottom, and truer words was never spoke. Why, you needn't only look at Gnessy's kids to know the truth of it, only God forfend I should speak ill of other folks, never mind abide such talk. . . . But there I go again, mixing up one thing with another. Though don't be paying it any mind now, for it's only my nature. Besides which, it's as you says: womenfolks inclines to be talking nineteen to the dozen anyhow. . . .

So say you have got your schmaltz. . . . Well, if you are looking to profit from your birds, your schmaltz won't give it to you. Why, no. For even your schmaltz turn out A-one prime, it won't return only what you have laid out for the creatures in the first place. On account your profit come only by way of what's call your "etceteries." Which first amongst these is the remainders in the way of breasts plus drumsticks, that's to say, the creature's flesh. For God send and the flesh has come up meaty and plump, and it also happen that your meat on the hoof is dear in town—why, then you are in business! Only supposing all your butchers is having conniptions undercutting one another and meat is dirt cheap; and what's more, the whole town is hell bent on spiting his nibs Our Squire, so they brung down a new slaughterer in place of the old slaughterer; and that one, that's to say, the old slaughterer, well *he* went and inform to the gov'mint on the new one; and God only knows what he said to them because, on top of everything, the old 'un, that's to say, the old slaughterer, let it be known that the t'other one, that's to say, the new slaughterer, wasn't only one your smart-alecky modren breeds; that's to say, he is a Zi'nist, which got to do with that pesky lot from the newfangled cheders as generly come down to shul prompt every Purim to solicit contributions? Well, now, Our Squire cannot abide Zi'nists, and he won't have any truck with them, on account they are troublemakers, he says. And such being the case, the new slaughterer's handiwork is now about as kosher as pork sorsages, saving the difference. So, you see, there's many in town which is unwilling to take a chance on poultry what's already been slaughtered and is supplied by poultresses such as yours truly. So I commence to argying with my customers, saying: "Oh, never fear about *my* birds, ma'am. For my slaughterer is the old 'un!" . . . Only they be saying: "Well, we don't doubt it, but it ain't exactly tattooed on their chests which slaughterer it come from!" . . . Says I: "What you mean, it ain't tattooed? If I says they are from the old 'un, then they are from the old 'un! Unless," I says, "Unless my word ain't good anymore; which if it ain't, well, I don't know what the world is come to!" . . . Says they: "Now, don't be taking on so. For we believe your every word. But if we can take our own geese to the slaughterer's, what we need poultry for, which we don't know who slaughtered them?" "Oh, pooh!" says I, "Goodness, but must I be repeating myself all the time? Well, now, I'll take an oath on my husband and children then. So now you know my word is got to be good!" . . . But they only says: "Gracious, but why be taking oaths if we believe you anyhow?" . . . Only I says, "Well, at least take a couple of breasts and lighten up a poor woman's basket some!" . . . So they says, "Why, we love to; only we can't, on account we don't know which slaughterer they come from." . . . Well, talk about pulling teeth!? I mean, you would of thought folks might at least put themselves in another's place. Show a little sympathy maybe? Not on your life! For here's a body which near kilt herself over only a bunch of geese, thinking how she be making a little money by it, and along come this hard winter and no firewood to be had and straw costing an arm and a leg, and the kids going to school barefoot and coming back blue from cold, and when they have clumb up on the stove, they all huddle up there together, like little bunny rabbits, looking out for their meal of hot spuds, which each spud's worth it's weight in gold because the crop's gone bad and most of it been left to rot underground. . . . Call this a city? Why, there ain't a soul in it take notice of poor folks perishing of cold all around, getting swoll up, dying of hunger, and the children what's cut down like grass, dropping like flies everywhere. Anyway, it's a mercy, you says, it's only paupers what's doing the dying, only God forfend I should ever speak ill of other folks, never mind abide such talk. . . . But there I go again, mixing up one thing with another. Though don't be paying it any mind now, for it's only my nature. Besides which, it's as you says: womenfolks inclines to be talking nineteen to the dozen anyhow. . . .

Yes, etceteries. . . . So if we was to depend on the creatures's flesh alone, that really put us in a fix, wouldn't it. So it's a good thing geese is got giblets. Of which there's your cracklings and your livers and craws and heads and feet and wings, also your gullets, tongues, hearts, and kidneys. Oh, and don't be forgetting your necks! Why, one my customers —Mrs. "Stuff Derma," I calls her—anyhow, this Stuff Derma woman, she always buys up *all* my goose necks. And even I was to offer her half a hundred necks, she still wouldn't rest till she got her hands on the whole lot. Her mister, she says—that's to say, Mr. Stuff Derma—well, he's partial to breast and neck, mainly. Only he likes his breast cold, she says, oh, and spicy, nice and spicy, she says, with pepper, lots of pepper, she says—and about goose necks? Well, he likes his stuffed with flour or grits or square noodles maybe, or say even livers and cracklings, which they been roasted separate, or like cooked up together with carrots. So what you think? Eat handsome, die handsome, eh? I mean, bless the man, but he don't look a day over thirty, though he's a good ten year older than my own mister. And even if my husband don't do much of anything either, at least he set and larn. And when he come home from his larnin', he won't be saying to you gruff, like other men do, "I'm hungry, woman, where's dinner!" Him, when he comes home from shul? Straightway he'll be setting down to a pious book and be letting on he's looking into it, don't you know? Only he'll be groaning under his breath the while. Which that's a sign he's hungry. But he never come straight out and say, "Where's dinner?" That be too much to expect of a body, wouldn't it. Only what? Oh, he'll be groaning on for a bit longer. And then he'll be pressing his hand to his breast, saying, "Och-och-och!" Which that's a sign he's good and hungry. Says I, "Perhaps you be wanting something to eat, dear?" Says he, "W-ell, now you men-tion it—." Now, I don't know how many times I told that man, "You got a mouth, mister, so why don't you use it? Just say you're hungry and be done! I'll be blest if I know how a grown man can set about the house groaning like that!" . . . Ever hear a wall talk? . . . Well, I got half a mind to see what happen if I didn't feed the man for three days running. Oh, you're not thinking perhaps the man ain't but a helpless fool? My gracious, but how can a Jewish gent what everybody knows for a prodigy of pious larnin' be only a helpless fool? Though if only—. Well, like if besides having that head for larnin' he might contrive also to be a mite better at cozying up to the right quarters? I mean, a man like that? Why, surely, a man like that might attain to the post of rabbi here. Well, you asks, but what shall we do about the old rabbi then? Only the question what bothers *me* is what we gonna do about our poor old cantor. Every think of that? Now, why they ever go and hire a new cantor for at shul? So the old 'un might starve? Like the man wasn't pauper enough before he was give the boot. And all on account of a rich old buzzard which he put on airs and got hisself a fool notion to hear fancy singing at shul. You want fancy singing? Go to the opery, you'll have fancy singing. Enough to bust both your eardrums, I only wisht! . . . Why, I tell you, if I was a man? Well, I'd give them rich gentry what for! Oh, I'd settle their hash, all right! Just you see if I wouldn't! You think I got something against rich gentry? Well, I got nothing against rich gentry, I only hates 'em. Specially parish squires! Why, a parish squire's a viper; he's a . . . only God forfend I should speak ill of other folks, never mind abide such talk. . . . But there I go again, mixing up one thing with another. Though don't be paying it any mind mind now, for it's only my nature. Besides which, it's as you says: womenfolks inclines to be talking nineteen to the dozen anyhow. . . .

Though about earning from geese. . . . Now, don't think because you have unloaded a whole mess of edibles, which that's all your schmaltz and etceteries and such, you can lay back and rest easy. For if it wasn't for the creature's down and feathers, there hardly wouldn't be any profit to the goose business. So early on, that's to say when I begun first with the cooping, I already commence plucking the creatures then, kind of picking away underneath the wings, nearby to the breast; like where

human folks generly got their armpits mostly? Which I then gather together the downy bits, laying them by the while. Later, though, that's to
say after the bird's been slaughtered, well that is when your actual plucking commence in earnest, with the down plumage put by separate and
the feather plumage put by separate. So now I got my work cut out for
the rest of winter. Well, the nights is long enough then, so it leave plenty
of time for plucking. So I pluck. Only there's help this time. Because girls,
well you know girls isn't boys. You see boys goes to cheder, but girls?
Well, girls is like geese. They sets at home and eat and grow, mainly. So I
gather round my gels and we set down together over the sifting sieve
then. "C'mon, dears," I says to them, "Less have us a plucking bee! For
you only lend me a hand now," says I, "why, then, tomorrow, an' God
willing, I'll pay you back with a bit of goose crackling or some that goose
fat dripped on bread maybe. Or, say! What you say to a nice bowl of
derma soup?" Gotcha! For you ought to see how their eyes will light up,
and they set to work. Well, I should think so! Derma soup's no small
thing, you know. I mean, none of them children generally catch sight of
meat for a whole week. Save on the Sabbath maybe. Why, if it wasn't for
the goose business? Well, I've no idea what I'd really do a whole week
with the children. This way I'm at least put in the way of a bit of belly
fat now and again or the odd gullet or say a head or a foot or a gizzard
or even schmaltz drippings sometimes. Why, the smell alone be sufficient
to keep them happy! Like once, when I use still to be living over at
Yenta's—an' Lord keep you and me, not to say all decent Jewish folks
from the same again—anyhow, I recollect the very thing come out of
Gnessy's own mouth herself then: "You know," she says to me, "come
Chanukah and you be puttering about over that Passover schmaltz of
yourn? Well, I declare, it do knock my bunch for a loop. For them
young'uns of mine, they honestly fit to believe they was actually eating
goose savories the while." . . . Well, you don't suppose it give me comfort, seeing how all them little ones which Gnessy got (an' Godpraise!)
was looking on at that great pot of schmaltz with the whole mess of
goose cracklings cooking away in it—and without so much as stretching
out a hand, and the poor things huddled together up above the stove,
staring down hungry as wolves, their mouths watering and eyes so shiny
then—oh, merciful God, it wrung a body's heart seeing what a state they
was in. So you put a crackling into a hand here, smears lips over with
schmaltz there. Only what more is a body to do? And how am I suppose
to feed so many mouths anyhow when Godpraise I got my own burden

of young'uns which wants feeding and my husband not earning two busted ha'pennies on his own account and what's owing on the geese still needing to be paid. And, oh, what wouldn't I give for the third part of what's owing, even we was both to share in it, what with that confound interest piling up like the devil's own mischief; which it's just got to be paid, for I've no wish to be a debtor permanent, end up a bankrupt, God forfend, like Yenta become, for instance, which she ain't paid her brother-in-law for the other half of her place yet, and all on account that boy of hern, which he's "tendin' classes," they say, "a-studying," they say, and which he writes on the Sabbath. . . . Least it's what folks say. Only I confess I wasn't by when he done it. And I do so hate saying what I don't know, nor I much hold with retailing ill of other folks behind their backs. Only answer me this: What's that boy of Yenta's got to be a-studying for? I mean, seeing as the boy's got . . . well, not to put too fine a point on it, he got—well, he got the TB, preserve us. All his people got the TB. Mind, though! I only wisht for her sake her boy live twice three-score years. For I'm her good friend, and what I got against the woman, anyhow? Though, now I mention it, she ain't done all that good by me neither. You don't go tossing folks which they is neighbors out on the street mid Foretide-to-Passover like that. And why she done it? Because that there Menasheh the Water Carrier can pay one ruble the week, and I can't. Well, she can crow when she get it! Word is, the man's in debt, anyway. Why, he even got his hair in pawn. And him carrying water to all the houses in these parts for the whole winter long and, notwithstanding, the man's still a dreadful pauper, and his missus, which she's call Pessy, you know, now she is some piece of goods all to herself, though God forfend I should speak ill of other folks, I'm sure, never mind abide such talk. . . . But gracious! . . . Wasn't I suppose to tell something? Now, what was it I wanted to tell? . . . Don't that beat everything? Dern if I can recollect what it was. Well, that'll teach you to mess round with womenfolks! Oh, I tell you, womenfolks is s-ome folks. I mean here I been mixing up everything in the one pot, apples and orangers, the kitchen sink, God know what-all. And see what come out of it? Well, it's only the truth what people say. Womenfolks does talk nineteen to the dozen. Well never mind. It'll keep. I'll only be telling that story next time round, I reckon.

The White Scape Hen

Monologue of a Woman of Breeding

Well! Now, I don't know about you, but speaking for myself, gracious, it could be the end of the world and I won't settle for any but a white scape hen. Oh, absolutely! Why, to tell the truth, I cannot even imagine myself sacrificing any but a bird of the purest white for the Yom Kippur. For I just know I should be put into the worst dread of dying for a whole year otherwise. You see, I've been accustomed to it from childhood. Matter of habit, really. But then everything's a matter of habit. Take mother, now. Now, Mummy's not what you'd call really observant, no more than myself, most ways. But that don't keep her from setting great store by such things still. Let's see, now: there's always borscht on the Passover, and there's bast on Feast of Weeks, oh, and white scape hens— always a white scape hen, and potato pancakes on the Chanukah, and exchanging dainties on the Purim—and, well, just a whole lot of pious duties of that sort, which she is as much a stickler for as any rabbi's wife. And Remembrance Prayers. Mummy absolutely dotes on Remembrance Prayers. And I cannot conceive of anything on earth would upset her more than if she missed hearing the shofar blown at synagogue. Much as I might take on, say, if, God help me, I was to miss hearing Mr. Chaliapin sing. . . . Though you would just never know it to look at her. I mean, who could possibly take her for anything but the genteel woman of breeding she gives herself out to be? You know, she's a wonder still for rattling off her Goethe and Schiller to you, oh, at just the drop of a hat. Come to that, she still entertains a great passion for Herr Zschokke. Why, to this day, the woman won't even think of retiring for the night without taking Zschokke to bed with her. But, then, First of Elul prompt, she will throw a white kerchief over her head and be keeping company with the rest of the pious biddies. Only I can't think what she finds in common with the old things to be chattering away so cozily with them about it. Braiding kosher candlewicks, I shouldn't wonder. . . . Though the High Holidays being over, the kerchief gets put away and she's back to her Goethe and Schiller and Zschokke again. Well, that's Mother all over for you, and it was how she brought us up to be as well. We were five girls and were all let to marry "for love," as they say. Well, we were pretty enough for it and uncommon well educated. So with fifteen thousand settled on us each at the bank, by way of dowry, I shouldn't think there was all that much to despise in us, really. Though I must say, it wasn't for our beauty so much, or being such uncommon accomplished young ladies, that we made our name in society as for being well brought up. Upbringing's mortal important, don't you find? Makes just a world of difference in a person, really. Though I'll have you know that Mother was awfully liberal in that way, and ordinarily she left us free to do pretty much as we pleased. Oh, absolutely! I mean we were let to talk to *whomever* we wanted, go *wherever* we wanted, and do *whatever* we wanted. But when the talk came to keeping to Jewish practices and such? Why, strict wasn't the word! Mummy was a perfect tartar on that head. The woman never gave an inch! Apropos, did you know that to this day you couldn't ever get me to take off my left shoe before taking the right one off? You can hold a gun to my head, and still I wouldn't do it. My Volodia though is always poking fun at me for it. But then if I was to be paying any mind to Volodia's poking fun, we'd be having *our* Pesach made over into *their* Pasch in very short order, wouldn't we, with colored eggs all over the place and not a shard of matzo to be had anywhere in the house for love or money. Now, about Volodia's views on things Jewish—well! . . . let's just say he inclines to be a mite contrary on the subject and leave it at that. I mean, it isn't as if Volodia was disrespectful because you couldn't be more wrong if you thought that. Why, he has only to hear about Jews being in trouble somewhere—say a pogram or such?—and the poor man's inconsolable, oh, just beside himself with grief, and he'll be going on about Jewish blood being spilt again and how awful it was. No, what he can't abide is only their unmannerliness. The way they walk and talk and behave. Their damnable impertinence, as he says. Jews are pushy, Volodia says, "uppity" as he calls it. . . . But, then, let a stranger say the least unpleasant thing about Jews, and he is quite ready to pull the fellow apart with his bare hands. Really odd, Volodia is. Very. You know, he'll be having, say, some of his fancy high-horse Russian friends over for a game of preference sometimes? Well, I don't know how many times I've heard him positively crowing to that lot about our own Mr. Herzl, that's to say, the great Jewish diplomatist, and how that famous man was such an honored guest at the Sublime Porte and received by the sultan of Turkey himself when he visits. But when some Zionist gentlemen came round the other day, soliciting for contributions, Volodia was the longest while haranguing them about how they were deluding themselves and it was bound all to turn out a mare's nest in the end anyway, so why bother! . . . Oh, and the money? Now, you'd have thought he might send them packing after that and have given not a penny. Not my Volodia! Gave handsomely, he did. Well, I did say Volodia was odd. You have simply no idea how many run-ins I've had with that man over the children! Now, mind you, my children are just the sweetest, cleverest, prettiest, healthiest, sprightliest children you'd ever hope to meet and touch wood! So what more could a parent wish for? Well, it's not enough for Volodia. No, *he* must have them know everything. I mean, knowing everything's all well and good, and I for one wouldn't have it any other way. For, my goodness, but don't everybody wish to see their children educated? But I won't stand idly by while their health is being ruined! Now, I don't set myself up to be the best of mothers—far from it—but I'm a mother, notwithstanding. So if there is one thing I know the value of, it's good health! You know, my Alex and Sophie while they were growing up? Gracious, wasn't it always touch and go then! And now that man has come along with nothing better to do than be wearing my darlings out. Wants them to learn everything, he says—just everything, mind. Even Yiddish. Yiddish, for goodness' sake! You'd think they hadn't schoolwork enough as it is, but there's also the music lessons and the dancing lessons and God knows what other torments the man hasn't inflicted on them besides. And now they must have this new misery thrust on them: Yiddish lessons! Well, I shouldn't so much mind if this was your normal sort of lessons—the kind you'd be likely to get if you settled for studying only German or French or English. Why, you'd at least expect a Yiddish tutor might be like the rest. Only the man is . . . well, God forgive me for saying so, but he's . . . Oh, I hardly know *what* he is! Even Volodia can't stand the smell of him. Why, every time the fellow leaves, Volodia throws open the window. "But, darling, why be keeping the wretched man on?" I pleaded with him. "It's the fashion now," he says, "Yiddish lessons are the fashion, so they will have to learn Yiddish." You hear that? The fashion! That's all it comes down to these days, don't it. Everything's the fashion. I suppose cards, too, is the fashion. Why, I don't believe the man knew tricks from trumps once. And now it's all preference and derda and sixty-six with him. You know, these days he'll sit himself down to a game on an evening and be playing straight through into the next night. Why, it's got so he can't seem to do without it anymore. It didn't use to bother me as long as he did his playing at home. And, mind, I won't say I'm not partial to a game of preference myself now and again—and come to that, I shouldn't say no to a hand of okka if I was asked, either. We used all to play okka at Mummy's all the time. No, it's his playing at the club bothers me. The club! Always at the club! Lord, how I wish the wretched place was gone to perdition! Firstly, it's the money has got me worried. Now, when Volodia plays, he plays meaning to win. Only he loses, you see. Why, the man's lost a fortune, simply a fortune, at cards! I can always tell when Volodia wins or loses. If he's terribly on edge like, when he comes in, and very irritable and complaining about everything and finding fault—it's a sure sign he has lost. And the time wasted! When I only think of all the lost time! And the nights! Especially the nights! I mean, at first, that's to say before I found out where he'd been disappearing to every night, oh, I was made frantic by it and just so beside myself I thought I'd go mad. And each time he'd be making up his fool excuses for me. Always it's to do with cases pending, arbitrations for three nights running, hearings, anyway, some such nonsense, or it's maybe only an old chum had insisted on dragging him away for a game of preference over to his place. Thing is, I know Volodia. I can always tell when he's lying or telling the truth. If he swears he's telling the truth and gets into a mortal great huff the while, it's a sure sign he is lying. Well, I began making a few inquiries here and there on my own, asking round a bit, don't you know? So that's when I learnt about the club. Oh, the relief! You've no idea! I thought, thank God, the man's not betaken himself elsewhere, at least. . . . "Volodia, darling," I pleaded with him, "Couldn't you as well play cards at home?" Only he said: "Why, dear, one gets to meet everyone who's anyone there. And there's no end of useful tips a fellow might pick up at the club if he's sharp."—Stuff! Believe that, and you'll believe anything! "But think, darling," I pleaded with him still, "you might at least show some consideration for me. It just isn't fair your leaving me on my own for nights on end like that. And when's the last time you saw the children? Why, it's sinful the way you've neglected them. Have you no shame, sir, even before God?" So he said he couldn't stand scenes and hated it when I spoke in God's name. So I started to cry. So he walked out, slamming the door, and only came back the next morning in one of his mortal great huffs again. Well, you see his game now? It's *him* that gets to go out again! And looking at him, I thought back to how it was once, when we were courting, you know? Oh, but didn't he dance attendance on me then! Waited on me hand and foot he did. Why, he'd always be walking on eggshells round me then, anticipating my every whim. And talk about watching your P's and Q's? Well, didn't he ever! I mean, of course, first he had to make certain to get on Mother's good side, letting Mummy recite from memory for him, oh, just pages and pages of Goethe and Schiller and Zschokke. Next he read books to her, novels no less, those awfully sentimental ones, don't you know, which nobody can get through whilst keeping a dry eye. And, mind, the while he'd be holding onto her loops of yarn for her, as well. Summertime he helped Mummy with cooking the preserves, and winter they played casino together. And he certainly had his work cut out where *I* was concerned. Why, the poor man simply pined after me then, padding about at my heels constantly like a little puppy dog. And don't think I didn't run him a merry chase either before he finally got the good word from me. Because I had three others I kept company with then besides, that's to say, other than his nibs, and each as good a catch as himself. Now, I recall one young man, in particular—well, he's a doctor now, you know —why, the fellow loved me to distraction! But they were all mad for me then. And today? Well, I dare say, I can still turn a man's head when I choose. Like Brennholz the pharmacist, for instance. He's certainly taken to fluttering about me lately, buttering me up, oh, just a treat, doing his best to persuade me I'm ten years younger than I am. And why do you think he is always coming round just at the time when Volodia happens to be out? . . . Well, now, perhaps I do encourage him, just a little. You see, I *want* Volodia to know, so he should fret over it. . . . Why, yes, I even tell Volodia about it afterwards. "Guess who came by today," I'll be saying to him. "Brennholz?" says he, not turning a hair. "Oh, and darling, about tomorrow?" I'll say next, "I'm going with him to hear Chaliapin tomorrow, just the two of us!" . . . "Oh, are you really? Who with?" says he, "Brennholz?" Well, I looked at him then, thinking, "You just wait, mister! I'll get your goat yet!" So I said to him, "What would you say, Volodia, to renting a summer cottage together with Brennholz?" "Oh," says he, "I shouldn't think that would present much of a problem." "But you know," I said, "Brennholz wants me to come with him to Marienbad next year, just the two of us." "Oh?" he says, "Sounds fine, dear, just fine!" Oh, sounds fine, does it? Well, not on your life, mister! No, I shan't go! If only because you want me to so much. . . . Well, I ask you! I mean, what's become of my Volodia lately? It's those chums of his, isn't it! It's them that's taken him in, haven't they! I mean, God knows what that bunch is capable of. Why, every night they go from there to . . . well, it so happens I know exactly where they go! Because I've been asking round, you see. From the club they go to Le Parnasse, L'Olympe, L'Arcadie, and other such places. Only we all know the sort of entertainment gets served-up there, don't we! . . . Oh, confound the club! And confound his cards! Why, time was, when me and Volodia used to stay up whole nights without sleeping, and we'd only be talking and talking the while and never once run out of things to say. These days, though, I doubt we are able to spend half an hour together. The talk's run out. So that's why we keep that pharmacist fellow around, Brennholz. It's only to hear him talk. Oh, about any old thing. Nothing special, really. Only talk. Well, you know the sort of thing: jokes, songs, funny stories. Oh, and the stories that man tells! Brennholz, that is. Hee-hee! I tell you he's a devil, Brennholz is, for making a body laugh. My gracious, yes. And Jewish stories, mind! Well, I declare, there isn't anything on earth I love better than a good story. Why, it's the one thing I never grow tired of. So Brennholz sits up with me all night, telling me stories. . . . Well, of course, I know I've set tongues wagging all over town! What is more, I know exactly what they're saying about me. Only I don't care. No, it's Volodia's not caring that bothers me! . . . Lordy, lordy, lordy! You know, in the old days, if Volodia was to learn someone was keeping me company into the wee hours, telling stories? Oho! And what've we here!—But now? Nothing! You know, sometimes he'll be coming home of an evening, late, and find the two of us out on my balcony? Nothing! The man won't even bat an eye. "Ah, Brennholz, old man! What news?" And Brennholz-old-man proceeds to tell him. And Volodia will be smoking away then, nodding his head, pretending to listen. Only his mind? Well his mind's elsewhere—oh, miles away! And I suppose you'd like to know where, eh? Well, wouldn't we all. It'd be a different story if we knew just where "elsewhere" was. I've wanted to, for longest time now. Well, I'm finally onto something, though. Oh, I'll say! I mean just recent I picked up a pair of his trousers lying about, and—Can you keep a secret? Yes, well, I picked the trousers up and a pink *billet* slipped out of the pocket. Rose paper it was, scented rose paper. Signed, too: "Masha"! Masha? Masha? Now, who would you suppose Masha was, I wonder? Well, I tell you I've been beating my brains out over it for all of a fortnight now, and I'm still at my wits' end to know. . . . Ah! And what if I was to find out? Well, there'd be no flies on me then! Oh, I'll give him Masha, all right! He'll have it up to here with Mashas! . . . But goodness, where've I got to? Now, what was I talking about just now? Why, yes. Scape hens. Well! Now, I don't know about you, but speaking for myself, gracious, it could be the end of the world and I won't settle for any but a white scape hen. Oh, absolutely! "As the sin offering is white, so shall the sinner be made white." That's what Mother taught us. And I always follow in Mummy's way. Always. So that's why I must always have a white scape hen. Mind you, not just for myself. But for Volodia's sake and for the children's. Why, I have even got a small white pullet all picked out for the baby, my little Lola. A little white scape hen she'll have, all to herself. Won't you, sweet? I'll be offering it for her this Yom Kippur eve. Yes, I shall be doing it for all of them. For God help me, I'm the only one left to do it. The only Jew in the house to keep the faith. The only one who knows even how. . . . I shall be taking out my prayer book and open it to the words: "Man which dwelleth in darkness, in death's shadow," and I shall speak the words of the prayer, whirling the creature over my head the while: *zoys khalifosi, zoys temurosi, zoys kaporosi*—"This my substitute, This my replacement, This my atonement!" And I'll feel a great burden being lifted from my bosom. For it will be a white scape hen, purest white, AS GOD HATH ORDAINED IT.

Holiday Dainties

Monologue of a Vilna Housewife

They say, your modern breed nowadays, that is, and I wish the whole cheeky lot in a bad place, that people will be happy if a mishmash is made, like mine's thine, thine's mine? . . . Well, I say the day such a thing come to pass, we'll be all at sixes and sevens. It'll mean mischief. Like with bells on if you take my meaning. Just listen to what happened to me a year ago this First of Tabernacles last. Well, as you may know, I live down what's called Gitke Toyba's Alley? Yes, so I got my lodgings inside Goody Nehama's bit of a courtyard there? Only that courtyard is about as much Goody Nehama's as the alley is Gitke Toyba's, or say you and me was kissin cousins. Well, the courtyard is what's called your "X-squeeze-doory" courtyard, that's to say, with God's bounty five brothers and two sisters share it original. So the brothers died and the sisters died and they left children, which these was quite a few, so you couldn't divide it nor sell it nor pull it down nor even burn it, which God forfend because the whole street would go then and probably half the town. So they are as much stuck with it as I am with my troubles: no roof, no stairs, no stove—it's a henhouse, for pity's sake, which you are supposed to keep a fourposter in and pay all of two and a half ruble the month for, not counting change. And why's that? Heat's included, they say. Well, you only hope your worst enemy keeps breathing as much as anybody ever get round to heating up the place, except Sabbath and holidays; it's body heat keeps the place warm enough, they say. . . . Well, it's warm, I reckon. Too warm! Specially you consider what a blessed sight of lodgers clutter up the one place. There's your glazier, Shmerl, so that ain't but one; and your butcher, Pini Meir, so that ain't but two; and your boys' tutor, Naphtali, what's from that dinky place called Shmargon in these parts, so that ain't but three; and, course, there's Moishke, the widow man, so that ain't but four. But that one's as much a widow man as you're the governor. He only gets called the widow man because, preserve us, that's what he was once. Only praise God he's a widow man no more. Because the good Lord bless him since with an ill-tempered shrew for a wife, he best keep to himself for God's sake. . . .

Oh, and I forgot the scrivener, Reb Yoshe, and his daughter-in-law. Though you notice I said daughter-in-law and not the son? Well, it's because the son went away to war, so he give up his place to that fortunate pair everybody calls "the Bunimoviches." And know why? It's that he's lame and she's blind, so they both got Mammon's millions. Work the streets, don't you know. Anyhow, word is they got nice capital laid by, handsome nest egg by all accounts. Well, what you expect with both earning the way they do! Though that proofreading gent Reb Leybe don't really count, I suppose, for he's never home, anyhow, except it's weekends Sabbath. Very busy man Reb Leybe. Got more sidelines than you can shake a stick at. I mean, not counting his employment at the printer's, he's your dealer in pious books, your Tenth Man for worship, your errands-boy dispatcher, your psalm-sayer, your cheder boys' six-of-the-bester, your shofar blower, and God forbid somebody's in a dying way, he'll get you up a quorum for deathwatch prayers, too, and, well, other work along such lines mainly. Never fear though, his old lady don't sit about idle neither. Dips candles and sells horsebeans, for all I know. Only notwithstanding, the man must have devils for friends because he's still a pauper, anyhow. So what's the count now? Say a baker's dozen? Well that's your worshipers' quorum of ten easy plus a bonus even. So you think everything was fine and dandy, wouldn't you. And so it would be, too, if everybody was to worship at the same shul. Only this one does his praying away over Wilejka way, and that one does his away over Chandrikowa way. Well, now, if our glazier prays over at the Glaziers' Shul, and our butcher's glad enough to pray in Butchers' Row, and our tutor prays at the Lubavitchers' concern—well, that's only to be expected. Every buzzard after his kind, as we say. Only you, Mr. Widow Man, what in the nation possess you to be doing *your* praying plumb over at the Old Shul? Just to hear the one and only Sirota cantoring there? And don't give me that guff about being such a cockalorum "cornersewer" of pious songs neither, Mr. Smarty Pants, because I know better! For when it come to Sabbath hymnings at home? Damn the man!

Got the voice of a slaughtered rooster and preen himself on it! Why, the old fool so bust my eardrums with his cock-a-doodle-doo grace after meals Saturdays, it set my ears aching into Sunday morrow. Only you tell me what bounty the man ever receive at the hands of that shrew to be praising the Lord so almightily about it. Except it's the dirt she make him eat and the fat ear she give him. But talking to her you must give the woman her due. For she's right, you know: "A husband's like the Jewish exile," she says, "a trial which becomes a habit." Well, you have to hand it to her. The woman's got a head on her shoulders. . . .

Because it seems to me if I do have a bone to pick, it's more with the One Who I Am Unworthy of Mentioning by Name. After all, my husband's one of them, uh, whatcher-call-'ems—yeah, "pious sheep." Not worth much as mutton maybe, but he sure got an uncommon knack for woolgathering. I mean, the man's never done a useful lick of work that I know of. Though mooching around shul, "a-larning and a-praying," as they say, is more in his line. It's called doing the Lord's work. Well, it's a very noble line of work, only where's it leave me? Tucked up with a spade baking bagels, I guess. Though God knows. It may earn me a chair in heaven yet. So I carry on like the faithful ass of the adage so the table may be set royal for his nibs on Sabbaths and holidays. Why Sabbaths and holidays? Because weekdays he must make do with "Deborah-Esther's charitable board." That's to say, he must put his trust in Providence. Only I don't waste any bother over it personal, nor much care to, I reckon. All I know is, come Sabbath and holidays, there's challah loafs with fish, plus what meat I manage to scrape up, with the whole blessed spread with all the trimmings laid out and ready at table for him. And Feast Days? There's got to be holiday dainties for dessert, Feast Days. It's the rule. Passover is prune stew; Tabernacles is carrot stew.

So you like to hear a story? Tabernacles last, carrots suddenly come very dear. Dickens knows why. Seems they wasn't brought in, some such thing. Anyhow, they was dear. A kopeck a carrot maybe. So you think that might be an excuse? Only my husband cherish his holiday dainties more than anything. He will give up his fish and meat both, the whole blessed spread with all the trimmings, if you only let him have his holiday dainty. Course, all that is only in a manner of speaking, as the dainties come last anyhow, so he can afford to be generous with what he already ate. . . . Well, I brung home a basketful of carrots that day and got the fixings ready and set the pot to simmer on the stove. Only talk about taste! M'mm! It's not for nothing your quality will make an everyday meal of such things on weekdays; quality isn't fools, you know. Your quality enjoys everything on a weekday which our lot is partial to only on weekends Sabbath. . . . Well, the stew being done, I put it away in my corner of the stove—because don't you know everybody got his own corner in the stove in our place—after which I covered it over in ash and slipped out to my sister's to see how she was getting on. My sister Beiltse, preserve us, she's paralyzed in both legs, which she hasn't had the use of these ten years now. Though she manage to get by on the labor of her own hands, notwithstanding. Plucks poultry is what she does. That's to say, summer she plucks poultry, winter she knits toddlers' stockings and woolly hats. Well, now she lives over by Jews' Street, in Leybe Leyzer's courtyard; which it's also one of your "X-squeeze-doory" courtyards, which there must be about a couple of hundred families at least occupying it besides. Only you tell me how it's my fault I stopped by my sister's for half an hour once in a holiday? And don't think I didn't take a challah loaf and some fish along so the woman might know the taste of a real holiday feast, for once. And only perish the thought I should ever bring her a stranger's cooking and not my own which I cook myself personal. Nor have I to answer to my husband for it, so who else got anything to say to me about it, anyhow?

Though, being as how we don't hardly ever see each other the whole week, except it's Sabbath and holidays maybe, we got to chattering away and lost track of the time, kind of. Well, next thing, somebody come to fetch me home straight away because he already come back from shul—that is, my husband come back—and, gracious me, I hoped the man wasn't too upset because he must have been good and hungry by then and missing his dinner. Well, I tell you it was a terrible state what I dashed home in and found the sixth couple was already at table in the Tabernacles' hut; because all of us we got only this one bit of a hut put up in the courtyard which we can't all be at table feasting at once in, so we take it in turns like. Thank God, though, he didn't say anything to me, that is, my husband didn't. Well, he's not one of your "saying" sorts anyhow, is my husband. The man's more by way of being your quiet kind of a gent, if you take my meaning. Only I could tell he was out of sorts. See, I can always tell by his look: if he is looking into a book, it means he is out of sorts. That's to say, he's always looking into a book, only there's looking and there's looking: the other kind is one kind of looking, and this is another kind of looking, which it's different. Besides which, being he's a mite blind in his one eye, he never have what I care to call the look of holiday cheer about him, anyhow. Course, I set in to making my excuses straight away: this, that, my sister, we don't see each other all week—Nothing! Man wouldn't give an inch. Never look up from his pious writ even once. Hand him the dipper as per usual, aforemeals handwashings, put the fish on the table next. Tastes a treat. Come the dish of boiled doughcrumbs, also the bit of meat—Fine and dandy all around. But now the time come round for dessert, I spoke up. I mean the gent's still a man of pious larnin, so it's only right he come in for being treated civil on occasion. "Know what, dear?" I says to him, "got a dainty waiting which make your mouth water sure thing," I says, "fit for a king," I says, "and know what else?" I says, "It's even carrot stew!" . . . Well, now, hearing talk of dainties and carrot stew, he perk up marvelous. Actually put his book by. Me, I make for the stove. I give a look—Why, bless me if that pot wasn't clean as a whistle! Not a lick of dainty inside! No dainty! Dainty-dainty, where's my dainty? So I run about amongst the lodgers, here, there, yonder, asking round, "Anybody seen my dainty?" Dainty? Dainty? What dainty, where dainty, never heard of such a thing, they says! My luck, a neighbor got to feeling sorry for me along the way and said she knew where my dainty was. It's a goner, she says. A dainty no more. Passed on, and Godrest! Been ate up, oh, hours ago. Only she didn't care to say who done the deed, she says. Because she wanted no trouble with "sighted" folks. So that's when I knew it was the blind party which done it. Though when I look over my husband's way, you think the rogue wasn't poring over his book again? Not much he wasn't! And back to playing the clam again as always, what's more. . . .

Well, you may be sure I made a beeline for that fortunate pair everybody calls "the Bunimoviches": "Goodnessgracioussakes, woman," I says, "what the dickens you want of my dainty?" Says she, "What dainty?" Says I, "My carrot stew holiday dainty!" Says she, "Bless you, what you talking about anyhow? I had me a frutkick." . . . Well, didn't that get my dander up, just. Nerve of the woman! And me knowing all along, you see, she hadn't a carrot in the house to save her neck, so she goes and says she had a fruitcake. Why, that only mean she had a better holiday dainty than mine! Says I, "So you had a fruitcake?" Says she, "Frutkick!" Says I again, "Fruitcake?" Says she again, "Frutkick!" . . . Only that really was the last straw. I mean, if she'd at least tried denying it, say it wasn't her which done away with my dainty, then I may have thought: Well, now, maybe so, maybe it wasn't her which done it, but somebody else. But letting on like she had a fruitcake? Well, that take the cake! . . .

I mean, what's there to say more? A nasty business, very nasty. . . . And whose fault is it anyhow, if you take folks and stuff 'em together higgledy-piggledy like they was hens in a henhouse saving the difference, and just you try to do anything that way! But you only talk to *them,* to your cheeky modern breed, the same lot what's rarin' to bring them newfangled changes into our Old Shulyard only so there be a proper mine's thine, thine's mine, share-and-share alike, lovey-dovey mishmash there—and they got the gall to say that clever folks opine it's all to the good! . . . Well, I say we'll be all at sixes and sevens then, it'll mean mischief, like with bells on, only you be sure and have yourself a happy holiday anyhow, hear?

Goody "Purishkevich"

Containing
An Account of How a Widowed Jewish Lady Called
Goody, Who Makes Her Living Selling Wissotzky Tea
Door-to-door, Had, after Laboring Long and Hard, for a
Full Three Years in the Third or "Black" Duma, Obtained
at Last the Release of Her One and Only Son from Military
Service, Causing Her Entire Local Council To Be
Brought to Book, Lock, Stock, and Barrel,
and Receiving in Consequence
the Unfortunate Moniker of
"Purishkevich"
from Her Own Townsmen.
As Reported in One Go by Herself in Person.

Gracious sakes! What all you folks come crowding round for anyhow? Shoo! Go Home! That's right, show's over! Where you reckon you are, the theayter? Well, you won't get no clowning nor any your cock-and-bull stretchers from me, hear? Except I'm told there's a gentleman about, calls himself Mr. Sholem Aleichem, which he writes? Oh, you that same Mr. Sholem Aleichem, which he writes? Well, you make sure and get it all down. Only don't be getting writer's cramp doing it! Just you write up the whole town, mister, top to bottom. And don't you worry, they got it coming. Specially the quality, God's own gentry what believes the world been created only for themselves alone. Our likes must sweat and toil, live in misery, and they have only to buy their way out of every calamity and affliction with money. And they dast yet to make fun of a poor widow woman, which she earn a living by Wissotzky Tea. Supply

44

Wissotzky Tea door to door, I do. Which it's paid for by installments and puts bread on the table for me and my one chit of a child, my one and only son, which they was set to take away from me, through no fault of mine but of others. Well, just you listen to what kind of wickedness goes on in this world. For I don't reckon it ever happened since creation that anybody took away an only son, a woman's one chit of a child and only provider a widowed mother's got in her old age, which please God praise Wissotzky, she is proud to say she lives in the world. If you can call it living. Though you can call dying living if you care to stretch a point. Because what kind of living so-called you expect for your pound of tea, with competition being what it is, and you can't scarcely find a pauper left, which he ain't took to selling tea door to door these days. For a body can take a considerable beating if the competition drop his price by ten, so you bring yours down by fifteen, so he come down level to your fifteen, so you drop by twenty. But how long before it end? I'm not Wissotzky! Not before the bitter end, what you reckon? So all I got in prospect is my one provider in old age, my Moishe. Well, I ain't got but the one chit of a child, an only son which my husband left me with by way of inheritance, so called. Now, he's even a very good boy is my Moishe, which I can't complain about, strong, handsome, your normal kind of a boy, even. Only he never did take much to larning. What I mean is, he didn't take to it at all! Because you might whup the boy, wallop him all you want, and still he wouldn't take to it. Gracious sakes, what's to become of you, Moishe, I says to him; if you don't larn, don't write, you don't even pray—why, then, all what's left is hiring out for dogcatcher! Ever hear a wall talk? So I give him over to be a prentice workman, to a tailor, which I settled express with him, that he should teach my boy the tailoring trade. Well, yourself, sir, has seed more of needle and thread than my boy ever done with that man. All the boy done was to look after the baby night and day, or help the missus peel spuds, or be disposing of family wastewater and house slops and such. Why, you'd of reckon it was a beholden privilege if the boy was let to heat up the man's pressing iron for him, even. So I went and took him away from that tailor and give him over to a shoemaker. Which it turn out the man was madder than a meat ax, and only the smallest thing went wrong, he'd pick up a hammer and throw it at the boy, so it like to knock the child's brains out. So I went and took him away from that shoemaker and give him over to a gawdelpus bookbinder as never seen a lick of business nor had a piece of work in hand. So I went and

took him away from that gawdelpus bookbinder and give him over to a
watchmaker, which he was even a worse gawdelpus, as didn't fix watches
but broke them instead. Everybody said so. Now, that's all I needed,
wasn't it, him turning my son into a botcher same as himself? So then I
went and took him away from that watchmaker and give him over to a
lacemaker, he should larn him tatting, that's to say, larn him lacemaking.
And I drew up the indentures with him myself, with the lacemaker, that
is, for a term of two years; that's to say, for two years the boy shall weave
lace for him without pay, and in the third year, that is, after the boy
already become good at tatting, he shall receive something by way of a
small wage as well. Well, with God's help I come on a proper workman
this time, one as even was partial to his drink. Which is why he also
larned my son to weave lace in considerable less time than I reckon I'm
standing here talking with you. Well, the boy took a real liking to the
work, and in half a year my Moishe become a sure-thing lacemaker.
Though what good it do me, anyhow, if the boy must work full two
years at no pay? But signed is sealed, I reckon. So with God's help, the
two years run out. Well, it's easy to say, two years run out! For if I got
through them two years, I must have an iron constitution to have done
it. And even I did get through that time, you think that was the end of it,
finish? It's only then you must look round for a job for him somewhere
or scare up custom for the boy somehow. Only where you got work these
days, anyhow? What you reckon, drunk loses sober finds? And here's
myself, a woman alone, trotting about with that pound of tea door to
door, and the competition being so fierce, and, why, I even gone bankrupt. Proper Jewish gent he was, too, family man. Which he went and
order three and a half pound of tea from me on account, that's to say,
paid for by installments. And then one night he up and done the moonlight flit, gone, they say, to America. Well, there's ways I rather have seen
the man gone which was maybe a sight more permanent! I thought the
whole world come tumbling down on me then. Thing like that? Three
and a half pound of tea, at two ruble twenty? And you must keep it dark
yet. Because if Wissotzky was to find out, I'd gone bust? Well, it do
wonders for my credit, wouldn't it! So what you reckon God do? He
says, "Goody, you think you got griefs now? Well, just you wait if you
looking for *real* griefs. Because you got a call-up notice coming next."
. . . Where call-up? What call-up? I mean, the one chit of a child a poor
widowed mother's got for a son, which please God praise Wissotzky—
but where in creation you ever hear the like, gracious sakes! Where's

God? Where's conchuns? Only go and cry mercy to the winds! And with all that trouble aborning, my boy Moishe got to be of an exact age with his nibs our parish squire's three grandsons, which is his by three daughters. Why, I only wisht their nibs was all brung low by the boils, the buboes, and the ague together and in such a place as they couldn't stand up nor walk about nor lie down nor sit down in it. Though folks did warn me, "Goody," they says, "you just watch out they don't make your boy the patsy for His Nibs's grandsons, hear?"—Huh, how you reckon, patsy? Why, my boy's the one chit of a son and only provider a poor widowed mother's got, which please God praise Wissotzky, whereas that one's the squire. Why, he's rich, he's pow'ful, he got millions! Unless, preserve us, you're saying there's no God in the world! Only talk about the power of money? For one by one they commence calling in each of His Nibship's grandsons. First the one, whonk "UNFIT!" Then the next, whonk "UNFIT!" Well, sure, I took to feeling uneasy, what you reckon? Because if that third party was pronounced unfit, then heaven help my Moishe! And just my luck, as if this wasn't grief enough, my Moishe bless him is what you call a great big strapping fella and never a pip nor blemish on him anywhere. Why, he's more in the way of being a man, really. Though that's not to say the squire's grandsons was lying at death's door, exactly. Only they got rejected by the doctor. Because the minute that man seed that it's a niblet what's come through the door, then it's whonk "UNFIT!"—next! And go do him something. Well, you reckon I take such a thing lying down? So straight away I hie me over to the county princident, and I says to him: "Your Washup!" I says, "Two items on our squire's bill of goods been rejected already. Now, God forbid, any more such item gets rejected, it may even come down to my Moishe, mayn't it? And my Moishe's the one and only provider a widowed mother's got in her old age." . . . But the man fell into a most savage rage and give orders to chuck me out of the county orifice. And sure enough, even before the last of the squire's niblets gets called in, the doctor went whonk "UNFIT!"—next! And my boy's led in, led out, shorn, sworn, and it's lefright-lefright-lefright! And, oh, lordy, my Moishe's already been marched off clear over to Kharkov ways, which that's only like good-bye, so-long forever, and don't forget to say your prayers, sonny! Well, you reckon I take such a thing lying down? So I hie me over to the county princident and whistle him up such a good morning as might set his ears ringing into next week: "So!" I says to him, "When it comes to His Nibs's little niblets you go ahead and reject them. But when talk's only of the one chit of a son and only provider a widowed mother's got, which please God praise Wissotzky? I mean, gracious sakes! Where's conchuns? Where's God?" Well, you don't reckon he didn't say, chuck the ole Jewbiddy out? Only this ole Jewbiddy never use the post when she can ride, even it's to the Govement House away over Kharkov ways, to see the govenor. Which straight away I come into him, I fell at his feet: Your Washup, I says, listen! The squire's all three grandsons been rejected, and my Moishe what's the one chit of a son and only provider a poor old widowed mother's got, which please God praise Wissotzky. I mean, gracious sakes! Where's God! Where's conchuns! Well, he heard me out, the govenor, but he said he wanted it on paper. Says I: "Your Washup! What you want papers for? I've made myself quite clear, I should think. So you just go ahead, make your inquiries, and you'll see what I told is God's honest truth." Says he, "On paper, on paper!" Says I: "Your Washup, sweetheart! I ain't one of your biddies as has got much to do with papers anyhow nor is given to informing on other folks, neither. All I meant was to tell my grievance: gentry gets rejected whilst poor, only sons gets taken. Gracious sakes! Where's God? Where's conchuns?" Says he: "God give me strength! What's the woman want of me now?" Says I: "She wants that truth will out, and her only provider be given back to her. Nothing more besides. Heaven and earth have swore the truth shall rise as doth oil on water." So then he got good and mad, the govenor, and ordered the ole Jewbiddy chucked out. Well, the ole Jewbiddy wasted no time and sold off what she had. And she set out to find the truth, making straight for St. Petesburg to do it. In Petesburg you got your mister of war and mister of interior and your synod together. And even if the czar must be seen, you reckon I wouldn't find the way? A body may even come before God with the truth. So I come to St. Petesburg. Only no sooner I arrive than the whole rigmarole commence, what with all the running round to obtain what's called your right of residence there. Well, I says to myself, I says, being chucked out of town don't scare me; I fear none but God, I says, and the czar, I says. Otherwise, I fear no man, for I walk in the way of the truth, I says. Only meantime a body has got to eat, as it wouldn't do to be hawking up my last in this place. Now, you know I'm not accustomed to handouts. Only question was, what to do? Well, I had me an idea. You see, St. Petesburg isn't what you call your average sort of backwater exactly as there's plenty of Jewish folks live there, thank goodness, and Wissotzky Tea is known in Petesburg even better than everywhere else, maybe. Well, seeing as I got so much to do with govement orifices and with govement 'ficials anyhow, I begun delivering Wissotzky Tea to their door, paid for by installments. And please God praise Wissotzky, I manage to scrape by on the earnings, just, and even put by a bit to send to my Moishe in the regiment, a ruble, even two, sometimes. Only that right-of-residence business was the one fly in the ointment. Now, you see, that was bitter. Be queen, I would, if only I'd of had that right of residence in Petesburg. But as I had only griefs and troubles, not right of residence, it was more bitter than death. It come to the point they was even set to deport me the way out of Petesburg for certain. And they'd of done it, too, bound me over in "chains and bilboes," as they say, right and proper! Except merciful Providence send me that fine noble creature, proper lady she was, as wrote on them papers for me, an' God grant her long life for it, too. More angel than human, really. Which besides getting me out of a considerable sight of troubles, she acquaint me with that Mr. Pargament. You heard of him, surely? At the Duma? One of them Parlorment gents as use to talk there? Heart of gold, that man, a real gentleman—which I only wisht him a bright Eternity in the next world. I mean, after all what he done for me? Why, the poor man fair kilt himself for me. Give me a letter, he did—and to such lofty gents as it was a beholden privilege only to be allowed to come into them, even. Which each one heard me out to the end and sent me along to the next party; which they sent me along to the next one after that; and that one, to a third party; and each time I be sent higher and higher. Till I finally come into the Duma. Which I begun going to the Duma regular every day pretty much, even twice a day, sometimes, listening to everything what was said there. Now you want talk? Prime talker, Mr. Pargament. Well, sure, everybody talk there, anyhow, but the best—that was Pargament. Him, when he stood up to talk, well, now, I tell you he'd pitch into the business with such a passion the walls was like to give way and the stones to melt. Wasn't no piker, that Pargament! Which it stirred up such enemies against him in the Duma that—well, what you want me to say? You never knowed such a bunch of atrocious agintators! And screamers? Why, they'd set on him like a pack of mad dogs and be kicking up such a awful monstrous din, I couldn't scarcely keep to my seat looking down on it (for I always had my own place in the Duma, away upstairs, looking down). It's enough to be only thinking about the man, for it to bring tears to a body's eyes even now. You simply cannot imagine what a rare gem, what a prince that Mr. Pargament was. And talk about your angels from heaven—

well, of course, that goes without saying. I mean, the man would drop
everything, business, guests, whatever, only to take the time to larn all
about what my boy Moishe been writing to me. Well, what the boy got
to write about, anyhow? My Moishe only write that thank goodness he
was coming along fine in the militree service, and his orificers was very
satisfy with him. But his sturgeon-major give him trouble. That fool goy
be the death of him yet, he says, all the time putting the bite on him for
money. Well, sure, the boy swear he got no money. Only that sturgeon-
major won't believe him. Says all Jews got money, anyhow, which I wisht
he only got the chills and fevers with Pharaoh's plagues together. So
how you like that for a sturgeon-major? So he laugh, that's to say, Mr.
Pargament did. Oh, he did like a good laugh. Always game for a joke,
that man. Like I recall once how I come to him, and he invite me to sit
and asks, as he was like to do, how I am getting on in Petesburg? So I
says to him, "Why, bless you, sir, I only wisht all 'postates was getting
on as I been." Well, he practically fall off his seat, laughing so hard.
"Well, it seems," says he, "you didn't know I was an apostate myself,
ma'am?" "Is that so?" I says. "Well, now, I shouldn't mind 'postates such
as yourself, sir, even if they was a million. Though, however many 'postates there may be in this world, I'd sooner see every one in Perdition
before one hair on your head come to any harm." So he laugh even
harder then. So how anybody reckon a man like that will up and die on
you? And so sudden, too! Well, what can I tell you, my friend? Though
I know I hadn't ought to say it, I believe that even when my own poor
husband Godrest was laid out, I didn't shed so many tears as on the day
they told me Mr. Pargament died. I shouldn't wish any father such grief.
I can only say when Pargament pass away, I just become sick and tired
of St. Petesburg and the Duma and the whole world together. If Pargament was around, it surely be different. Well, sure now, your Messers
Nusselovich and Friedman are mighty fine gentlemen, too. That nobody
can deny, nor should I, either. Only Messers Nusselovich and Friedman,
they wasn't no Pargament. No, sir. Like when I come pleading to that
Mr. Nusselovich or Mr. Friedman, all they say is they cannot do anything
for me because it's the law, and they cannot go against the law. Says I,
now, where you got a law as says of a squire, which he's rich, which he's
pow'ful, which he got millions, that his precious by-blows gets rejected,
one after the other, the while a only son gets took instead to serve in their
place, which he's the one chit of a child and only support a poor widow's
got, which please God praise Wissotzky? Well, go on, I says, I'm game!

You just show me where you got such a law. A Duma, I says, gracious sakes, a whole blessed Parlorment, I says, with such a lot of folks and all of 'em talking and all of 'em shouting and all of 'em name-calling. So why, I says, isn't there one amongst them as will take a poor widow woman's part, I says, which please God praise Wissotzky? Got nothing to say, eh? What's wanted of you is another Purishkevich, I says, a Jewish Purishkevich, which *he'll* larn them gentry a thing or two, all right! Why, it's been pretty near three years since I come to St. Petesburg and been knocking about in the Duma, I says. And in all that time, I says, has anybody thought to speak up even once about this mortal wrong, I says, of taking away a poor mother's one measly prop, which please God praise Wissotzky is her only support in old age? Fact is, it happened only once, in all that time, that some nobby Rumanian actually up and come out with a whole rigmarole concerning "militree conscripshon," as they calls it. Well, naturally, I only hear "militree conscripshon," and I'm all ears. Oho, thinks I, thank God! Truth will out. High time, too! Only what? They dish out such a load of fool rubbage, you bust a bladder hearing it. Well, I only reckon it come from all the fuss I kicked up when I got in to see that pair of govement misters, the mister of war and interior. Only what come of it in the end? Big fat goose egg, that's what! Try this one on for size: "What's wanted," the man says, "is a special conscripshon for Jews, which it's by money." Hear a notion? "Jews," he says, "ought to be let to buy their way out of militree service. You wants out, you pays up!" . . . But that only mean their poxy nibs, the gentry, will benefit all over again, don't it? And won't poor wretched paupers be serving again instead, which they are poor widows' only sons besides? Gracious sakes! Where's God! Where's conchuns! Then it happened. The Almighty God wrought a miracle, and all blazes broke loose with everybody shouting and stomping, so you thought they all gone crazy. And the man who raised the most cain, as per usual, was Purishkevich. Well, that atrocious villian, which God only mend him to aitch, was all set to show, with witnesses and evidence, he said, that Jews don't serve in the militree. No, sir. Not one Jew in militree service, he says. Well, that was the last straw! It stuck in my craw, and my dander was way up. Gracious sakes, my one and only support already been serving in the militree upwards of three years—even got a decoration to prove it—and along come that dern high-strutting cockerel, Purishkevich, which he dast to declare such a thing before all the world and to all them misters of state. Now, you don't reckon I take that lying down? So I straight away heaved myself up on my hind legs, calling out, from away upstairs, in the gallery, good and loud, so the whole dern Duma might hear:

WELL, I NEVER!? ....
....

So what happened, you like to know? Oh, nothing much. Except they seen me the way out of that Duma, right enough. Even marched me down to the police station. And they was set to bind me over in chains and bilboes to deport me out of Petesburg, too. Only I said to them, I says, being chucked out of town don't scare me one bit. I fear none, I says, but God and the czar. Otherwise, I fear no man, for I walk in the way of the truth. I got the same right to the Duma as any of you, I says. You talk about militree service, but that's all it is, talk. Whereas my boy serve the czar, notwithstanding he's an only son. Well, they'd met their match, all right. Their luck, though, I didn't bother hanging about Petesburg over the Passover, whilst there was that big to-do at the Duma over the blood business—you know, about Jews using blood on the Passover? Because I'd of larn them a thing or two about who has got blood on his hands: us, or them? Only they got off easy, this time. For I had to go back home for the holiday as word been sent round to me express just then, from the Mister's of War Orifice, that my boy Moishe already been sent home from the regiment. Plus word was that Their Washups, the county princident and the doctor, fact the whole dern Local Council, lock, stock, and barrel, been brought to book and was bound over for trial. Seems one of them 'ficial govement audits was held. And turn it out they was running a regular factory there—for making them "white cards," for militree exemptions, don't you know? And pious Jewish and Christian gentry—which it happened they was also flush—was declared unfit for militree service. Whereas poor, unfortunate folk, even such as is one and only sons, was made to serve. Well, that's all finished with now. No more privileged gentry! The party's over. Because everybody be equal in this town from now on. But you are a man what writes, sir, so *you* tell me. No, I mean it, mister, you tell me yourself! Am I deserving of being made a joke of by everybody, and any time two folks set to jawing, they must drag my name into it and make it a party of three? Which I shouldn't mind so much, anyhow, because they can laugh themselves silly for all I care. Only gracious sakes! What did I ever do to deserve being called Purishkevich for, which I wisht all of my ills was on that evil man's head instead? "Goody Purishkevich" is what they call me. Ever hear such cheek? I mean, you'd think at least they'd have the decency to say "saving the difference"! Oh, I tell you, Mister, it's a town of jokers, naught but pudd'nheaded fools and ne'er-do-wells. So don't you reckon they all deserves to be written up about, top to bottom, big and small together? Well, just you make sure to write 'em up good, Mr. Sholem Aleichem. Write 'em up, so the whole world may know them. Write 'em up, so nary a one be left which been unwritten up about!

The Squire's h'Omelette

Lithuanian Dialogue

"**Hinda, know wot?** Pawn my besht Shabbath coat, for I am pow'ful determine to be rich!"

"Wot brung thish on, I wonder?"

"Been over to Hish Washup the Squire's is wot. Y'know, when they brung in his h'omelette, oh, it do look a handshome treat!"

"Coo! Wot they do it up in? Shequins and shpangles?"

"Cahn't shay I notish. Do tashte a treat tho' . . . M'm!"

"Gwan! Yuh din't ate it?"

"Yeah! An' mebbe I'm Hish Washup's son and law?"

"So how you reckon it tashte a treat?"

"Got eyes, don't I? Tell a mile off it melt in y'mouth like putter in the pan!"

"Shquires! Wot don't such folksh *not* got, I wonder?"

"Headaches, I s'pose! Know wot I like to shee y'make for once, Hinda? . . . M'm! . . . M'm! . . . Just for once shee y'make me a h'omelette!"

"Zat so? Well, try another!"

"Aw, why not? Only thish once, please?"

"You took mad recent—or what?"

"M'm! . . . M'm! . . . Oh, I'm sure I shall perish otherwise, Hinda! Do make me a h'omelette, please?" . . .

"Godelpus! What from? Got any idee?"

"Me? How'd I know?"

"So wot y'talkin' for? Fu'sht off, they—that's to say, your shquires —they bung in who knows how much putter!"

54

"Forgit the putter, long as it's a h'omelette!"

"Worse luck! Wot of milk, where I git milk from?"

"Forgit the milk, long as it's a h'omelette!"

"Fine! And eggs? No making a h'omelette without puttin' eggs in fu'sht, is there!"

"Eggs? Where's it say 'eggs'? Besides, it don't take only one egg which to beat up to make a h'omelette."

"Done! So where I git it? There use to be a egg about, excep' half the yolk'sh gone on shtuffin' and a bit of the white on the Shabbath loafs." . . .

"Now, now! If only you set y'mind to it, Hinda, I'm sure you'll find wot from to make a h'omelette!"

"So, wot from? The shell? Half a egg!"

"Well, I dunno. Tho' I should think you was a bit more the houshwife than me."

"Houshwife, he says! Tho' praps with a bit of flour?" . . .

"Sold! Flour's prime, long as it's a h'omelette."

"Oh, ain't you a wit! So where I git flour from?"

"Aw, wot's a bit of flour to find for such as yesse'f?"

"For such as yesse'f, y'mean! . . . Tho' praps buckwheat?"

"Sold! Buckwheat's prime, long as it's a h'omelette."

"Worse luck! No buckwheat. Tho' praps a onion?"

"Sold! Onion's prime, long as it's a h'omelette."

"Lordy, forgot! Ain't none. Do got a bit of garlic tho'." . . .

"Sold! Garlic's prime, long as it's a h'omelette."

"A h'omelette he says! Tho' wot shall I grease up the pan with?"

"Whatever! long as it's a h'omelette——"

● ● ●

"There, have y'fool h'omelette! . . . Mebbe it put a cork on that sinful hankerin' awhile . . . Saw it at the shquire's, he shez! An' I shpose if Hish Washup went and cut off his nose, you be havin' yours off too! Monkey sees, monkey does! Go ahead have your h'omelette, all of a sudden. . . . Here's the pitcher! Wash y'hands already, y'h'omelette's done!"

"——Wot? h'omelette done, already? Now y'see, Hinda, that's why I love y'so! . . . Rich folks thinks they are the only ones wot enjoys h'omelettes. Handshome, just handshome! M'm! Garlic shmells a treat, too! Prime, Hinda, just prime! Wisht I had one every day . . . M'm! . . . M'm! . . . Tho' y'know wot, Hinda? . . . M'm! . . . M'm! . . . Y'h'omelette ain't quite . . . wot's the word? Well it sheem a mite sour, y'ask me, nor nearly shalty enough, and shticky as well, come to that. . . . M'm! . . . M'm! . . . Well, you'll forgive me for shaying so . . . M'm! . . . M'm! . . . But my God it tashte foul—*ph'too!* . . . Devil knows why rich folks ever pother workin' up a passion over sich a thing!"

Men's Talk

Advice

"Oh, by the way, my dear, there's a young man been coming round every morning, noon, and night for three level days now and finding you always out. Just frantic to see you, he says!" That was the greeting waiting for me upon arrival once from one of my trips away.

"Writer, with a 'creation,' no doubt!" was the thought that immediately came to mind, and I sat down at my desk and set to work—when, hark! sure enough, there was the doorbell, door opened, somebody shuffling about out there, dropping his galoshes, coughing, blowing his nose—yes, all unmistakable signs of a writer in the offing. Oh, I do wish the fellow would quit dawdling and show his face! By and by, though, he came in. And, making me a pretty reverence, that's to say, retreated a couple of paces, bowing from the waist, and, rubbing palm in palm, introduced himself, giving out a contrived fanciful name of a sort that, once it is uttered, gets promptly mislaid and slips irretrievably out of mind!

"Yes, well, do sit down. How can I be of service to you, sir?"

"I come to you on an urgent errand, sir. That's to say, urgent as regards myself, most urgent, really, you might even say, vital, and only you, sir, so I reckon, will understand it. I mean, seeing as you write such an awful lot, sir, I should reckon you must know everything, sir, must surely be knowledgeable in all things. So I reckon, anyway. That's to say, not reckon, sir, but I'm absolutely certain of it."

I sat, contemplating the person of my visitor. Your very type of a provincial Jewish gentleman of letters. Your author. Your pale sort of a young person, with great saucerlike black eyes, always begging compassion, pleading with you: "Oh, please, please, kind sir, take pity on a poor lost soul." I do not like eyes of that sort. Eyes of that sort scare me: they

59

never live, are never merry, are always a sight too much in an introspective reverie. I hate eyes of that sort.

"Oh, very well, show us what you've got," I said to him, and I leaned back in the chair, waiting for him to pull out a fat roll of manuscript from his breast pocket: doubtless one of your tedious stretched-out three-decker novels that go on forever, or a play in four acts with a cast of characters all called Murtherson, Goodfellow, Piousheart, Bittersprig, and other such names that are a dead giveaway about the sort of folk you are being asked to have any truck with. . . . Or must it be another cycle of New Songs of Zion that we are in for:

> Yonder towards the Mount he hies him,
> Yonder where the eagle flies in,
> Yonder where the olive thrives in,
> Yonder where the Prophets bend an humble knee
> Before Divine Eternity. . . .

I dare say I'm familiar enough with such verses and rhymes that repeat on you like a bad meal, make your eyes swim and your ears buzz, and leave behind an awful emptiness in the heart and a strange barrenness in the soul.

But do you know—this time I was dead wrong. The young man had *not* reached for his breast pocket nor did he pull a roll of papers out from anywhere else nor even suggest an inclination to read me out a novel or a play or a New Song of Zion. What he did do was set his shirt collar right and give me a couple of propitiatory coughs before addressing me so:

"Well, you see, sir, I've come here to see you, that's to say, I only came to talk to you about my troubles, sir, heart to heart, and obtain your advice. Because you write such an awful lot, sir, I reckon you must know everything and are the only one that can advise me, I mean, properly, so whatever you may tell me, I'll be sure to do it, you have my solemn word as to that. Only your pardon, sir, truly, do I presume on your time, sir?"

"Oh, it's quite all right. Do go on, do go on," I soothed, feeling now genuinely relieved of an intolerable burden. And my young visitor edged his chair nearer to the desk and proceeded to pour out his troubled heart to me, in an easy manner at first, and ever more passionately then as he progressed.

"Well, you see, the fact is, sir, myself, I'm from what you call a small town. That's to say, not all that small a town, but more in the way of a big town, really, more of a city, you might say; only living here as you do, sir, I reckon by your lights you would incline to call it only a small town. I have a notion, too, that you must know the place pretty well, only, I am not naming names because it wouldn't take only that much for you to be writing about it, and that wouldn't suit me for all sorts of reasons. . . . What line I'm in? . . . H'm. . . . Well, I'm in . . . well, the fact is, I don't do much of anything, really, still board with my in-laws, you see, that's to say, not so much board with them as we live together with them, lap of luxury, you might say, because, what with her being an only daughter, that's to say, her being their one and only offspring, sir, and them having no other children besides, but only the one daughter, they can afford to keep us for the next ten years, pretty much, because you see they are quite prosperous, you might say rich, even, and down our ways—well, they can pass for being very rich there, more of monstrous rich, even, because nobody can touch them for being rich down our ways. Only I have a notion, too, that you must certainly have heard of my father-in-law. So I reckon, anyway. Only I am not naming names as it wouldn't be proper. Fact is, though, he is your sort of gent that is partial to making an almighty splash everywhere, so people might know him. Like the time there was the big fire which burnt down half Bobruisk two years back, that's to say, back in 'ought-two? Well, he gave away a bundle that time, and then, last year, when they had themselves the big pogrom over in Kishinev ways, he went and put his name down for the biggest donation of just about anybody. At home he won't give even a mite of charity, for it's only abroad that he likes making a big splash where folks are sure to hear it. I mean, after all, the man is nobody's fool. He knows everybody in town kowtows to him as is, anyway—so why waste any bother on their account? Which is why he reckons he can get away with cocking a fig at the whole town and give nothing away besides. He is not your giving sort is my father-in-law. He cannot give. Says so himself, even. I cannot give, he says. Anybody comes to him for charitable donations, he goes dead stiff and says: 'What, again? Come for handouts again? Well, here's the keys, gentlemen, and there's the cabinet, help yourself, take all you want!' . . . Only you really don't suppose he takes the keys out then? Because, with respect, sir, you'd be wrong! Keeps the keys to that cabinet hid away somewhere in a desk drawer anyway and got the key to the drawer tucked well away somewhere else besides. That's the sort of person my father-in-law is. Well, it's only as you'd expect. For the name you earn is the name you get. Because between you and me, sir, pretty near everybody in town calls him the Old Hog. . . . But generally only behind his back, though, because it is sickening the way people will suck up to him to his face. Though he reckons it is all only honest coin, anyhow, and pats his belly preening himself on it and living on velvet the while. Did I say, on velvet? On velvet, and how! Because there's living and there's living, and a world of difference between. I mean, judge for yourself: the man never lifts so much as his little pinky, lives like a lord, eats like a horse, sleeps like a top—what more could anybody want? Done snoozing, he'll order the buggy hitched and brought round so he can take an idle afternoon's turn or two over the mud with it. Come evening then, his clutch of cronies from town will forgather, repeating outrageous old slanders and retailing new scandals which nobody believes anyway, telling black lies about everything and everybody in town, and generally having themselves a high old time all round clowning at everybody else's expense. And then the big samovar gets wheeled in, and the time's come for His Nibs to sit down to another game of dominoes with Shmuel Abba. That's Shmuel Abba the town kosher slaughterer, who is a young chap that notwithstanding he has managed yet to hold on to his original side curls and face whiskers, has fallen pretty well in with the new ways and wears spiffy white shirt collars and walks about with a high shine on his shoes and is never one to shy away from the ladies and has got a way with a song, as well, and takes out subscriptions to Russian newspapers and plays a crackerjack game of chess and is the world's absolute whiz at dominoes. And when them two sit down to a game of dominoes, they will be at it all night into next morning with the rest looking on and yawning fit to yank your jaw off its hinges! Well, you'd think any damn fool would know enough to get up then and make for his room and sit down to a book or read the paper there. But no! And why? Ain't fitting. I mean, you can't just get up in the middle like that and be walking out on a guest, now can you. Because a thing like that only gets his back up. My father-in-law's back, that is. That's to say, he won't say anything; only he'll puff himself up and glare daggers, and then you can be talking yourself blue in the face and you won't get a word out of him. Nor from his wife, either—because she only follows his lead anyway. And that loving pair being now of one mind anent yours truly, then it's *her* turn to be glaring daggers—well, after all, her being their only daughter, mummy

and daddy's one and only offspring, sir, and them being the light of her
life, as is she of theirs, to say nothing of being the apple of their eye,
forever petted and fretted over, so if she is ever feeling off color or goes
the least bit queer—then it's always, oh, my God, go and fetch the doctor,
and heaven help us all! So it's no wonder a creature such as herself
reckons the whole world must be made only for her own pleasure and
nobody else's. And her being short on wit don't help matters any. That's
to say, talking to her, in only the ordinary way, you would think she was
no fool, no fool at all, clever you might even say, sharp, even, and I mean
really sharp, got a man's head on her shoulders, that woman! Trouble is,
she is spoilt, spoilt rotten, a wild goat that won't browse where she is
tied. All day long and half the night it's hee-hee this and ha-ha that, and
next thing, she's thrown herself down on the bed and is bawling like an
infant. 'What's wrong, dearest? What's ailing you? Why are you crying,
darling? What do you want?' Not a word! . . . But never mind. Because
if that was all there was to it, it would be only half a misery. For if a wife
is set to crying, she'll cry until she has cried herself out. But then, you
see, you haven't reckoned with the fly in the ointment—the mother-in-
law, that is. Because the minute that woman gets wind of the business,
she'll come swooping down with her Turkey shawl thrown over her
shoulders and her handwringings and that godawful deep-voiced yammering singsong she'll be putting on when she's on about something—
got the voice of a man, that woman has—and be saying: 'What is it,
child? Is it that wretch again, that awful brute, that wicked, wicked man?
Oh, woe is me! What cares he that I've only the one good eye left in my
head? What's eating him now—stomach giving him trouble again, got
the nosebleeds maybe?' . . . blah, blah, yap, yap, on and on, like meal
pouring out of a sack! And it seems to me it won't ever stop, won't ever
end, sawing away at my heart, gnawing at my soul, and I get the sudden
urge then to snatch that Turkey shawl off of the woman's shoulders,
crumple it up in my fists, jump up and down on it, shred the thing into a
thousand bits and pieces. Only now I really think of it, I'm sure I can't
say why I should have anything against the woman's Turkey shawl,
anyway, in particular. I mean, it's only your ordinary variety of Turkey
shawl, which it's brought over from Brody, mainly. Know the kind I
mean? Those big checkered, polka-dotted old things which come all
painted up gaudy in black and red and yellow and green and white
checks and polka dots and have got these very, very long fringes all
about." . . .

"You'll forgive my asking, young man," I said, interrupting him at full flood, "but it seems to me you wanted my advice about something?"

"Your pardon, sir, truly," he said, resuming after catching his breath. "Do I presume on your time, sir? But rest assured it was all necessary to the matter in hand, sir, for it was done so you may be the better acquainted with the family, sir, with the sort of people they are, because it is only when you have some acquaintance with the family, with those people, sir, that you can understand my situation exactly. . . . So the minute she goes the least bit queer, that's to say, when my wife goes queer, preserve us, then the mother raises a clamor, and my father-in-law orders the buggy out and sends to fetch the doctor, that's to say, sends for the new doctor—because that's really how we call him back home, the new doctor—though, naming no names, I might sooner have wished the devil had fetched him away instead! . . . So there, sir, is where my business with you really begins, that's to say, the matter I have been meaning to tell you about and obtain from you such advice and good counsel on the subject as you may have to offer."

My young visitor paused now to mop the perspiration from his face and edged himself a bit nearer, picking up something on the way to hold in his hands, for there are people who cannot talk without holding something in their hands because they are otherwise incapable of telling you a story. I keep a collection of handsome *objets* and pretty little curios set out on display on my writing table, among them a little bicycle, which is also by way of being a cigar cutter. It is a very great favorite with visitors, so anybody coming in to see me must inevitably seize upon it and begin toying with it. My young visitor, proving no exception, also picked up the little bicycle with which he was evidently much taken. At first he contented himself with contemplating it while he talked, then he took hold of it, then tried spinning its wheels, till at last the little bicycle never left his hands, and, thus, he took up his narrative again.

"Yes, now about the new doctor. You know, it is hard to say which there is a greater abundance of in our town, dogs or doctors, for we have plenty to spare of both and then some. Because there are your Christian doctors and there are your Jewish doctors and then there are your doctors in only a small way of business and, lest we forget, there are your Zionist doctors, as well, that's to say, doctors whose first order of business is Zionism. But the doctor I'm telling you about in particular is still only a very young doctor yet, hometown boy, don't you know, son of a tailor, that's to say, that his father used to be only a tailor—only he really isn't a tailor anymore because how would it look him being only a tailor with a doctor for a son? Or so *he* thinks. Only what I say is, how would it look with the son being a doctor and having only a tailor for a father, and not just any old tailor, but what's called your 'tailor amongst tailors'? That's to say, taken all in all this is only your pint-sized, loud-mouthed, runty sort of a Jewish gent that likes walking about in a cheap padded-cotton caftan and has got a cast in one eye and a finger out of joint and with a clapper in his head for a mouthpiece that is set to clapping nonstop for, oh, just four-and-twenty hours, day and night, jabbering on about 'Coo, you oughtta sheed wot practish my doctor got yeshtiddy! Lordy, wot practish my doctor got! Ain't no flies on *my* doctor!' And if that wasn't trouble enough, the doctor happens also to be a male midwife, that's to say, the town obstetrician, so if there is ever a domestic secret anywhere, it won't keep long but is instantly noised about all over town by that walleyed tailor with the crooked finger, and woe betide either wife or maid who should fall into that doctor's hands, for she must surely fall into the tailor's mouth as well. . . . Because, you know, it once happened that a girl in town. . . ."

"You'll forgive my asking, young man," I said, interrupting at full flood again, "but it seems to me you wanted my advice about something?"

"Your pardon, sir, truly, do I presume on your time, sir? I only started out by telling you about the doctor because it's him that has brought about my ruin! If it wasn't only for that man, I'd be wanting for nothing in this life. Because, look, what do I want for otherwise of the good life? I mean, here I've got me a sweet little wife, what's called a "real looker," sir, a great beauty you might even say, nor have we got any children, so what with her being an only daughter, that's to say, their one and only offspring, sir, why then in the fullness of time, of which I wish them nothing short of a hundred and twenty years, which is only their due, sir, she stands to get all of it, that's to say *I* stand to get all of it, to say nothing of social position, sir, because thank God that in matters of precedence, sir, the son-in-law of a town squire, that's to say, of the richest and most powerful Jewish gentleman in the neighborhood, never wants for any of it—touch wood—neither when it comes to first recitals of the Prophets at shul upon the Sabbath or holidays nor receiving first collations at circumcisions, and come Feast of Tabernacles, with the citron fruit and willow branch, I am always first behind His Worship: that's to say, naturally, the cantor always comes first, then the rabbi, then my father-in-law, and then myself with all the rest tagging along behind. And even at the bathhouse (saving the difference!), when I have taken my clothes off and come in naked (saving your presence!), the bathhouse keeper will make a great show of running before me then, bellowing, 'Gangway, gen'men, all make way for His Washup's Son and La-a-a-wr!' But I swear to you that it does embarrass me, sir, because I hate it! Though hate is maybe a bit strong. Because everybody likes being flattered, and I don't know as anybody ever turned down a privilege. Only trouble is, it has just gone too far, sir. I mean why all the fuss, anyway? Just because of being his worship's son-in-law? So let them be sucking up to him and welcome to it, let them be slobbering all over him, only begging your pardon because, truly, sir, they are all savages, plain ignorant savages, but I am made to sit with them anyway on account of not being allowed to keep company with just anybody because how can any son-in-law of His Worship be allowed to keep company with just anybody? And it's no use talking to him, you know. Why, the man is downright common, sir, dead common, absolute ignoramus, you might even say, for which craving his pardon for saying so—only what he don't know won't hurt him anyway, so why bother? As for herself, she's a wild goat, sir, a one-and-only daughter, as I already told, always laughing one minute and crying the next, one minute it's hee-hee and ha-ha and the next she's thrown herself on the bed and the new doctor must be fetched —who I wish the devil might fetch away instead! Because believe me, sir, it makes me that miserable only to be thinking of him. Why, sometimes I want to snatch up a knife and butcher him on the spot or run down to the river and drown myself because that's how miserable that doctor has made me!"

My young visitor lapsed into thought and grew sad.

"So are you saying, sir, you entertain some suspicion in her regard?" I now said, stopping short of speaking more plainly.

"Gracious heavens, no!" he exclaimed, jumping up with a sudden start, and he edged even nearer to me then. "Suspicions regarding her? Why, sir, she is an honest woman! Come of pious Jewish stock, sir! . . . No, it's only him I meant, that blasted dandy doctor. Nor even him so much as that walleyed daisy of a tailoring daddy of his in the padded cotton caftan, blast him! Goes about four-and-twenty hours, day and night, noising it about all over town. Think there's a word of truth to his twaddle? Why, no! It is all rubbish, sir, pure rubbish! Creature's got a tongue, so he lets it rattle on regardless! Now, I shouldn't ordinarily pay his croaking any more mind than a bullfrog's in high summer. Trouble is, sir, folks have ears, and ears are partial to listening, so if you listen good you are apt to hear things you would rather not hear. Specially in our town, sir, which I tell you is a town which everybody knows, when it comes to folks having long tongues and being mad for scandal, has every other town in the world beat, hands down. Ask anybody, sir, and they'll tell you! Because when a man's reputation falls into people's mouths down our ways, sir, he may as well say goodbye to it forever. Oh, around me they trod ginger enough; only behind my back I had heard such things, sir, it made me take a good look about me, keep a weather eye open, pick up a word here, a word there, and, well, what can I say? Just wasn't anything in it, sir, not a blessed thing—except I noticed one thing, though. Whenever he came round, she'd be a very different person, sir; face had a different look about it, different sort of look in her eye. That's to say, she was the same person, really, same face, same eyes; only the look was different. Know what I mean? A different look, different sparkle, somehow. Think I didn't ask her, "Why is it, dearest, whenever *he* comes round, you are a different person some-how?" Well, now, you try and guess what she answered me then. Laughed out loud is what, giving out with such a monstrous ha-ha-ha, I thought I was being put into the ground and tucked up in it whilst still among the living! And promptly she was done laughing, she threw herself down on the bed with such a great wail it brought the mother-in-law running in with that Turkey shawl on, trying to buck her up, and then she, of course, started in with that awful yammering of hers, which only caused my father-in-law to have the buggy brought round to send for the doctor, and who do you reckon was sent to fetch him, sir, if it wasn't my own self, and the minute the doctor came in, she took an instant turn for the better, and the color came right back into her cheeks, and her eyes began to sparkle again like a pair of brilliants in the sun. . . . And imagine the fine position I was put in by it; why, having to step into that house was like a journey beyond the grave. Because surely even a descent into hell might have been more agreeable! And having to look the fellow in the face yet! I mean, you ought to see it, sir. Handsome mug he's got, too, I must say. Kind of a beet-red coloring to it, though maybe more of a blue, really, and talk about your pimples, sir, why, he has got the things all over, so even his pimples have got pimples! Chap likes smiling a sight too many as well, and what a smile it is, too—like a corpse laid out before planting! Thing's a fixture, whether it's wanted or no! I mean, it just never leaves his face. Always smiling, sir, affable with everybody to a fault, no matter who. Never mind with myself! Why, the fellow is so constantly sweet and gentle with me, I may as well bottle him to cure my boils with. And there is no end or limit to it, either! Like, just recent, when I wasn't feeling what you'd call in the pink, exactly? Come down with that newfangled whatsit, influenza thing? Well, you should have seen how that man laid himself out for me then. Why, it wasn't human, hardly. Remarkable thing, though! The more he goes out of his way to be nice to me, the more—though God spare me notwithstanding—the more I hate him for it, just can't bear the sight of him, sir, especially not when he sits amongst us and they are all exchanging knowing looks with her! . . . Seems to me if I took him by the scruff and tossed him out, it would do me a power of good! Because it's his way of looking at her I cannot tolerate, sir, his way of grinning at her I cannot stand. So I am resolved once and for all now—let there be an end! How much humiliation is a man to take? Why, it's reached a point where the whole town has made my business its own! So there is no other course to follow—but divorce! Seems to me it is the only recourse I have left. Ah, but! . . . But is it practical, sir? Rich father-in-law? One and only daughter? Another hundred years she stands to get all of it, that's to say, I stand to get all of it? That'll be the day though, won't it! Only what did I do before, anyhow? What do lots of young gents in my shoes do? No other recourse, though, is there! So, what you reckon, sir? No other recourse but divorce?"

Here my young visitor stopped to draw breath again and mopped his face, waiting to hear what I should say.

"Why, I hardly know, sir. But I am inclined to agree you've no recourse but to divorce. Most particularly as the love between you appears not to be so very strong, nor I understand are there any children, so with the town talking, well, what need have you to persist in an unfortunate business you're best out of anyway?"

The whole while I talked my young visitor kept spinning the wheels of the little bicycle and watching me mournfully with his saucerlike deep black eyes, and when I finished he edged nearer to me still and heaving a sigh he replied:

"You say, love. . . . Well, I can hardly say I hate her, sir. I mean, why should I hate her? Because I do really love her—no, I mean, love her really, sir! . . . And what you said about the town talking? Well, let 'em talk, is what I say! Because what really burns me up, sir, is *him;* that's what really burns me up! I mean, why must she always be making such a monstrous fuss over his coming anyway? Because, well, now, you tell me, sir, why don't she go all red and joyful when she sees me? I mean, in what way am I worse than him, sir? Just because he is a doctor and I am not? Because maybe if they was to teach me the same as him, I should be a doctor, too, maybe even a better doctor than him! And believe me, sir, as regards pious book-learning, I am his match on any day of the week, and when it comes to knowing the Sacred Tongue, that's to say, Hebrew, sir, well, I just reckon what that man knows wouldn't make small money for my change purse! So, on second thoughts, sir, I have reconsidered: because, I mean, what fault did I see in her that was so terrible that I must divorce her anyway? You say, the new doctor! Well, as to that, what would I do if it wasn't the doctor but who knows what plaguey no-account instead? And where does it say that a wife must be unacquainted with a doctor anyway? So that's one away. And two, there is the practical side wants considering. I mean, what's in it for me if I was to divorce her. Because you may not know it, but I am an orphan, sir; that's to say, I'm on my own, not having a single close relation or good friend in all the world. So just you try and go back to being only a poor boy again and remarry and start all over again, that's to say, begin everything from scratch again! And who's to say I'd do better this time, anyhow? Because I could as well end up in a worse hell than even now, couldn't I? I mean, better the devil you know because at least I know what troubles I've got. Besides which, I am what you call Crown Prince anyway, sort of, being I'm His Worship's son-in-law, and another hundred years she stands to get all of it, that's to say, I stand to get all of it. . . . Don't you reckon? I mean, why be taking chances anyway, why just speculate? Otherwise it's all only a gamble, just a lottery really. So what you reckon, sir? Ain't it all a lottery? Just a gamble, really?"

"Yes, quite," I said, "I am inclined to agree. It is a gamble, a lottery really. And yes, of course, a reconciliation is preferable to a divorce."

I was now happily congratulating myself on having tipped the scales in favor of reconciliation and thought to be done with the fellow at last. When suddenly he picked up the little bicycle again and had edged quite near this time so he was speaking directly in my face.

"Reconciliation? Well, yes, I reckon you're right. But then I think of *him*, blast him, of that doctor, that's to say, with the pimply red face! Because that walleyed daddy of his has been going around noising it all over town anyway about His Washup's precious daughter getting a divorce. I mean, how lowdown can you get, even for a tailor? If, at least, the old fool hadn't noised it about! Because now that the whole town knows anyway, what have I got to lose? I mean, what's the saying? If the pot's broken it won't get more broken. Because as long as it was kept secret, there wasn't anything to it, really. Put a brave face on and brazen it out—that was the ticket. But the whole town is talking about divorce now, so digging my heels in seems awfully crude, even to me. So there isn't any choice left but divorce, I reckon. Eh? What about you, sir? Don't you reckon?"

"Yes, well, I am inclined to agree," I said, "as everybody is talking openly of divorce anyway, it does seem a bit crude. So I really don't see that you have any choice but divorce."

"So, what you are telling me," he said, edging his chair nearer still, so he was almost on top of me now, "so what you are telling me is I must divorce her forthwith? Now, think carefully, sir. I mean, say you was the rabbi, and I was to come to you with my wife asking for a divorce, so you ask me, 'Tell me, young man, why do you want to divorce this woman?' So what answer you reckon I might give? Now, just for the sake of argument, say I was to tell you it was because she looks at the doctor and the doctor looks at her. Well? I mean, where's the sense in that? Because, now, I ask you! What am I supposed to do, run and blindfold the woman? Only think how that would make me look! I mean you judge for yourself, sir. Because here I have just gone and divorced a woman what's called a 'real looker,' sir, a one-and-only offspring, sir, another hundred years she gets it all, that's to say, I get it all. . . . Eh? What you reckon people will say then? Mad, eh? Wouldn't you reckon? Stark raving with bells on, eh?"

"Oh, I am inclined to agree—with bells on, absolutely!"

Here my young visitor edged himself so near as to leave no distance at all between our faces, to say nothing of the inextricable confusion resulting to our feet in the consequence, and having also by now quite demolished my little bicycle, he drew my inkstand toward him instead. And uttering a sigh, he resumed his argument.

"Oh, sure, it's easy for you to say somebody else was stark raving with bells on. Only I'd like to know what *you* would do if the shoe was on the other foot. Because what if you had a father-in-law who was rude and ignorant and a mother-in-law with a Turkey shawl who won't leave off nagging and a wife who notwithstanding she was as healthy as a carthorse has took to being doctored all the time and then having the whole town pointing a finger at you and singing out, 'Ho-ho-ho, there he go, li'l miss nanny-goat's handsome billy-bo'!' Well, I reckon you'd be out of bed before half the night was done and be lighting out to where the hills are sugar candy and hens lay hard-boiled eggs!"

"Well, yes, I am inclined to agree. I suppose I should be lighting out to where the hills are sugar candy and hens lay hard-boiled eggs."

"Oh, sure, it's easy for *you* to talk," said he, "of lighting out to where the hills are sugar candy and hens lay hard-boiled eggs. Well, lighting out is all well and good. But lighting out how, sir? And lighting out to where? To blue blazes I reckon! . . . And what of her being an only daughter? . . . A one-and-only offspring, sir. . . . Another hundred years she gets it all, that's to say, I get it all. . . . Well, don't that count for nothing in this world, sir? . . . Besides! What do I have against the woman, anyway? No, you tell me, sir, what do I have against her?"

"Yes, well, I am inclined to agree. What *do* you have against the woman, anyway?"

"Man alive!" said he, "What about the doctor!? Seems you forgot all about the doctor, sir. Because as long as I see the doctor, I cannot stomach looking at the woman!"

"Well, if that's so," I said, "you really must divorce."

"Well, yes, I reckon," said he. "Only what of the practical side? Seems you forgot all about the practical side, sir. I mean, what's a young gent such as myself to do in hard times like these? Well, go ahead and tell me, sir, because I should like to know!"

"Well, in that case," I said, "I suppose divorce is out."

"Divorce out? But the doctor! Because as long as. . . ."

"Why, then, divorce it is!" I said, thinking to make an end.

"Divorce? But the practical side! Man alive. . . ."

"Well, then, for God's sake, don't divorce!"

"But what of the doctor?"

I don't know what came over me then. For the blood had suddenly rushed to my head and I was in a blind rage and I had taken my young visitor by the throat and was pressing him against the wall and screaming uncontrollably at him:

"Divorce her, you horrible little man! Divorce her! Divorce her! Divorce her!!!"

. . . .

. . . .

Our outcries had brought the entire house rushing to our side. "Goodness, what is wrong? What has happened?" "Oh, nothing! Really, it was nothing!" Though catching a glimpse of my livid features reflected in the glass, I scarcely took them for my own and was next apologizing profusely to my visitor, pressing both his hands in mine and craving of him over and over to put the unpleasantness between us out of his mind. "It happens sometimes," I said, "that a man may be put out of humor." My young visitor, still shaken and confused, allowed as how if a man loses a grip on himself, he is sometimes put out of humor. . . . And executing the same mincing reverence he had made me upon entering, he took his departure now: the same retreat of a couple of paces, the same bow from the waist, the same rubbing of palm in palm: "Your pardon if I have presumed on your time, sir, but I am most beholden to you for your advice, sir. . . . Deeply beholden, sir. . . . Well, good-bye, sir!"

"Not at all, sir, not at all. . . . And Godspeed."

At the Doctor's

See now, doctor, what I'm asking is for you to hear me out. That's all
I ask, sir. Now, I don't mean about hearing out what's wrong with me.
About what's wrong with me we'll talk later. See, now, I intend to set
you right about that very thing myself. No, what I want is for you to
hear *me* out, that's to say, to hear *myself* out personal. Because it isn't
your every doctor cares to hear a patient out. It isn't your every doctor
lets himself be talked to, sir. Doctors, they got this habit. They do not let
themselves be talked to. All they know is to feel your pulse, look at a
timepiece, make out a prescription, and collect their fee. Now, what I
hear tell about you, sir, is that you are *not* that kind of a doctor. What I
hear tell is you are young, sir, a young physician, sir, one as ain't yet
grown so greedy, as ain't so passionate fond of his lucre as the others is
generally. See, now, that is why I have come to consult yourself, sir, about
my stomach. Now me, I'm your man with a stomach, sir. Well, now,
your medical science will have you believe *everybody* has got to have a
stomach. Stuff, sir! I mean, where's the sense in it, sir? If one's stomach
is a stomach, why, then, all well and good, but if one's stomach is no
such thing, sir, if it is no stomach at all, sir, then what good is there in
living, sir? Oh, now, I suppose you'll be quoting pious writ at me next:
"Perforce thou livest," is that it? Well, that won't wash because I already
know it! Know it as my own backside knew the rebbe's cane at cheder,
sir. See, now, what I'm saying is, so long as a man lives, he is not partial
to dying. Though I'm bound to tell you, sir, the truth is, for myself, I fear
dying not at all. Because, firstly, sir, I'm already past my sixtieth year.
And, secondo, I'm your kind of a gent, sir, as accounts living and dying
as being pretty much the same party, sir—six of one, half a dozen of the
other. That's to say, of course, living is better than dying because who

wants to die anyhow? And most particular a Jewish gentleman, sir. And more particular, a husband and a father, sir, with eleven daughters, bless 'em, and a wife, sir, which true she's really my third, but a wife, notwithstanding. Well, now to cut a long story short I'm a Kamenets man myself; that's to say, not from Kamenets proper but from a small town not far from Kamenets. In the way of being a miller I am, God help me; keep a mill I do; that's to say, it's more the mill keeps me than the other way round because once you are planted, sir, you generally stays planted, as you might say. Well, it isn't as if you was given a choice now, is it? It's a wheel, sir, and a wheel generally turns round, now don't it. Well, you just consider, sir, your wheat must all be paid for in cash, and your flour parceled out on credit; why it's all IOU's, sir; and your custom, sir, see now, it ain't as if you was dealing with civilized folk, it's all to do with ruffians, sir, coarse ruffians and women. Now, sir, you care particularly for women? Well, you just try to explain anything to them: why's this, why's that? Why don't the challah come out right? I mean, where's it my fault it don't, anyhow? Well, now, ma'am, I says, maybe your heat was a leetle mite low? Or maybe, ma'am, your leaven was bad? Or maybe, I says, your wood was wet? And don't think they won't have at you then and be making you eat your peck of dirt and promise next time you'll have the loaf slung at your head. . . . Well, sir, you much fancy having a challah slung at your head? So that's the housewives, my retail trade. Only maybe you're thinking my wholesale custom was any better? Why, no. When such a gent comes into the mill first time, looking to establish credit, why, he'll be so hail-fellow-well-met with you then, don't you know, sucking up to you, oh, just a treat, and covering you with compliments and generally shedding so much sweetness and light you are dead certain you really must have that fellow patented for a poultice and cure boils with him. Only later, when the time come for payment, well, don't the complaints come rolling in then: delivery come late, sir, the sacks come torn, sir, the flour come bitter, sir, tainted, sir, grown spoilt from being left to lie around—why, it's all bother and vexation then, just carp, carp, carp! And money? "Send me the bill!" the man says. Well, now, at least that's halfway to settling up, you think. But send over to collect? "Tomorrow!" the man says. Tomorrow—"Day after tomorrow!" Yesterday, day before yesterday, yesteryear—no money, nix! So you start threatening the man with a protest, and you actually go file a protest. Well, now, say you have filed against him, what you think come of it? You get out a writ, and you come to execute the writ, only the gent's got all his property under his wife's name anyhow, so you can go whistle for your money, or crack his lice if you want, or whatever, because ain't nothing will help. So, now, I ask you: With dealings like that, how you expect a man not to have a stomach? So it's not for nothing that my own wife up and says to me, which even she ain't my first, sir, but my third, sir, and a man's third wife, why, sir, that's as you might say, a sunbeam in winter, sir; yet for all that, she cannot be ignored, sir, as she's a wife, notwithstanding: "Noah," says she, "now, why can't you just throw over the mill business altogether. Oh, I wish that mill of yours burnt down, Noah, and the business with it, for at least I should know you was alive and this side of the grave yet!" "Oh, my! Good gracious, woman, if that mill ever set to burning? Poof! Why, the thatch alone would go up like tinder." . . . "Now, now, Noah," says she, "that's not what I'm saying at all! What I'm saying is," says she, "you're on the fly all the time; running about here, there, yonder; never a Sabbath nor holiday; never time for wife nor children. What for? Why run about so, Noah?" . . . Hanged if I know why. Go ahead ask me, sir, and still I couldn't tell you why. I mean, what the dickens can I do if it's my nature to be running about so? . . . See, now, I *like* business. Love the hurly-burly of it, sir! . . . Though now maybe you think a body get anything out of it? Troubles, sir, nothing but. I mean, you put any kind of business my way, no matter what, and I'm bound to take it, sir. No brandy what's bad brandy in my book: you offering sacks?—I'll take sacks; you offering timber?—I'll take timber; you offering auction lots?—I'll take auction lots. Now, sir, you wasn't maybe thinking apart from the mill I have no other businesses besides? See, now, sir, if you'll forgive me for saying so, but that is where you are dead wrong! Because look at me, I'm your lumberman, as well, sir, which I got a partner in the business what owns the land, and we do the lumbering for him; and I'm also your prison victualer, sir; and I've a hand, too, in the kosher meat tax, sir—though every year I'm put out of pocket on account of it; which you'd only hope to earn the half each month of what I lose in tax farming because I'm a man with a heart, sir, and not your bloodsucking sort of tax man, sir. So why do I even bother? Cussedness, sir, just plain cussedness! See, now, I am a contentious man, a perverse man, sir, an ambitious man, sir: because once the battle's joined, sir, why I should cheerfully see the whole town brought to ruin and myself go down with it—just so long as I get my own way! Now, you take me all round, and you won't find me a bad sort, really, only I have got what you call a "short fuse," sir, that's to say I have got a bad temper, sir. Because for myself, sir, you only let my honor be slighted in the least, and there'll be the devil to pay for it! Which on top of everything, I have got something of a stubborn streak in me, as well. You know, there was a time once, but I was then still in my salad days, sir, when I was ready for war to the knife, sir, to actually draw blood, sir, over only the mere privilege of leading "Unto thee it was shewed" prayer at synagogue, on the Simchas Torah, sir. Hauled the whole concern before the court, sir—and don't think I didn't get my way in the end. Well, what can I do? Runs in my blood, you know. See it's my nerves, that's what they say, the doctors, which that's to do with my stomach, they say. But it don't really stand to reason, now does it? I mean, what's nerves to do with stomach anyhow? Well, it does beg the question that, I should think! Because, now, where's your nerves, sir, and where's your stomach, sir? Well, now, nerves, sir, well, at least I should think your medical science will bear me out here, sir, your nerves, sir, is generally where your brains are mainly? And let's see now, your stomach, well now it's kind of away over to—why, that's like from here to the North Pole! . . . Eh? Why, where's the fire? Now, now, I'm nearly done. So spare a gent another minute, sir. See, now, what I want is to spell it out for you exactly, so after you've heard me out, you can tell me where this misery come from in the first place. I mean, sir, about my stomach. Now, maybe it's all to do with my being such a traveling man, always on the road and never at home, sir, and even when I am, sir, I ain't really, sir, if you take my meaning. Upon my word—but you know it's a joke, a really shameful joke, sir—why, I couldn't begin to tell you how many children I've got, nor even their names. Well, I say it's not right, sir, a house being without master nor father. You should only see my home, sir, an' touch wood. I mean, you wouldn't believe the state the place was in! Ship without a helm, sir. Pandemonium, that's all it is, sir, nothing but ruckus day and night, an' God save us! Why, it's no laughing matter, sir, having eleven children, bless 'em, of three wives. Whilst this one's having tea, the other's having dinner; whilst I'm at my prayers, that one's calling to be taken to bed. This one's mangling a roll, that one's all for herring, this one's hankering for dairy, that one's only yammering "Meat, I want meat!" And it's only jump at aforemeal handwashings that it come out there's not a blessed knife in the house for a body to cut his bread with. The meanwhile that pack of young'uns is all in an uproar, noising, fighting, raising the roof, so all a body want to do is run out the door and never, ever step over that threshold again! And pray tell why is that, sir? It's all because I've got no time, sir. Though it must be said in her favor, sir, that's to say in my wife's favor, that she is a very good person, well, maybe not so much good as tender, sir, a mite too tender, for she seems not able to get along with children, sir. It's a knack, sir, getting along with children. So they walk all over her. That's to say, she does whack 'em, sir, does larrup 'em, sir; why she even beats 'em black and blue, sir. Only what good come out of it? Why, she's only a mother, sir. And a mother ain't a father, sir. A father unbreeches a child, throws it over a bench and thrashes it. I know my father thrashed me, sir. Now, perhaps your father thrashed you as well? So what you think, sir? Why, I warrant it done you a world of good, sir! Well, now, I'm not at all certain you'd have been better off if you wasn't thrashed, sir. . . . Eh? Why, where's the fire, sir? Be done in a moment, anyhow. See, now, I'm not telling you this for no reason; it's so you'll understand the kind of life I lead. You think maybe I know how much I'm worth, sir? Well, now, perhaps I'm rich, very rich, sir, or perhaps—now, I trust this to remain strictly between ourselves, sir—or perhaps I'm ruined, a bankrupt, sir! . . . I mean, who knows? Why, sir, it's all only patchwork, now ain't it, patchwork night and day; pull out a stone here, fit one in there—only come the crunch, you think you won't be made to cough up anyhow? Willy-nilly, sir, a child must receive her dowry, don't she. And the more, sir, if God hath blessed you with daughters and such as are come of age to boot. Well, now, you try to have three grown girls at home, bless 'em, sir, which you must bring them all under the wedding canopy, sir, all three on the same day, sir, and we'll just see if you'll feel like hanging about the house then, for even a level minute, sir, never mind every blessed day! So you understand now why all this hurly-burly, sir, all this running about and being always on the fly? And the while you are hurlying and burlying so and running about and on the fly, sir, you're bound to catch your death on the road, ain't you, and submit to rotten meals at inns, sir, such as you are constrained to recover from it later on. To say nothing of the villainous smells you must breathe in, sir, from all that dainty air around, so I reckon a body may by now have earnt his right to a stomach! Piece of luck, though, I'm not by nature one of your ailing sorts, sir. Sound as a bell, sir. Always have been. Even whilst I was young, sir. Oh, don't pay it no mind, my being so uncommon scrawny and dried-up looking. It's only wear and tear what's pared me down. Besides, we was all like that at home, sir, lean and lanky. Had a couple of brothers, and they was all like myself, don't you know—an' longer life to the living—that's to say, to myself, sir. Notwithstanding, I am a healthy man, sir. And would, sir, I may continue so. Why, until recent, I never even knew of stomachs, sir, nor of doctors, sir, nor any other such misery in kind, sir. Only of late, ever since they begun stuffing me with cures, with their pills, sir, with their powders, sir, with their herbs, sir; and what with each one of them gentlemen pushing some notion of his own: like the one tells me I must keep to a "diet," in other words, to keep *no* diet, because I must try and take as little food as I can, and another tells me not to bother taking any food at all, in other words, sir, I'm to fast. So you think that be the end of it? Why, no, because along comes a new gift to healing, and *he* orders me to actually eat, eat up hearty, mind! Though I suspicion the man himself was, anyhow, partial to eating. Doctors they all have this habit, sir. That which they do not themselves despise, sir, in other words, that which they positively relish, sir, they prescribe to their patients. Though the wonder is, sir, they don't have us all swallowing money. . . . Why, they are enough to drive a body mad, sir! There was this one medico, I recollect, who prescribed walking a lot, oh, just hiking about all over the place to no purpose, sir, and to do it apace, yet, but then another come along and he recommends bed rest, sir. Well, now, it do set a body to guessing don't it, which of them two dunderheads might be the bigger fool. . . . I mean, what proof you need more? There was this one fellow kept feeding me nitrate of silver, sir; for pretty near the whole blessed year I was on nothing but nitrate of silver! So then I take myself over to another doctor, and he says: "Nitrate of silver? Good grief, man! Why, that's poison, sir, it'll be the death of you!" And he proceeds then to prescribe me some kind of a powder, a yellow powder it was, which I suppose you may know what kind of a powder it was? Anyhow, I come in with that same yellow powder to a third doctor; well, now, you don't perhaps reckon that fellow didn't straightaway snatch the powder away from me nor tear that prescription up into little bits nor write me up a new prescription for herbs instead? Well, them was *some* herbs, sir! Because before I become accustomed to taking them, well, sir, I swear I must have bust a bladder, near wretching out my innards on the floor! Why, I should hope that man, that doctor, sir, might be plagued by half what I wished on his head every time I'd be taking the whole kit of them herbs of his before meals! Why, I stared death in the face each time, sir. But what foul potions won't a body imbibe, sir, if his health is at stake. . . . Anyhow, what come of it in the end was I went back to that other one, that's to say to the first doctor, the one which he kept me on nitrate of silver, and I commenced telling him the whole story of them wretched herbs and how they was making my life such a misery —well didn't that fellow take on, though! I mean, you may of thought I'd made a tailor's botch of his bespoke overcoat, he was that steamed up about it: "But I expressly prescribed nitrate of silver for you," he says, "so why be running about from one doctor to the next? Why, it's sheer madness, sir!" Says I: "Whoa, steady on, now! What you reckon? You got the market cornered, or something? Well, now, I do not recall as we signed a contract, sir; besides, your competition got as much right to their livings as you do, being as they too is family men and got mouths to feed, same as yourself." Well, you should of seen that man carry on then. Like I'd said God knows what to him! Well, the short of it is, he said I may as well go back to the other doctor. Says I: "Well, I've certainly no need of your counsel on that head, for I am well capable of going on my own if I've a mind to." And I put a ruble down. Now, you don't think the man threw that ruble back in my face? Fat chance, sir, fat chance! Because their sort, sir, they cherish their lucre far too much for that. By heaven, but don't they, sir! Much more even than any us ordinary folks do. Believe you me, sir. Much more! But you catch any of them, for instance, hearing a patient out proper, as they ought to—that, never, sir! Not on your life! Because they won't tolerate so much as a word which *they* think is unnecessary. Why, only the other day, I dropped in at a doctor's, one as you are familiar with him personal, sir, so I won't bother naming him. Well, I come in, and I had scarce got two words out by way of preamble when—aha! you guessed it; by golly if that gent wasn't already ordering me to strip naked, saving your presence, sir, and bidding me to lay down on the coach. Why, whatever for? Wants to have a listen, he says. Oh, want to have a listen, is it? Well, now, I'd say that was handsome of you, most generous, I'm sure. But if you're so fired up about listening, why won't you let a body speak? I mean, what good is it to me, all of that tapping of yours, all of that thumping of yours, if you won't even let yourself be talked to? Sorry, running late, says he. Got no time, says he. There's others in the waiting room, waiting their turn. "Patients' roster," don't you know, says he. Well, it seems to have become quite the fashion among you people lately, I notice. I mean all that business about "rosters" and "waiting turns" and such. Like queuing for tickets at the train station or for stamps at the post office—though pardon the irreverence, sir. . . . Eh? What's that, sir? Got no time? Running late? Oh, no! Not you, too, sir? Y'don't mean to say you have got a roster as well? And here I thought you was a young physician yet. Now, how'd you ever come by rosters so soon, anyhow? Well, now, of course, if you insist on ordering things *that* way, it'll all end in grief and you'll have no practice. . . . Tut, I shouldn't be getting into such a huff neither, sir. Why, it never once crossed my mind, being treated free of charge! Good gracious me, sir, I'm not your sort of a Jewish gent as expects to be treated gratis, anyhow. And even if you didn't hear me out to the end, that's hardly the point, is it? Because, after all, consultations must be paid for. . . . What's that, sir? You say you *won't* be paid? Ah, well, please yourself, I'm not one to use force. . . . Well, I suppose you're well enough off anyway. . . . Cashing in coupons, I bet. . . . Dividends growing, sir? . . . Well, that's all right, then, and God keep you too, sir, *and* your dividends. . . . Adieu! Oh, by the way, I hope you don't take it in bad part, sir, about my having taken up your time? After all, what are doctors for, anyhow, eh?

Joseph

The "Gent's" Story

Oh, have your little joke. Go ahead, do a lampoon of me, make it a dashed whole book, if you wish—because you don't scare me. I want that made clear at the outset. Because I'm not the sort of a chap that scares easily. Writers don't scare me, I'll have you know. And, no, I don't go all grovely and weak-kneed in front of a fella only because he's a doctor, nor truckle to him because he's a lawyer, and if you was to tell me a chap's been studying to be an engineer, I'd be the last to drool over him on account of it. Because I've put in my time studying, too. Was a student myself once, y'know. Not that I finished. But that's only because of a scrape I got into over a gel. Fell in love with me, don't you know. Head over heels. Well, I'm a good-looking enough fella for it, always have been. Swore to do herself in, she did, if I didn't have her. Swallow poison, she said. But I wasn't any more interested in marrying the gel than, say, you might be. Well, now, it wasn't as if she was the only fish come to net, if you take my meaning. . . . But the thing had got out of hand, and one of her brothers stepped in then. Fella was a licensed chemist at a pharmacy, don't you know. Said if his sister was to swallow poison, *he'd* know what to do. Had just the thing to splash me with, he said. . . . So I had to take the gel. Worst three years I ever spent. Wanted just two things of me: keep at home and keep the old eye from roving. . . . So how d'ye like that for a bargain, eh? Well, it's not my fault God made me with a face that drives all the women and the gels wild. What's that you say? . . . Good God, no! . . . Why, no, there isn't "any more" to it! Fall in love with me, y'see. End of story. Finis. You know, wherever I go—I mean to say, I'll be getting off the train at some place? Well, they'll

81

be all over me, like bees at the old jam jar: marriage-broker chaps, oh, just hordes of 'em, buzzing about, pestering the life out of me. And why's that? I mean, here I am your progressive, modern young chap really: good looks, good health, good name, good income, scads of the old ready, which I don't much mind parting with, nor miss any if I do, et cetera, et cetera. So it's only to be expected I'd be fair game, now, isn't it? Well, y'don't suppose I intend to let them have their way? "Leave off," I tell 'em, "Already got my fingers burnt once." . . . But they only persist then, saying, "So where's the harm in looking a new gel over?" . . . Well, now, what chap turns down an offer like that? So here I am, looking gels over in the meantime, and the gels look me over, all of 'em at each other's throats, always clutching at me, clinging to me like limpets, hanging on for dear life, I tell you, for that's only the God's honest truth. They all want me, every one of them. But what good is it to me, all of them wanting me, if I don't want any of them? Because nobody but myself knows of the one *I* want. . . . So that's my trouble, y'see. It's what I've been meaning to tell you about. Ask a small favor first, though. Keep it amongst ourselves. Mum's the word, eh? You, me, the lamppost. Much the best way. Oh, not on my own account! Good God, no. I've already told you. Don't give two hoots myself about being "characterized," as you fellas call it. Not much point, though, in letting the thing get about, now is there. . . . Well, that's settled, then. So I'll get down to telling my story.

Now, I'm sure you appreciate why I shall say nothing to you about who the gel is or where she is from. I'll allow, though, she is female. Young. Beautiful. Mind you, no money. None whatsoever. Half an orphan, you see. Lost her dad. Lives with the mother, don't you know. Your young widow-lady type. Quite the looker herself, by the way. Keeps a Jewish restaurant. Kosher. Oh, about that: well, I confess, for all I'm your progressive modern chap really, good income, scads of the old ready I don't much mind parting with nor miss if I do, et cetera, I make it a point to eat kosher. Oh, it's nothing to do with being observant. Good God, no! Don't entertain the least scruple anent your grunting livestock myself. Sensible regard for the old tum is all it is, really. That's one reason. Besides, you'll agree Jewish dishes are far and away the tastiest. . . . Anyway, keeps a restaurant. The widow, that is. Does all the cooking on the premises herself, don't you know. Daughter serves. Though what cooking, what service! I tell you it's a song! It sparkles, it gleams! Sheer paradise, eating there. But the pleasure's not in the eating so much as in feasting your eyes on the mother and daughter both. Toss-up, don't you know, which one is the more beautiful. Eyeful, if ever there was one, that woman. Seeing her standing at the stove, cooking, bustling about, don't you know, never a hair out of place, always as fresh as the morning dew. Face as fair as the newly fallen snow; hands and arms, gold and silver; eyes, burning coals, passionate, fiery. . . . Oh, you can take my word for it, a man might easily fall in love with that woman still. . . . So you can only imagine what that little gel of hers must look like. . . . Well, now, I don't know how well-versed you are in the subject yourself. That's to say, in the subject of gels. Though as for the daughter, now there's a treat! Perfect little face, don't you know: peaches and cream complexion; soft dimply cheeks like two cream puffs; eyes like black cherries; silken hair; teeth like orient pearls; neck, throat, alabaster; sweetest little hands, with fingers, knuckles, palms, wrists all made for kissing; rosebud mouth, with that sort of a Cupid's bow upper lip, has that delicious little lift to it, don't you know, like a child's—oh, surely, you must know the sort of thing I mean! Gel's a picture. Perfect picture, I tell you. Chiseled is what I call it. Everything prinked out and polished smooth—exactly like one of those dainty porcelain figures that gets set out on the mantelpiece as if to say, "There, bust a gut feasting the old peepers on that awhile, sonny!" . . . And to boot, she has got her own kind of a tinkly laugh that sets her dimples a-playing bo-peep in her cheeks, which alone is worth the price of a meal. Because, when she is set to laughing, everything laughs along with her: you, the table, the chairs, the walls—why, life itself laughs along. That's the sort of laugh she has got. Well, you try an eyeful of that for a spell yourself sometime and see if you can learn to hate it!

But why should I go on boring you with this when the simple truth of the matter is that, nearly from the first afternoon I began taking my meals there, I just knew I was done for. Goose cooked, so to speak. Spitted, basted, and roasted, don't you know. Smitten. Head over heals! Though, concerning myself and gels? Well, I suppose you know all about that by now, anyway, without any of my prompting. I mean, I'm not exactly your sort that goes about putting gels on a pedestal, now, am I? And as for that silly business about "love"—or "romance," if you prefer —well, never took any stock in it myself, I'm afraid. Bagatelle's all it is, really. Just so: it's there, so why not have a crack at it, is what *I* say. I mean to say, all's fair in love and war, and all that. But for a chap to blow his brains out over such a thing—pish! Now, that's plain foolish.

Sort of thing a schoolboy will go and do, don't you know, not a grown man.

Well, now, seeing as how I was smitten, I took the old mum aside. Mind you, not to, as you say, "ask for her hand." Oh, nothing like that. Good God, no! Y'know, I'm not your precipitious sort of a chap, to snap a thing up first instant it's offered. . . . Nothing wrong, though, is there, with taking an idle turn now and then round Ye Olde Shoppe, as it were. Give the merchandise the once-over, don't you know. . . . Anyway, had a word with the mum, looking to get the lie of the land, so to speak, test the waters, and so forth, "So how do matters stand anent your daughter, madam?" said I. "Well, now, that would depend on what you meant by how matters stood, wouldn't it, sir," said she. "What I meant, madam," said I, "was practically speaking. Future, and all that, don't you know." . . . "Oh, well," said she, "not much to worry about on that head, I shouldn't think. It's quite settled, you know." . . . Well, I confess, hearing that gave me quite a turn. So I said: "What do you mean, it's quite settled?" . . . "Why, sir," said she, looking past me then, "you can judge for yourself about how matters stand, as you say. For here's our little worrywart now.". . . And no sooner were the words out than *she* appeared, the daughter herself, that is, in person, just lighting up the whole place, don't you know, like the sun in the morning.

"Mummy, have you seen Joseph?" she said. And when she said the name, Joseph, she pronounced it with that odd sort of a tuneful glide. Like a song. The way a gel might call to her "intended," don't you know. . . . At least, so it seemed to me; no, that's to say, I'm quite sure it was so. And not only this one time I'm telling of, but always, whenever she said the name, it came out with that same tuneful little glide: "Jo-seph." Know what I mean? Not plain: "Joseph!" More like: "Jo-seph."

Well, I mean, it seemed all you ever heard that gel say was "Jo-seph," over and over again, "Jo-seph." I mean, here we'd all be sitting down to table, and the first thing out of her mouth was "Where's Jo-seph?" . . . "Joseph won't be in today" . . . "Joseph said" . . . "Joseph wrote" . . . "Joseph came" . . . "Joseph went" . . . "Joseph sent" . . . Joseph-Joseph, Joseph-Joseph! Well, I must say, I was grown pretty impatient by now to get a look at this "Joseph" fella for myself, finally take the chap's measure, don't you know.

So not unnaturally I came to detest this "Joseph" chap. Oh, absolutely hated the fella sight unseen, don't you know. Though, what had I to do with him, anyway? God knows! Some perfectly horrid little twit, no doubt, boon companion, probably, to that set of snots that always hung about the place, one of the "bu-oys," as she used to call 'em, with that tinkly laugh of hers. "The bu-oys"! title quite suited them, y'know. Oh, to an absolute T. I mean, that's all they were, really. Bunch of schoolbu-oys! Queer little chaps, though, most of 'em. The sort that likes letting their hair grow and favors those vulgar long black peasant blouses. You know, with the high collar which buttons at the side and the shirttails hanging out and that silly cord knotted round the middle? Just the sort of getup I hate. . . . Oh. Meaning no offense! Though I see where you, too, seem to like wearing your hair long and have got the same kind of black blouse on. Well, if you think that's stylish, you are dead wrong, sir. Dinner jacket and white waistcoat's the thing. Infinitely nicer, I'll have you know. Take my word for it. Wouldn't trade them for all the blessings in the world. . . . Now, speaking for myself, whenever I catch sight of chaps wearing long black blouses like that with their shirttails flapping loosely about their bottoms (asking your pardon), the first picture comes into my mind is a worn-out trouser seat. . . . Think I didn't tell them so to their faces? I most certainly did! Because I'm the sort of a chap that prefers being above board, don't you know. Oh, absolutely. None of your bootlickers, I! Why, you'll never catch *me* sucking up to a fella. Not ever. And if, say, you had something bad to say about me? Well, you'd be free to spit it out, say it right to my face. One thing I won't abide, though. That's being called "bourgeois." Because anybody calls me bourgeois risks getting a pretty stiff biff in the old mazzard. . . . I mean, in what way am I bourgeois? Why, I am any man's equal in that department. I am up on everything, and I keep abreast of everything. Why, I'll have you know, I read all the the latest magazines and take in all your modern, progressive type newspapers, like everybody else—so how am I bourgeois then? Is it because I happen to have on a neat white waistcoat and dinner jacket, while you go about in that black blouse with your shirttail hanging out? Oh, not yourself! Good God, no. I didn't mean you, but only that unsavory lot of "bu-oys" I've been telling you about and their ilk, and that "Jo-seph" chap and his. . . . Anyway, held converse enough with the lot of 'em, whilst at the board together, so to speak, by way of table talk, as it were, and of a kind which gave me pretty well to understand they were about as taken with me as I was with them. You know: "Heart to heart e'er listeth," that old song? Well, never you mind. Because as far as the business of baring one's soul went —well, I didn't much see myself as being under any obligation in the way of such intimacies. Anyway, not vis-à-vis that lot. Though, apropos, I will confess to doing a bit of cozying up, used some of the old largess to buy my way into their good graces, as it were, try and get myself in with them, so to speak. Oh, not on their account! Good God, no. More on account of that "Joseph" chap, and not so much on his account either, as on account of her; I mean to say, on the gel's account. Well, it did eat away at me considerably, y'know, her mooning over him all of the time the way she did. Anyway, made myself a promise: if it was the last thing I did, whatever the cost, whatever the reckoning, come what may and damn the consequences—I must, no, shall! make the acquaintance of this "Joseph" personage. And don't think I didn't manage it, what's more. Because, now, I'm the sort of a chap, when he sets his mind to a thing, will allow nothing to stand in his way. Though, mind you, money's no object with me, either! Well, now, I mean, after all, here I am your young man of commerce, prosperous chap really, good income, scads of the old ready I don't much mind parting with nor miss any if I do, et cetera.

Though, now, pretty obviously, the business of buying my way in with that lot wasn't as easy as you may think. Had to proceed in easy stages at first, don't you know, one step at a time. So I set things rolling by sticking the occasional oar in from the sidelines, as it were, though always mindful of giving out with the mournful sigh or cluck of sympathy now and again, anent parlous times—oh, you know the sort of thing: days of trouble, public weal, and so forth—and letting it be known that in *such matters,* when push came to shove, money was no object, certainly not where I was concerned, no, sir, because, well, after all, I mean to say, it was only right for a chap to toss out a bit of the old ready if it's in a worthy cause. Well, I expect you know what I meant just now by "tossing out" a bit of the ready. See, now, there's your sort of a chap that will "toss" his money out whilst another only *takes* his out. Well, I mean, you'll agree there *is* a difference there. Y'see, "tossing out" the old ready is when a chap will dig down for a bit of Ye Olde Coine of the Realm, giving it a careless toss with an air as if to say, "Here y'are, my good fellow, *pas de quoi,* I'm sure—and dash the cost!" See, now, that's how *I* like going about things. Oh, but don't get me wrong, now! Not always. Good God, no. No, what I mean is, only when it's wanted. And when what's wanted is, say, for you to be forking out a twenty-fiver or half a century or, say, a cool hundred, well, you absolutely cannot allow the old hand to tremble. No, sir. Not a tremor. Well, I mean, suppose you are dining out with a party of chaps, say, it was for lunch, or supper maybe, and the reckoning's been brought round, and you pick up the tab. Well, now, what you must do is flash a quick look at what's called your "bottom line," the while talking airily of this and that, don't you know, and then when they bring round your change next, well, you must never stop to count it, like a market woman selling onions out of a basket, but must sweep it up without looking and toss it into your pocket straight away. End of story. Finis. Y'see, life's a school which you must get through, learn to make your way in, so to speak. I mean to say, one has got to *know* how to live. And if there is one thing I pride myself on, it's that I know how to live. Because it's all a question of knowing when to do a thing and when not to do it and how much. I mean to say, you won't ever catch *me* overbidding my hand, and I defy anybody to read my cards from my face, so to speak, make fish or fowl of me, as it were. I mean, you ought to have seen me amongst that lot of "bu-oys" then. Why, you'd never in a million years have guessed I wasn't one of the "bu-oys" myself. Oh, absolutely looked the part! Not that I ever let my hair grow long or took to wearing peasant blouses or anything like that. Good God, no! Had on the same trusty old dinner jacket and white waistcoat then as now. Only difference was, I let on like I was interested in everything they were interested in, and talked about the same things they talked about: "Proletariat" . . . "Bebel" . . . "Marx" . . . "Reacting," and so on . . . anyway words of that sort, which I bunged into the conversation every time they got to talking. Funny thing though. The more I tried cozying up to them, the more they seemed put off by it. I mean to say, any time I'd try on some of that patter, you know: "Proletariat" . . . "Bebel" . . . "Marx" . . . "Reacting," and so on, anyway words of that sort, I noticed how they'd suddenly go very quiet then and be exchanging funny looks and pick away at their teeth the while. . . . Oh, and another thing! I noticed, too, how when it came to money, they would all take from me gladly enough. Like on Mondays and Thursdays, when they'd be putting one of their concerts on, don't you know? Well, without fail, I was always the first brand snatched from the pyre, as it were. "Now, surely," they'd say, "the Gent wishes himself to be put down for a front-row seat tonight. Usual three rubles, sir?"

"The Gent"—that was the only name they ever knew me by. So, naturally, "the Gent" had to fork out three rubles every Monday and Thursday for a ticket. Well, I mean, it wasn't as if I had any choice, now, was it? Which, I suppose, is why every time the "Gent" walked in on the "bu-oys" in the middle of one of their powwows, a great hush would fall over the proceedings then. Mum's the word, don't you know. Could have heard a pin drop! . . . Well, pretty obviously this got the "Gent" fairly pipped, oh, just seething, if you know what I mean, mad as all get out, in fact. Problem was, though, what to do about it. But, as I said, I'm the sort of a chap, when he's got hold of a notion, never counts the cost. Sky's the absolute limit then. So I pulled all the stops out this time, plugged away for so long and hard at buttering 'em up, don't you know, until I managed finally to work myself in amongst them, or at least sufficiently anyhow, for them to consent to letting me attend one of their "discussions," as they called it—at which time, they said, this "Joseph" chap himself would be holding forth before one and all then. . . . Now, you have no idea how happy that made me. I mean, to be allowed to see the fella at last, and actually to hear him speak!

Though about when and where this discussion was supposed to take place—you'd never have got a peep out of them, even if you asked. And I can't say I much cared to ask, either. Because I only reckoned they'd come round to telling me in the fullness of time anyway, sooner or later, so why bother? I mean, these chaps set very great store by secrecy. Throve on it, you might say. Had their own special word for it, too: "conspirashun." That's what they called it. Made a point of memorizing the word myself. Here, see? Even wrote it down in my notebook. Because, see now, I'm the sort of a chap, when he hears a fine word, will jot it down straight away, make a note of it, don't you know. Well, maybe you can't really tell if it will come in useful or not, only neither will you lose by it either is what I say.

Anyway, upshot came one fine summer's day, Saturday it was, when two of the "bu-oys" breezed round without warning, beetled in by the front door, in black blouses, as per usual, and tipped me the nod: "Come!" they said. "Where to?" I asked. "What's it matter to you?" they answered. "Just follow along, and we'll see you get there." . . . Well, that was that. Had to tag along with them, you see. . . . So we all pushed off then, trudging along together to way past the edge of town and, fetching up at the woods beyond, we plunged in amongst the trees and then trudged along some more together, and every so often we'd come across one or another of the "bu-oys," seated under a tree alone and staring off into space, making out he wasn't paying us any mind, you see, though the instant we got abreast of him, he'd shoot us a side-mouthed whisper, "Go right!" or "Go left!" . . . Now, I'd look pretty foolish, saying I was scared then. I mean, after all, what harm could come to a fella at the hands of only a couple of Jewish chaps, anyhow? Safe as houses, really, when you come to think about it. Thing is, though, it did put me off. Wanted dignity, don't you know. Well, I mean to say, here I am your young man of business, chap of substance, really: good name, good income, scads of the old ready I don't much mind parting with nor miss if I do, et cetera, letting myself be led about by a pair of snotty school kids, mere "bu-oys"! if you get my drift.

Well, cut a story short, we walked and we walked and we walked some more, and then we walked some more after that. And, just as I was beginning to wonder if our little woodland jaunt should ever end, we struck a very considerable hill. Which it was only after we clambered up to the top of and had cleared the rise and then begun our descent that I beheld such a great crowd of heads as fairly blackened all of the ground below: oh, just a sight of "bu-oys," don't you know, young chaps in black blouses, squatting down on the bare earth, and gels, too, who had got themselves up in the feminine variety of the garment and then a whole bunch of just ordinary young people mixed in with them. I mean, you wouldn't believe the turnout! Must have been all of three thousand there, easy. Maybe more. And quiet? Not a whisper! Even the flies had quit their buzzing. And we crept in amongst the crowd of heads then and sat down on the ground, and I took to searching the faces, thinking I might spot this "Joseph" chap in the meantime. And then I saw. . . . Well, I mean, you'll never guess! Chap who I dare say I was acquainted with well enough by now. One of that lot of "bu-oys" I'd been eating at the widow's with all along. Damndest thing, y'know!

I remember thinking, This it? . . . Nah, can't be! . . . This all of him? This, the "Joseph" fella? . . . And here all along I'd thought he had to be God knows what. Horns maybe! . . . Though, if you must know, it was a sight that almost gave me pleasure—no, I mean *real* pleasure, at the way things had turned out. . . . Y'see, I began stacking myself up against him. Mind! Not that I have such a high regard of my own person as to think there wasn't anybody handsomer than myself. Good God, no! Well, I mean to say, I'm not so blind as all that! I know very well that you are apt to find chaps handsomer than myself around. Only compared to *him*. . . . Well, I suppose you know what I'm driving at. . . . I mean, if you like, I can describe for you exactly what he looked like when I first caught sight of him. Stood leaning against a tree, I recall. Slight, pale little fella on the whole, mainly: gaunt, wasted, narrow chested, with hollow white cheeks that were a mite flushed, you know, like high-

colored about the bone, and a growth of tiny fair-haired stubble about
the chops; impressive high forehead, though, broad, absolutely white;
oh, and gray eyes, like a cat's, except they were het-up, intense, don't
you know; and a mouth—my God, how it talked! But dammit, I'm
hanged if I know where the little fella got his strength from to talk so
loud and so fast and for so long and with such a heat and such fire and
such passion! I mean, this wasn't any of your ordinary talk. Inhuman,
that's what it was. Devil's work. Had to be, or some dashed infernal
machine someone had wound up to talk like that somehow or they'd put
up a device overhead, which the words gushed out of and it shot flames
into the air, or maybe it was really the tree that was doing the talking.
. . . And the whole while I kept imagining how any minute this runty
little bagabones with the hollow flushed cheeks and gray eyes might
work up such a terrific head of stream with his talking as suddenly to lift
up off the ground and then phut! go hurtling off somewhere into the
blue, words and all. . . . No. You may say what you will! For I tell you I
have been privileged in my lifetime to hear some of the best lawyers in
the country plead before the bench and never have I heard anything to
beat it, or even come near, nor I ever shall, I suppose.

I can't say how long he talked. Never even looked at my watch. I
only looked at him and at the crowd of heads seated on the ground,
gulping down every word the same as it was meat and drink to the
hungry and thirsty. . . . But nobody who hadn't seen *her* on that day can
truly say he ever saw something fine and splendid in all his life. I picked
her out at length from amid all that crowd of heads, sitting on the ground
with her feet tucked underneath her and her hands folded, palms down,
on her breast: her face shone, her cheeks flamed, and her upper lip parted
from the lower with a little lift, like a child's, and her black cherry eyes
were smiling only at him—smiled only at *him* y'see. . . . No, I won't deny
it. I became jealous of him then. Oh, not just because of how he talked.
Good God, no! Y'see it wasn't his gift of the gab so much, nor even the
rattling reception afterwards with all the cheering and hand clapping he
got when he was through. No, it wasn't for any of these things that I was
so jealous as for her way of looking at him then. I mean, *how* she looked
at him. Oh, I'd have given anything for such a look from her! Because
that look spoke words, you know. For it seemed to me I heard her voice
in it, speaking with that same tuneful glide it always had, when she said,
"Jo-seph!" Though, as I said earlier, I'm not your sort that goes about
putting gels on a pedestal. What I mean is, well, after all, I have known

my fair share of gels, y'know, seeing as how I'm not half bad-looking, as I think I can safely say, as being also your progressive, modern chap, really: good income, scads of the old ready which I don't much mind parting with nor miss any if I do, et cetera. . . . But even my wife had never looked at me in such a way as *that,* not in our salad days even, when she still loved me, worshiped the ground I walked on, so to say. . . . I had a mind then to get up and walk straight over to her, plump myself down beside her, which I in fact did, or sat down close enough, anyhow, to be bobbing and twitching about in plain view of her the whole while, like a fly buzzing at her ear or a mosquito maybe—only the lady wasn't buying! No such luck. Because twitch and bob as I might, her eyes never once strayed from *his* eyes, hanging on to them, sucking at them like a pair of leeches, and his eyes, too, only hung on hers. And it seemed to me that both of them, that's to say, *he and she both,* saw nobody but each other then, *needed* nobody but each other. Oh, it was agony! I can't begin to tell you what a rage I was put into. Though I hardly knew who it was I was raging at so. Was it at "her" or at "him" or at them both? Or was it myself I was raging at. . . . And at night, when I came home, my head hurt awfully, and I went to bed, promising myself I should never cross the widow's threshold again. I'd as soon see all of them in perdition as go back! Because who needed these people, anyway? I mean, am I right, or am I right? . . . But when I got up the next morning it was all I could do to wait for the hour, no, the very minute, when two o'clock rolled around again, so it might be lunch time once more. And don't think I didn't go back either nor run into the same crowd of "bu-oys" there at the board together, same as always, and *him* amongst them. . . . I don't know about you, but me when I see a celebrated "artiste," say, or a government minister or just some famous person or other, well, even if we all may know he's human, like everybody else, that he eats and drinks, as it were, like everybody eats and drinks— only no sooner I am told the same chap is an artiste, say, or government minister or just some famous person or other, than I immediately think he is *not* like everybody else, that there is something special about him which you cannot really put your finger on, if you follow me. . . . Well, that was how it was with me when I saw *him* again, that's to say, after that tub-thumping oration; seemed pretty much the same old fella on the whole, just another of the "bu-oys" same as before, yet not *quite* the same. Something about him. Like maybe an air or special mark of favor stamped on his face. Anyway, something. Though, as to what that something was exactly, hanged if I could tell you what it was even now! Still, I'd give anything to have it. Oh, not that I need it! Good God, no. Dashed if I need it! I mean, why would I want such a thing for, anyhow? No, the reason I wanted it at all then was only on account of *her,* because she couldn't keep away from *him* for a minute, you see, and even when she came over to talk to me for a bit, it was always only *him* she was thinking about anyway, never about me. Well, see now, I'm an expert about such matters, I'll have you know. I mean, God knows, I've paid dues enough for it by now. . . . Anyway, I was in hell all over again. Because earlier, you see, that's to say before I actually knew who Joseph was, I'd painted him up in my mind as being this great big handsome strapping chap, *manly,* don't you know; yes, that's the word I want, definitely manly. Couldn't stick the fella then, y'see. Envied and hated him at the same time, I mean to say. Only now that I'd found out just *who* this fine figure of a man so-called really was, that he was only another "bu-oy," no different from the rest of the "bu-oys," if you fellow me—well, it absolutely gave me the pip. No, I mean *really* upset me. . . . Though I can scarcely say who I was upset with most. I mean was it with *her,* for idolizing him so (because you'd have had to have been half blind not to see how she absolutely idolized him!), or was it with *him,* for God having so bounteously bestowed on him such a great thumping power of the gift of the gab, or was it really myself I was so upset with, for not having the same gift of the gab as him? . . . Not that I have a great need of the commodity myself, mind! Good God, no. I mean, what would *I* be wanting it for anyhow? Well, I mean to say, it's not as if I was altogether helpless in that department. Far from it! Me, when I want to hold forth —well, you just see if I can't do it. Why, I even spoke before a pretty fair-size audience once, and that was at a meeting of the Merchants' Club, I'll have you know. And just about everybody that was there said I hadn't spoken badly at all then, not badly a-tall! . . . Though about me being so upset. Well, now, I can't really describe it for you in so many words. You have got to experience it—no, you have got to *feel* it, for you'd have had to be in my shoes then, have gone into that establishment every day, have watched *her* every day, have seen her go about every day in that trim little white apron that shimmered when she walked, have seen her bright pretty face, seen how it glowed, how it sang, have heard her sweet voice that perked up a body like a healing cordial, heard her tinkly laugh that went all through and through you and then just settled in amongst your vitals, and to have seen *him,* then, and have known that the whole performance first to last had been only for *his* sake all along, all for his sake and for no one else! No, he'd have to be got rid of somehow, got out of the way. But how to do it, now y'see *that* was the question. Well, of course, I wasn't about to poison him or shoot him. I mean after all I'm no murderer, and it's not exactly the sort of thing a Jewish chap goes about doing anyway. . . . Challenge the fella to a duel? Faugh! Storybook stuff. It's what they do in novels. Don't believe a word of it myself. I mean, it's all only done "for effect," now, isn't it? Makes the story more interesting, don't you know. . . . Anyway, that's my opinion. . . . But I finally did come up with an idea. Pretty fair one, too, I thought. Now, what if I took him aside, had a word with him in private. Like, what's the adage? "Make a thief keeper of the key." . . . Sharp, eh? I mean, what could be safer? Anyhow, you may be sure I didn't waste any bother thinking it over—because frankly I don't much hold with thinking too long about things, anyway—and first opportunity after dinner once, I said to him:

"Y'know, I've a proposition I've been meaning to put to you. Matter of mutual interest, so if you'll oblige me?" . . .

But him? Fella never moved a muscle. Oh, not him! Just dumb-quizzed me with that set of deadpan gray eyes as if to say: I'm game, son, so what's the pitch?

"No," I said, "No, no, not in here. Keep it amongst ourselves. You, me, the lamppost, eh? Much the best way."

"Come!" he said, and led me out into the street and turned around facing me, waiting as if to say: Well? Come on, out with it, son.

"Not out here," I said, "Oh, I say, when are you usually in?"

"I can be at your place," he began; but then pulled up sharp and said: "Though if you'd rather. . . . All right, my place, then, say——" and he pulled out his watch, "say, morning, nine thirty, half past ten, tomorrow? . . . Here, take my address."

And so saying, he clasped my hand, gripping it, and he looked me straight in the eye as if to say, "conspirashun," eh?

"Oh, absolutely! Conspirashun it is." I said, "You may count on it!" And with that we parted, each to his own repose, so to speak.

Though you can well imagine I hardly got a wink of sleep. Put me in an awful fret, y'know, thinking what I should say to him. Where would I even begin? I mean, what if he was to say:

"Now, see here, Sir Gent, or Mr. Whatsyerface, where do you come off butting into business that's not your own? And what sort of a suitor are you anyway, Sir Gent Mr. Whatsyerface, to be courting a gel whom one of us 'bu-oys' has been pleased to regard as his intended since away back when?"

I mean, what can you say to a thing like that? Or suppose he laid violent hands on me and heaved me down the stairs. What would I do then? Mind you, not that I was scared. Good God, no! I mean why would I be scared of him, anyway? All I meant was to put a proposition to him. Take it or leave it: Y'want? So take!—Y'don't? So don't! End of story. Finis. No. Hardly a cause for mayhem, though, is it!

And that's how I spent the night in tortured musings anent this and that, and nine thirty prompt the next morning found me clumping upstairs to a poky, dashed-to-all-dammit garret somewhere on a top-floor landing where he lived—I mean, there must have been all of two- no, maybe three-hundred steps to the thing, easy—and, presenting myself at his door, I saw I was in luck and he was in. Him plus a bonus of two "bu-oys" besides, who were exchanging funny looks, as if to say, Now, what business d'ye suppose the "Gent" might have here? But my little bird tipped them the wink, which the "bu-oys" were quick enough on the uptake to accept, and they took up their caps and made themselves scarce.

So the pair of us being alone, just him, me, and the lamppost, as it were, I commenced pouring it on, full tide from the pulpit, so to speak, giving him an earful: Well, y'know, blah blah, this, that, anyway in a nutshell, I'm a chap on his own, single fella, don't you know, though, notwithstanding, I'm only your commercial sort, simple man of business really, good name, good income, scads of the old ready I don't mind parting with nor miss if I do, et cetera, still and all I keep abreast, right on top of things, your *progressive* type, if that's the word I want, modern chap really, know everything, read all the latest newspapers and magazines—and I went and unreeled the whole spiel of funny words then: "Proletariat" . . . "Bebel" . . . "Marx" . . . "Reacting" . . . "Conspirashun," and so on, anyway, words of that sort. Well, he heard me out. Though I must say he was dashed civil and polite in answering. Modest, you know. None of your high-flown talk, came straight to the point, saying,

"Yes, well, how can I be of use to you?"

"Oh, a small matter," I said, "I want your advice."

"Advice? . . . From me? . . . You?"

And so saying he dumb-quizzed me with his deadpan gray eyes as if to say, Where does a li'l bit of a chap as myself come to be giving advice to such a swell Gent as yourself? . . . Y'see, he was beginning to feel a mite, what's the word I want? Yes, ill at ease. Distinctly ill at ease. Come to that, so was I feeling ill at ease. Only what was I to do? Die already cast, so to speak. I mean, I'd already plunged in, so I had to follow the thing through to the end. So I commenced unburdening, laying my griefs at his feet, confessed all that was in my heart from the minute I laid eyes on her, even to this day, my life has been an absolute agony, haven't known a moment's rest, y'see, that's to say, *she* won't give me any rest! . . . "I mean, I should never have believed," I said to him, "not in a million years, that over a mere gel, I mean to say, even if she was the Grand Duchess herself, that I should be so, so—now, what's that word I want?—yes, should be 'Reacting' so, because, well, dash it all, notwithstanding I'm your modern sort, that's to say progressive, still and all I'm a man of business really, commercial chap pretty much, good income, scads of the old ready I don't much mind parting with nor miss any if I do, et cetera.

Well, he heard me out. Though dashed civil and polite in answering, I must say. Modest, y'know. None of your high-flown talk, came straight to the point, saying,

"Yes, well, if you want my advice, I think you might start by talking with the girl yourself." . . .

"Yes, but what about you?" I said.

"Oh, I don't want——" he began, but then pulled up sharp and said, "Well, I can't, you see, I haven't the time to concern myself with such things."

"Oh, I say, you don't think——" I said. "No, but that's not what I meant at all! I'm not asking you to have a word with her on my behalf. I mean, how could I? I only wanted to know what *you* have to say about it."

"Yes, well, what *can* I say?" he said. "Should your feelings towards her be reciprocated, why, then, I imagine. . . ."

And so saying he came straight to the point and pulled out his watch —none of your high-flown talk, mind, only civil like and polite, as if to say, Well, I did so enjoy our little chat. Though as regards that business with the watch, I dare say I'm familiar enough with it. Should be, y'know. Apt to use the same dodge myself when I want to get shut of a fella. Trouble is, some chaps never take the hint. Slow to catch on. Well, as it happens, I'm not, and, getting to my feet, I beseeched him to keep this little matter amongst ourselves, under the old hat, mum's the word, eh, that's to say "conspirashun," and took my departure. Well, what can I say but Glad's a dirty dog next to what I was feeling then. Joyful? Pooh, not even close, I was in seventh——no, by God, in seventieth heaven! I tell you, I felt like hugging and kissing everybody I met along the way. Everything and everybody seemed to me all at once to have the most extraordinary charm I never noticed before. To say nothing of Joseph! Because I came to love him like a brother that day, no, really, as dearly as my own brother. Why, if only I hadn't been so shy, I'd have turned round and gone back and kissed him, and if I wasn't afraid of offending him, I should have brought a present along, a gold watch with a smart *breloque* and a chain.

But my good spirits got the better of me in the end, and I went to the club. I like looking in at the club in what's called the shank of the afternoon, mainly. Not that I like playing cards myself. Good God, no. I never play cards myself. Though I like watching others play, and once in a great while, that's to say very-very occasionally, I take a sporting interest in a chap's hand and will put down what you call your "kibitzer's stakes" on him, in which case it's one or the other: either you win big, or you lose big. Well, this time I won handsomely. Oh, absolutely on velvet. I mean, you talk about the cards coming a fella's way! Well, I gathered up my winnings and gave ye olde "Bummer's Mob" a hail—which is the name chaps at the club go by who have been relieved of their pocket money—and stood champagne dinner all around, had the good stuff brought up, too, that's to say, Rederer's Champagne Wine, and when I came home it was well on to midmorning, and there was a telegram sitting on my desk calling me away urgently on business. Well, you know how it is with us "gents-at-trade" chaps. The minute we get the summons, it's over. End of story. Finis. Drop everything and dash the rest, as we like to say. Off like a shot, y'know.

Well, I left thinking I'd be gone for two days, but, of course, I was away for three weeks, and first thing I got back I made straight for the restaurant to eat and found the place in a turmoil. Of the "bu-oys" there wasn't a sign, and such as were still about looked considerably short of their usual chipper selves, if you know what I mean: distraught mainly, uncommonly so, all of a dither, don't you know. Made short work of their meal, too, eating on their feet, as you might say, and then moped off separately with their heads down, like dogs after a rain, one going this way, the other that way.

But the thing that really set me to wondering, though, was where Joseph was. Why wasn't he around? And looking the "bu-oys" over then, I observed they certainly were acting mightily standoffish for a change, all of a huddle shushing each other the while: ssst-ssst! ssst-ssst! . . . Well, this wasn't just your ordinary conspirashun anymore—it was what you'd call "conspirashun to beat all conspirashun"! . . . And herself, well, she, too, appeared strangely quiet and pensive, quite "conspirashunal" on her own account, I thought. . . . The flame was gone from her cheek and the smile from her black cherry eyes. And her bo-peep "kiss-me-sweet" dimples were gone, and her tinkly laugh which when she laughed everything laughed with her: you, the table, the chairs, the walls, life itself laughed along!

Though I suppose you may have already guessed, I wasn't missing this Joseph chap all that much, anyway. . . . Still, I was at my wits' end to know where had he got himself to? And was it for a short time, or was he now well and truly gone? And had he written, or had there been no letters from him at all? Well, you try inquiring about such things of the "bu-oys"—see if they'll favor you with a civil answer. Because they'll only gawp and be picking away at their teeth, as if to say, "Listen, son, you'll grow old pretty quick if you go on wanting to know everything."

But then arriving at the restaurant in the early morning once, I found the "bu-oys" all forgathered there already, sitting around the table, and one of them was reading from the paper and the rest listening raptly to him as he read. Well, I reckoned it was news of Joseph. Knew it right off, y'see. That's to say, I knew it on account of her. Standing apart from the rest, y'know, black cherry eyes and trim white apron, with her hands folded palms down on her breast: her face shone and her cheeks flamed and her upper lip parted from the lower, with a little lift, like a child's—the same as in the woods. . . . Only difference was that her pretty black cherry eyes had gazed upon Joseph then, whereas now they groped for him somewhere far off, but always for him, always for Joseph! . . . Well, cut a long story short, I couldn't wait for the paper to be put down, and I tore it open, and I knew then: MY JOSEPH WAS IN THE SOUP, NECK OR NOTHING NOW!!! . . . Though I'm bound to say I always knew he'd come to a bad end, known it all along, y'see, if not today, then tomorrow—anyway, someday soon he'd be landing himself in the soup, just had to, y'see, inevitable. . . . Though, of course, you couldn't really tell how it would turn out yet, I mean to say, know the *exact* outcome, but it was pretty much a foregone conclusion, wasn't it, that he wouldn't be let off with just a pat on the head, as you say, never mind being allowed to lick honey or breathe the fair fragrances of Araby for it.

I couldn't even begin to describe to you how I felt then; well, I won't say I was greatly upset because, after all, he'd stood in my way, been an awful thorn in my side, hadn't he. . . . But if I said I was overjoyed, that wouldn't be the whole truth either, now would it? I mean, it's not exactly what you'd have wished on your worst enemy, now is it? No, believe me when I say that I really wished him well with all my heart, wished for his sake that God wrought a miracle somehow, and they wouldn't. . . . Well, you couldn't very well expect that he'd be let off scot-free, could you, because that couldn't be allowed, now could it? Only—well, maybe they'd let him off easy, oh, I don't know, give him a light sentence just for form's sake, maybe? . . . I mean—anyway, I expect you must know what I mean, now don't you?

Well, for the next few days I went about in a fog, not knowing what to do with myself. And when I learned that the business was finally over, thank goodness, and the sentence would be announced on the following day, well, I give you my word, swear solemnly, on my life—which rest assured I hold dear—that I did not, no, could not fall asleep but lay tossing restlessly in my bed for half the night, till finally I got up and tried looking in at the club, not so much for the cards though, good God, no, as thinking maybe it might help me forget, even if for a minute, that . . . Because, y'see, I had had a premonition, a feeling, no, I knew, almost for certain, *that it was all up with him now.*

End of story, finis. I went along to the restaurant at the usual hour, and as I approached, two "bu-oys" came tearing out of the door looking greatly discombobulated, I must say. Quite nearly knocked me down! Coming inside, I met two strangers seated at the table, eating. She didn't appear to be serving, for her mum had taken her place. Nor was mum looking any the better for it either, because I'd have laid odds she'd been crying. Well, I'm never one to stand on ceremony, so I called her aside:

"Just wondering, madam, where your daughter might be keeping?"

"In her room," said she, giving a nod over at a hole in the wall with a door hung on it.

We'd been playing an amusing little game me and the mum all along, y'see. Oh, nothing was actually *said* amongst ourselves about the real business in hand, not outright anyhow, I mean, not in so many words. But I took it as read that she wanted the match: y'know, modern chap, good name, good income, scads of the ready I don't much mind missing, et cetera, so why shouldn't, I mean, why wouldn't she? Well, I should think she would! I mean, I'd already dropped several hints to her, *broad* hints, mind you, that I had conceived quite an interest in her daughter, quite a considerable interest, in fact. Well, I mean, what surer proof was there than I couldn't bear for her to be serving at meals. . . . So what answer you think she made me?

"Can't bear her serving? Well, perhaps serving yourself may suit you better!"

Her very words, the mother's, that is, whipping a naked elbow across her face to wipe it as if to say, "And you can like it or lump it!"

Yes, so where was I?—Hole in the wall with the door. If you were to ask me about letting myself into that small bit of a room she had, how I up and walked in suddenly, and the first thing I said to her, directly when I came in—well, I couldn't say, because I'm hanged anyway if I can recall any of it. No, what I meant to say is I only recall seeing her still wearing the trim white apron she always walked about in, sitting by the window, with her hands folded on her breast, palms down, her face gone pale and her cheeks white without a drop of color in them, and her upper lip parted from the lower, with a little lift to it like a child's, and her black cherry eyes without even a tear but misted over as if groping for something far-far off somewhere, with an air of dumb mourning all about her sweet white brow, wrinkling it a mite with a thoughtful, broody sort of a ripple you'd otherwise never have noticed in it. Oh, I give you my word, sir, swear it solemnly on my life, which rest assured I hold dear, that in that instant she appeared to me so beautiful, so, so—what's the word I want?—so divine, so absolutely divine, I was fit fairly to fling myself down on the ground before her and smother her feet in kisses! . . . Though, catching sight of me, she took no sudden alarm, as I thought she might, nor rose from her place taken aback nor even asked to know what I wanted. So unbidden I took up a stool and sat down facing her and I commenced talking away, talking without pause. The words seemed to come of themselves, came in torrents then, and I just talked, and talked, and talked. Hanged if I even know what I said, only I suppose the gist of it was mainly this. I wanted to console her, buck her up, let her know that it didn't make any sense, her "reacting" so. . . . In plain language, she mustn't take it to heart because, in a word, she was still too young, too fresh, too beautiful for that just yet. . . . I urged that no one could say for certain what the future had in store for her. . . . Well, now, take me, for instance, because here I am your young man of business, modern chap really, good name, good income, scads of the ready I don't much mind missing, et cetera. . . . I mean, what better proof did she want than that I should be prepared instantly, at her mere word, if she but declared herself willing to forget all that had heretofore transpired, as if none of it ever was, none of your Joseph, none of your "bu-oys," none of your "conspirashun" had ever even existed, all of them gone, end of story, finis.

You know, I haven't a clue as to where I had got such a power of the gab from then. But you think she gave me an answer for my troubles? Oh, forfend! Perish the thought! No, all she did was to only just sit and stare, sit and stare, sit and stare. Though it really beats the daylights out of me what all that sitting and staring signified anyway. Was it: "You really mean it? Oh, it's too grand to be true!" . . . Or, "I shall want the time to think it over, you know," . . . or "Go away!" or maybe really what it was, was: "Jo-seph" . . . Know what I mean? Not plain: "Joseph!" More like: "Jo-seph." . . .

I mean, you simply cannot imagine what a complete ass I felt then. Why, I was too humiliated to show my face for days afterwards! . . . Never mind feeling simply too wretched for words, almost as if I had had a personal hand in any of that ghastly business myself. . . . I mean, try as I might to get the fella out of my mind, absolutely to forget him, that's to say the Joseph chap, it was simply no go—just couldn't do it! . . . Now, it isn't as if I took any stock in dreams myself, because I don't, and certainly dead people have never scared me any, and I most emphatically do not believe in witchcraft, but I swear to you, by all that is holy, not a night has gone by since, that he hasn't appeared to me in a dream, that's to say, Joseph hasn't, and woken me up, pointing with his hand at that, preserve me, that mark like a blue ring, going round and round his throat. . . . You don't *really* think there might be anything to dreams? Because I know for a fact——Well, it did happen to an uncle of mine once that. . . . Oh, let it go! I don't take any stock in dreams, anyway! . . . It's only that I wasn't quite myself, off my feed, don't you know, just couldn't sleep. . . . You wouldn't be thinking I was scared, maybe? Good God, no. But, I mean, after all, chap I knew personally. Broke bread with together, shared the same table with for so long. Well, I mean to say! Anyway, I thought better of it, let the chips fall where they may, so to speak, and directly I'd worked myself up to it, I made straight for the restaurant where I knew I should find them.

Though, coming up to the restaurant——What restaurant? Gone!

Premises vacated! Absolutely no sign of the place! "Oh, excuse me (sir, madam), but where is the restaurant?" "Packed off a couple of days ago!" "How do you mean, packed off? Packed off where to?" "Packed off's packed off! Where to's another thing!" . . . Well, so I went round to the front gate and rang: Ding-a-ding! Gate was opened; went in, looked up the landlord: "Where's the restaurant? Dash it all, man, but where have they removed to?" Oh, lots of luck! Nobody seemed to know; couldn't say where they had gone. But that only fired up the old ambition, and once the old ambition gets fired up, it's heads up, for I'm the devil! So I went dashing about all over the place, looking here, there, everywhere, intent on leaving no stone unturned. . . . And the "bu-oys"? Well, wouldn't you know, but they'd gone and made themselves scarce; out of spite, as I've no doubt, now I needed them. Because I couldn't find hide nor hair of them anywhere. Not a trace! So, wanting to leave no avenue unexplored, I next went down to the police station, *pour faire des recherches,* that's to say, make official inquiries. Well, coming into the station, I got what you'd call your standard-form salutation: "State your business!" So I says, "Well, y'know, blah blah, this, that, so where's the restaurant?" So they says, "Which restaurant?" So I says, "Well, y'know, restaurant at blah blah, corner blah." So they says, "State your business anent said restaurant!" . . . Well, I mean to say! Would you believe it? I mean, about wanting me to tell them what *my* business there was? . . . Well, I clammed up, I mean who wouldn't have done? But they wouldn't let up, and kept putting the same question to me over and over again. . . . So, to cut a long story short, I'd landed myself in the most awful kind of a mess, and that's the truth. I mean, you simply have no idea what a runabout I got from them on account of it with the devil bringing up the rear! . . . Though, on the other hand, thinking back? I mean, what had I to be scared of anyway, seeing as how I am your commercial chap really, good name, good income, scads of the old ready I don't much mind missing, et cetera? . . . Because I'm not the sort to get himself mixed up in such business in the first place. I mean, after all, *si l'on ne mange pas de.* . . . Well, pardon my French, but there's no smoke without fire. I mean, you cannot eat garlic and expect your breath to smell like roses. Thing is, though, I hate it! No, I mean, ABSOLUTELY HATE IT. End of story, finis! . . . Well, I was fed up to the back teeth with the lot of them and heartily wished them all to the devil: dash the restaurant! dash the gel! dash Joseph! . . . Nor should I welcome anything more than to be over her finally. Make an end of it, basta! But, you see, the damnable thing is, she simply won't be gone from my thoughts. I keep picturing her in that trim white apron that shimmered whilst she walked and her cherry black eyes like cordials and her Cupid's bow lip with the little lift to it like a child's and her "kiss-me-sweet" dimples a-playing bo-peep and her tinkly laugh going right through a body and settling in amongst his vitals. . . . And often, at night, when I'm asleep, I'll suddenly hear her voice calling: "Jo-seph! Jo-seph!" . . . And I'll awaken in a cold sweat and with a start. For no sooner I'm reminded of her, than I'll be thinking of *him*.

See? I never wait for a chap to pull out his watch. Because I know well enough that all good things must come to an end. . . . And you do forgive me for taking up so much of your time? Here, give me your hand, then. There's a good chap! All to remain amongst ourselves, agreed? Like, what d'ye call it: "conspirashun," eh? . . .

Adieu!

Chabne

In Odessa it was. As it happens we were all sitting about having us a
party, a whole bunch of us, all literary types, don't you know, writers
with a bent for writing, readers with a bent for reading, and a mess of
just ordinary young folk, a couple of university boys were there too, oh,
and a girl was there, come down to Odessa to study, not bad either, a
real looker, built along remarkably strapping lines, nice rosy cheeks, as I
recall; there were also the occasional odd man out, that's to say, your
Jewish young men on the periphery, none of them belonged to our set,
but seeing a party of Jewish chaps jawing away sociably, they fall into
listening in, gradually inching their way forward with their chairs ever
closer and closer, till pretty soon one big companionable circle has been
formed, with everybody switching glasses on top of the table, and inter-
changing feet underneath it—and, suddenly, it's the Jews, all for one,
and one for all. . . . Now, mind you, it wasn't even a Friday night, nor
anywhere near the Sabbath then, just a regular weekday. The fact is
nobody had even mentioned the Sabbath because we were all talking
about something else entirely; the subject under hot debate then, if I'm
not mistaken, being Zionism, Territorialism, Ahad ha-Amism, Klausnerism, that sort of thing, and nobody was paying the least bit of mind to
the subject of money at the time nor thinking about any backwater called
Chabne, for that matter. Why, no one brought up the name of the place
even in passing. But all at once, I haven't a clue as to why or how, one
young man was up on his hind legs—it was one of the young gents on
the "periphery," redheaded chap with white eyebrows, and he swept the
table with his hand calling for silence, and was suddenly set to talking
away at us, so:

"Ssh, quieten down! Here, you say you want proof? I can tell you a

103

whale of a story that happened to me back in Chabne. You know Chabne? Well, there is a small town called Chabne. Now, Chabne is your sort of a place that has got everything you expect of a small Jewish town: post office, crown rabbi, a river, a real rabbi, a telegraph office, cemetery, town constable, talmud torah, synagogue, a whole parcel of pious Jewish folk, two tiny shuls, both of them prayer-and-study concerns mainly, and a great many paupers, with only a couple of exceedingly rich folks thrown in to garnish up the monotony; in other words, pretty much your down-home, run-of-the mill, average small Jewish town. Well, it was just my rotten luck to be passing through Chabne one afternoon of a Friday, when it was getting on towards the Sabbath. So listen to this. It won't take a minute to tell, and it's a pretty good story. Who knows, it may even come in handy, someday. I mean to say, as I am sure you already know, if you ever arrive in a small Jewish town for the Sabbath, then you had better act in a Jewish small-town way yourself; that is, if you know what is good for you. Thinking of continuing on your journey? Forget it! Chabne is not Odessa. Not in all Creation has anybody profaned the Sabbath day in Chabne. And if you are staying there for the Sabbath, you must first go to the bathhouse for ritual immersion. Though what else is there to do, anyway? Write a book? Never mind going to shul, saving the difference! You think otherwise, God forbid, they will do you an injury? Forfend! Nobody will lay a finger on you. All they will do is *stare* at you; all of Chabne will gather round to *stare* at the Jewish gent who has come to town for the Sabbath and won't go to shul. And what of your landlord, what sort of an impression do you think you will be making on him? What sort of pleasure do you think you will receive of a meal brought to your room to be eaten apart from everybody else? And who is to say they would agree to bring your meal up to your room, anyway? I mean, what do you take yourself for—a Russian *pomeshchik,* some high-nosed Russian country squire, not to be sharing the Sabbath meal with your landlord, not to be reciting the benediction ringingly at the man's table, not to be sociably hymning Sabbath anthems with the rest of the household? See, if you happened to be a *pomeshchik* (save us!), that would be something else again because they'd be bringing everything to your room then: your meat, your drink, a cigarette, even throw in the samovar; and all of it done on the q.t. so nobody knew, on account of it was the Sabbath. I suppose you want to know why. Well, don't bother asking. For once you start in to asking why—why this, why that, there just won't be an end to it. Cut a story short: you have come to Chabne? Then you had better be a Chabnite!

"So what happened to me is this: I was traveling to see the *pomesh-chik* who had an estate not far from Chabne and was delivering a roll of money to him, and a hefty couple of thousand it was too (save us!). Made for a mighty tight fit in the old inside breast pocket, I can tell you! So anyone not knowing I was carrying money would have guessed it straight away. Just by looking at me, I should think. Because when a man carries money on him he has an altogether different look about him: he walks different, stands different, talks different. Why, everybody knows money has power in it—it's, well, it's money! . . . The point is, though, what to be doing with it. I mean, first of all it was the Sabbath, so one couldn't very well be carrying it about on one's person without profaning the day. Chabne is not Odessa. Besides, I will confess it made me a bit jumpy staying the night at an inn, and all of that cash on me (save us!). Not, heaven forbid, that I was afraid of the inkeeper. As it happens the landlord was an excellent, God-fearing gentleman, quite respectably pious, too, by the look of him, what with that extremely handsome caftan he went about in, which he kept decently girdled round his middle and all. Nor was I afraid of robbers: Chabne did not (save us!) have a reputation for being a town of thieves and kidnappers. There has never been a case of anybody having his throat cut yet in Chabne nor of being robbed of his money there either. Oh, there had been a progrom or two, but that sort of thing only happened while it was on. Besides, where don't you run into progroms these days? . . . Anyway, I'll stake my name on it, you can walk about Chabne all alone even at the stroke of midnight, and nothing will happen to you. You have my personal guarantee as to that. So what had I to fear then? Well, naturally, I was afraid of only one thing: it was such a lot of money (save us!) and somebody else's money besides, not mine. . . . I mean, what if? God knows things did happen all of the time! . . . Well, I kept mulling it over, this way and that —truth to say, it looked bad. So I had a word with the innkeeper. 'Who,' I asked him, 'are the most reputable gentlemen in the parish, your richest men in Chabne?' So of course he asked me, 'For what purpose, sir? A business matter perhaps?' Well, I was damned if I'd reveal my predicament to him! It was all very well, his being an excellent, God-fearing gentleman, with an extremely handsome caftan he kept decently girdled round his middle and all, and Chabne (save us!) wasn't a city of thieves and cutthroats, but this was money, and such a lot of money besides, and somebody else's, not mine. . . . Anyway, I asked him one thing, he asked me another, so I said 'rich man,' so he said 'business'; this, that, one way or another I winkled out of him what I wanted to know: namely, that

Chabne had all the paupers you could want, and then some; that's to say, there were rich men in Chabne, too, but they were a bit thin on the ground. Well, actually, there was only one man you could really say was rich, without necessarily stretching a point, very rich even, maybe even rich as Croesus. That's to say, nobody bothered counting his money; still the man did have money, a whole sight of money, tons of it. Had considerable properties as well, houses, a marketful of shops, owned a wood or two—two huge tracts of timberland, actually. Nice chap, too, by all accounts, good heart, they said, openhanded; enjoyed throwing his money about in a philanthropic way, handouts, charitable loans, doing folks favors; never turned away a soul—didn't matter who came to him; all of it done to obtain public esteem, of course, because rich men like being held in high regard by ordinary folks; though he was quite unassuming on his own account, personally modest, hated being made much of (supposedly); in other words, a pretty honest gent on the whole; no saint, mind you, but he stopped short of doing what one oughtn't to do in public; anyway, not while anybody was looking; so they wouldn't really know, would they; I mean, who can vouch for anybody else, anyway? Although, come to that, if talk is of honesty, why be thanking the man for it? Because if such a person isn't honest, then who on earth is? . . .

"Well, from our talk, I knew that here was an individual I could entrust with my little hoard of money until the Sabbath was out. So I went to see him in good time, eve of the Sabbath, before taking ritual immersion in the bathhouse, and I found him at home sitting over a pious book. And a very presentable gent he was, too, I must say, serene, grand manner and all that, every inch your small-town rich gentleman to the dot. Well, coming into his study, I gave him good day and put my whole case to him, about my being on my way to see the *pomeshchik* who had that estate nearby and my carrying money to him, but having stopped the night here to keep the Sabbath; though I was anxious lest . . . well, I mean, God knows, things did happen all the time, didn't they, even if Chabne was not (save us!) a city of thieves and cutthroats, and my landlord was such an excellent, God-fearing gentleman, with a handsome caftan he kept girdled round his middle and all; only thing is, this was such a lot of money (save us!), and somebody else's money besides, not mine! . . . So he gave me a funny smile, and said, 'Well, what is it you want of me, young man?' So I asked him if he wouldn't please take my little hoard and keep it in his strongbox for over the Sabbath; because I

heard tell he had an iron safe, and I'd rest easier then. That's to say, God
forbid I should harbor any suspicions because, as I said, Chabne was not
your city of thieves and cutthroats; but it was such a lot of money (save
us!), and somebody else's besides, not mine. . . . Well, he heard me out,
and said smilingly, 'Young man, you don't know me, you've never laid
eyes on me before, so how can you trust me with so large a sum of
money?' So I says, 'A good name, sir, lets itself be known; and besides,' I
says, 'I am sure you'll give me a receipt of some sort; such a lot of money,'
I says, 'and somebody else's besides, not mine!' . . . So he smiled, saying
he never gave receipts. . . . So I says, 'All right, then, let it be without a
receipt.' So he answered that he didn't care to. So I asked him what was
to be done. So he says, 'As you think best.' So I says, 'So what about
witnesses?' So he says, 'Please yourself.' So I says, 'Who should I bring?'
So he says, 'Who you will.' So I says, 'Aren't there any reputable people
in your city that can be relied on?' So he says, 'All our people are reputable.' So the minute I heard that, I says, 'Well, in that case I'll run right
out and find a couple of reputable householders who can be relied on.'
So he says, 'Run out and bring who you will!' . . . Well, now, I could see
he was put out by the notion. So I excused myself to him by saying I'd
certainly not be doing such a thing, did I but possess as my own that
which I was entrusting to him; but as the money wasn't mine, I said,
being God's first and somebody else's second, I can't be be too careful.
'So don't you agree, sir? One cannot be too careful, can one, eh?' . . .
Well, he heard me out and smiled, but said no word besides. So I gathered
he wasn't too happy. But as I had told him I would run right out and
bring him a pair of reputable householders, I reckoned I'd better run out
now and bring him a pair. And so I quickly returned to the inn, and
proceeded to question my landlord once more about who in Chabne
were the most reputable householders. Though I couldn't get a thing out
of the man. For he insisted on being apprised of one thing first; because
if it was matrimony I had in mind, he said, that was one thing, but if it
was credit I was after, well, now, that was something else again; but even
if, he said, I was asking for no particular reason, he would still want to
know why. . . .

"Well, it was like pulling teeth, before he finally allowed that all
Chabnite householders were, without exception, reputable. For if you
want, you can remit them what they fall short of in reputability; because
what does being reputable have to do with anything anyway? Why, sir,
says he, if you will, you might call everybody reputable on his own

account, and if you will, there wasn't anybody on earth who was reputable. See now, says he, it rather depended on what you were looking for in a person in the way of reputability: was it money, was it lineage, or learning, or good breeding, or all of them rolled into one? But as there was nobody who possessed all of these qualities together, says he, then everybody in Chabne was reputable; but if, says he, it was top-drawer, sure-thing *quality* reputability I wanted, why, then there were only two reputable persons in Chabne: Reb Leyzer and Reb Yossi. For in the case of these two gentlemen, what we were looking at was the honest-to-goodness genuine article!' 'Ah, and who,' I asked, 'are Their Worships Reb Leyzer and Reb Yossi?' So he said to me, 'Now, really, sir, what's it to you, anyway? Why, suppose I was even to tell you, would you be any the wiser for it?' So I said to him, 'How do you mean? Everybody has his character.' So he said to me, 'Now, you *are* a wonder, sir, for wanting to know everything! Reb Leyzer is a Jewish gent called Leyzer, and Reb Yossi is a Jewish gent called Yossi. There, feeling happier now?' . . .

"Cut a story short, I went around to Reb Leyzer called Leyzer, and to Reb Yossi called Yossi, making the acquaintance of both these gentlemen; and quite a pious pair they made, too, both of them fairly up to their eyebrows in pious whiskers, and I chatted sociably with them about this, that, and the other thing, for as long and as windily as it took to get to the reason for my visit; which I then proceeded to explain to them without further ado, telling them all about the whys and the wherefores of my being on the way to see the *pomeshchik* who had the estate nearby, and of how I was carrying money for him, and was anxious lest . . . well, God knows, things did happen, even if Chabne was not (save us!) a city of thieves and cutthroats; but it was such a lot of money, and somebody else's money besides, not mine. . . . Which is why I was asking this favor of them. So if they'd be so kind as to spare me a minute and do me the honor of accompanying me to the house of the Wealthiest Man in Chabne, all I wanted of them was their estimable presences while I deposited my money with His Worship for safekeeping until the end of the Sabbath. Having heard me out and stroked their whiskers thoughtfully, Reb Leyzer who was called Leyzer and Reb Yossi who was called Yossi rehearsed each particular of my narrative with me several times over, and, satisfying themselves as to the whence and whither and what and when of the matter, they didn't wait to be asked twice, and we all went together to see His Worship the Wealthiest Man in Chabne, craving of him, if he would only be so kind, even if Chabne was not (save us!) a city of thieves and cutthroats. . . . And I unlaced my pockets in high style, retrieving and counting what tidy hoard I had been carrying, and I wrapped it all up in a piece of paper and put the entire bundle directly into His Worship's hands, to be deposited in his safe until the Sabbath were out; and then I craved of him again, if he would only be so kind, for even if Chabne was not (save us!) a city of thieves and cutthroats, this was after all money, and such a lot of money, and somebody else's money besides, not mine. . . . And His Worship received my bundle of money as tenderly from me as a boy-child at a birth might change hands from godmother to godfather, with my two gents looking on and stroking their whiskers like a pair of cats eyeing a slab of butter. . . . And then I took my leave of all three gentlemen, craving their pardons once more all around, if they would only be so kind, even if Chabne was not (save us!) a city of thieves and cutthroats, and I wished them all a good Sabbath, and there was an end of the business at last.

"My inside breast pocket being emptied, I felt half a ton lighter; and my mind being set at rest, I went along now to shul and heard a very fine cantor who was inclined to overdo the wobbly-voiced bits, and went in rather too much for extravagant cantoring, warbling the 'Lechoh Dodi' as trickily as a nightingale, and belting out the 'Mizmoyr-Shir-Leyoym-Shabbos' like a tenor at the theater (saving the difference!), but when he wound down finally, the style was purely Jewish, and done so feelingly, and in a manner so mournful and sweet, you'd have given anything to hear it done all over again—it was years since I had heard such a cantor, as in Chabne, and years since I had heard such a Sabbath blessing and Sabbath hymnings, as in Chabne, and years since I had tasted such savory hot peppered fish and noodles and Sabbath meat stew, as in Chabne, and years since I had slept so soundly as on that Sabbath night, to say nothing of sleeping into the following day as luxuriously as a king in the royal four-poster. And having slept roundly enough to do me for a month of Sabbaths, I arose refreshed and went out for a few idle turns on the Chabne High Street, taking in the Chabne sights, and the Chabne gentry and Chabne ladies, and the young Chabne bucks and young Chabne maidens all done up and prinked out in the 'latest fashion'; and after banqueting on the Sabbath-day cold cuts, and hymning the Sabbath-day anthems, and attending the Sabbath evening service, and coming back home to assist at Sabbath-end blessing, I settled my account with the landlady, knocking at least thirty kopecks off the reckoning, as per usual, and then went around to His Worship the Wealthiest Man in Chabne to collect my couple of thousand from him.

"Arriving at the house, I met my wealthy gentleman of Chabne parading up and down in his parlor in his best holiday silk caftan and wearing his best holiday silk waistcord with tassels. Which last items he had set to twirling around and around, and was passing from one fore-finger to the other, while cheerily bombinating along and hymning in his best holiday voice, so:

> Eleeyohoo Hanovee!
>   Elleeyohoo Hateesh-bee!
>   Ellee-yo-hoo Ha-ghee-lah-dee!
>   Beem-heyroh-oh, beem-heyroh-oh,
>   Beem-heyroh-oh-oh, bee-yo-meynoo! . . .

" 'Well,' says I to myself, 'if the man is in a hymning mood, then by all means, be my guest; I can wait to say my piece when he's finished.' But milord of Chabne never finished bombinating and hymning and twirling his tassels and passing them from one forefinger to the other. I was beginning to feel like I was sitting on hot coals and kept jumping up to ask him about that small matter needed attending to, but it was no use: he went on bombinating and hymning and twirling and passing his tassels from one forefinger to the other and pitching his voice ever higher and higher:

> Elleeyohoo Hanovee!
>   Eleeyohoo Hateesh-bee!
>   Elee-yo-hoo Ha-ghee-lah-dee!
>   Ai-ai-ai-ai!
>   Ai-ai-ai-ai!
>   Beem-heyroh-oh, beem-heyroh-oh,
>   Beem-heyroh-oh-oh, bee-yo-mey-noo! . . .
>
> Eleeyohoo Hanovee!
>   Eleeyohoo Hateesh-bee!
>   Elee-yo-hoo Ha-ghee-lah-dee! . . .

" 'Lord! when will it end?' I remember thinking, and I finally plucked up courage and went over to him and told him outright I was going away today (God willing!); that's to say, I was leaving directly, so about that small matter we have to settle between us? . . . Eh? . . . But all the fellow did was lift his forefinger with the tassels into the air, and pitch his voice higher still:

Eleeyohoo Hanovee!
  Eleeyohoo Hateesh-bee!
  Elee-yo-hoo Ha-ghee-lah-dee!
  Ai-ai-ai-ai!
  Ai-ai-ai-ai! . . .

" 'God! this is what I was dreaming the night before and last night and the whole blessed week!' That was what came into my mind then. 'Why, the man has gone completely round the bend over Elijah the Prophet and won't leave off singing that wretched tune!' . . . Cut a story short, he went on bombinating and hymning for just as long as it took until he finally stopped bombinating and hymning. 'And a very good week to you, young man!' he said to me then, 'Here, pull up a chair!' And we both sat down companionably at his table and he offered me a cigarette, ordering two glasses of tea to be brought, one for me and another for himself. Then he said to me, 'Now, young man, what good news do you have for me, eh?' 'Well, sir,' says I, 'what can I say but that I am going away today. I mean, I'm leaving directly, so if you don't mind,' says I, 'what of the little hoard I left behind?' 'Oh? What hoard was that, young man?' 'Why, the couple of thousand I gave to you.' 'What couple of thousand?' 'Why, sir, my money!' 'What money?' 'I mean, sir,' says I, 'the money I gave you to keep for me until the end of Sabbath.' 'Are you saying that you gave me money?' . . . And he shot me a look as though I had just told him the nose on his face wasn't his own but mine. . . .

"You can imagine how I felt. I mean, here was a fine how-d'ye-do! Oh, it's all very well your saying Chabne is not (save us!) a city of thieves and cutthroats. . . . But presently I thought better of it. Maybe he was just having himself a leg-pull at my expense? I began to laugh. 'Ha-ha, oh, that's rich, sir,' I said, 'You really had me going awhile, didn't you!' So then he says to me, quite seriously, 'How do you mean, had you going?' 'But surely, sir, you were pulling my leg!' This time he answered rather more sternly. 'Young man,' he said, "I am not your equal and I am certainly *not* pulling your leg!' . . .

"I felt my face convulse, I saw spots before my eyes, my ankles began to tremble, I thought I was falling through the floor! But I didn't let on. No, I persisted still in taking the whole thing for a practical joke and said, 'Now, really, sir, there is such a thing as carrying a joke too far! So won't you please give me my money and let me be on my way?' But his nibs of Chabne just sat opposite looking me in the eye, his gaze never flinching from mine, not by so much even as the quirk of an eyebrow or the flicker of an eyelash. He did nothing else except to stare, quite as though I had lapsed into lunacy (save us!), gone mad. 'Young man,' says he to me next, cool as a cucumber, 'I think you are mistaken, you are somehow out of your reckoning.' I confess I grew pretty hot under the collar at this, and I said to him, 'If you are not joking, Your Worship, then quite frankly I don't know what your game is!' . . . My mouth had gone dry and my tongue faltered and I fought for breath and a whistling commenced in my left ear so I thought any minute I would fall down in a dead swoon. 'Well, young man, I really can't imagine,' says he, 'what you can be talking about.' 'But didn't you,' says I, 'receive money from me the other day?' 'Me?' says he, 'receive money from you? Well, as to that,' says he, 'can you show me anything in writing?' . . . Here I despaired in earnest; I now understood why he had refused to sign any receipts back then! . . . 'God alive!' says I to him, 'but there were witnesses, what of the witnesses?' So he says, 'Witnesses? Which witnesses?' 'But there were two gentlemen present yesterday,' says I, 'Reb Leyzer and Reb Yossi!' Reb Leyzer, you say? Reb Yossi, too?' 'Good heavens!' says I, 'can't you remember, why, I even said I would run right out and bring them to you!' 'For my part you can run whither you please,' says he, 'just so long as you stop pestering me; for it seems to me, young man,' says he, 'that you aren't quite right in the head!' . . .

"But as I ran out looking for my witnesses I began to have doubts myself: suppose, now, I really was out of my mind? Had I conjured all of this out of my imagination? A dream? Maybe I wasn't even in Chabne? I went pounding down the street and my thoughts pounded away inside my head so I believed my skull would burst open and shatter into a thousand pieces. Only the devil himself must have induced me to stop at Chabne for the Sabbath. Dear God, what was I to do, what was to become of me, was I accursed, utterly ruined then!? . . .

"Some way or other I reached Reb Leyzer and Reb Yossi and told them of my calamity. 'For pity's sake,' I pleaded, 'I beg of you, sirs, you must come, quickly, if you have any mercy in you, it's such a lot of money, and not mine even, oh, save me, sirs, save me!' . . . And all three of us hurried over to see His Worship of Chabne, who, observing our arrival posthaste, came forward to receive us with an odd smile playing on his features and addressed himself to my two pious companions, so: 'Well, sirs, what make you of our pest here? This young man has somehow got hold of a ridiculous notion. He alleges to have given *me* money to keep for him, a very substantial sum, he would have us believe, and names you two good gentlemen as being witness to the proceeding. Damned impertinence, don't you think?' . . . But my two companions, my pious pair of witnesses, stood there up to their eyebrows in pious whiskers, merely glancing at me and at each other. 'Go on, gentlemen, why don't you speak?' His Worship prodded. 'Have you ever heard such damnable drivel in all your life?' 'Lord protect and save us from such a thing!' answered my pair of pious gents of the pious whiskers, exchanging glances the while. 'He claims, too,' continued His Worship of Chabne, 'that a great deal of money was involved, some outrageous sum I was supposed to be keeping under lock and key for him over the Sabbath. All poppycock, of course! I am afraid the poor boy is a bit, well, a bit tetched, God a-mercy!' 'Oh, yes, certainly, quite so . . . a bit tetched, God a-mercy!' echoed my two pious companions, glancing at His Worship and at each other and stroking their pious whiskers. . . . I wanted to protest, to cry out—but I couldn't! My tongue clove to my mouth, stopped up my throat somehow, like a bone, and I thought I would die. . . . My two companions now quietly withdrew, glancing oddly at His Worship and at each other. Their faces looked as white as the moon, but shone brightly, and their eyes were lit up as if the good Lord had just blessed them with a week's worth of profitable business. . . .

....

"Would you believe it? God only knows what would have become of me hadn't His Worship of Chabne come over to me just then and put his hands on my shoulders and opened his safe, saying to me, 'there, now, there, young man, don't be taking on so. Here is your money. I just wanted to show you *what* Chabne was and just *who* her pious folk were. . . .'

"Since then I never go to Chabne, and if I do go to Chabne, I never carry money with me, and if I do carry money, I never keep the Sabbath there, and if I do keep the Sabbath. . . . Well, I reckon by now I know what to do. . . ."

•   •   •

And when the redheaded chap with white eyebrows had finished telling his story, he drew his chair off to a side a bit, and sat down facing us, looking us all over to see what impression his tale had made. But we were all pretty well struck dumb. Our discussion had been cut short as with a cleaver. Finally one of us (I don't quite remember who; me, I think) did venture to inquire of the redheaded chap with white eyebrows, asking him:

"So, apropos of what did you tell that story?"

"Apropos of what?" returned he, perplexed. "What do you mean, apropos of what? Apropos of nothing, that's what. It's just a story is all it is. I just now happened to think of it, so I told it to you."

Three Widows

A Cautionary Tale
Told by a Bitter Old Bachelor

Widow Number One

Ah, but you see you are dead wrong, mon cher petit prince! Not all old maids are unhappy, nor all confirmed bachelors egoistical. Oh, I've no doubt that seated here in your study, with that seegar in your mouth and a dainty book in your hand, you think you know everything, believe yourself to have plumbed the human soul even to its depths, and all knotty questions are now resolved for you and lie prostrate at your feet. Never mind having with God's help discovered that true humdinger of a word *psychology!* Psh-sh! Who, sir, dare hold a candle to you now. Certainly no piker, that word *PSY-CHO-LO-GY!* . . . Shall I tell you though what sort of word psychology is? A fine word to butter parsnips with! That dish looking and smelling good enough to eat and tasting well enough to swallow, but it lies ill in the bowels, sir. Ergo, naught but hot air! So butter me no parsnips and spare me your talk about psychology. Though if you want real psychology, sit back and put your mind to what a body has to tell you. You shall afterward have, I assure you, time enough to make your opinions known (if any) as to the root of unhappiness and wherein does egoism reside. Now, in me you have living proof of the confirmed bachelor, and a confirmed bachelor I shall certainly die. The reason why? Ah! Now you see, there you have it! The moment one begins asking for reasons why and is prepared to listen *that's* real psychology! The main thing is not to be interrupting me with questions of why and wherefore and the rest. Quite hate being interrupted in the

115

middle like that. Myself, as you well know, sir, I've always rather inclined a mite to tetchiness; add to which, my "nerves" have recently taken to acting up. . . . Oh, no, not going mad, gracious me, no! You needn't fear that quite yet. That is rather more in your line, I should think; you've a wife. Myself, I cannot afford it. Have to have a clear head, you know. Keep in the pink. Surely you see that. In a word, no questions! And when I have finished with my story, and there is a point or two want clearing up, perhaps not quite accounted for, then ask away. No, really, be my guest. I shan't mind. Agreed? So, then! Though first take my seat. Y'don't really mind if instead I deposit myself on your rocker? Ah! Yes, I confess to rather liking it soft and comfy like this. Oh, by the way, you're really better off there, anyway. Not too likely to be caught napping on that thing, are we.

So, then! Get down to the story straight away. Quite hate introductions, unnecessary palaver. Paya was her name, but what she was known as at large was "the young widow." Why? There you go again! Why, why! Honestly, some people never learn. Stands to reason she'd be called "the young widow," doesn't it, if she was both young and a widow? Though, mark you! I was younger. How much younger? Does it really matter? I told you I was younger, which is quite sufficient for you to know. Younger *tout court*. And so there were people about with loose tongues who said that because I was young and unmarried, and she being a young widow—well, I suppose you know what I'm driving at. . . . Others went so far as even to congratulate me, wishing me all the happiness in the world in the liaison. Now, you can choose to believe me if you want or not, but if you don't, I certainly shan't loose any sleep over it. Mark you! I stand in no need of boasting to you; I was as much of a couple with her in that way as you, sir, are with me. Good friends is all, fond of each other. So what is new in any of that? Well, I had known her husband, you see. Oh, not "known" in the sense of only being acquainted, but friendly. Now, mark you, I don't say we were friends. I say we were *friendly*. That's two quite different things, you know, being friendly and being friends: one can be friendly without being friends, and the reverse, be best of friends and not be friendly. So *I* think. No, I don't want your opinion! So, then. We had got to be very friendly her husband and I, played preference together, chess occasionally. You know, it has been said of me that I am quite a famous chess player. Mark you, I myself make no such boast to you. I allow there may be better chess players. I only repeat what others say. . . . Quite a remarkable young man, though, her husband. Extremely accomplished fellow, you know. Rather learned, too, very much so, in fact. Complete autodidact, though. Oh, entirely self-taught, I assure you. No; no schooling whatsoever. Never at university, nor even secondary school, come to that. Hadn't a diploma to his name. But then we know all about diplomas, don't we. Give you a plug Russian trey note for the lot. What, not interested? Ah, well, suit yourself. Do quite hate contradicting a fellow! Oh, and wealthy, by the way. Quite wealthy, even. Well, I'm not sure what *you* may call wealthy. But in the circles I move in, any Jewish gentleman who has got himself a house and *ménage* to look after with a neat phaeton which to ride to town in and thriving businesses besides is accounted to be wealthy. Our sort don't much go in for cracking whips and rattling about the country hither and yon, do we! No, I dare say we don't. Casual saunter's more our style. So, then. His affairs throve, and he lived well. Absolute pleasure to be calling on 'em, you know. And didn't much matter when either, always made to feel welcome, quite one of the family, really. Not like some others who first time around will be all over you trying to please. Though second time, of course, your reception cools very considerably. Till by the third visit the temperature's become so chill you end up catching cold. . . . Oh, you needn't be looking so amused. Wasn't for a minute suggesting anyone *we* knew, I should hope. . . . And once let in, you weren't let out without being properly feted and fed. But why waste words, when an example will say all. A button need only have come adrift of your waistcoat, and nothing would do them but to have it sewn back on again for you on the spot! Ah, that amuses you, I see. Pooh, a button, you say! What's a button in the great scheme of things? Well, my good friend, to a bachelor a button more or less can make a world of difference. Reminded of a story, apropos. Frightful tale, really. Seems a young man went to look a young lady over before paying his addresses to her. Well, they took one look, found a button missing, and what d'ye think? Laughed at him that's what! So he went home and hanged himself. . . . But let it go. Quite hate digressions, anyway. . . . And as for their life together, perfect idyll. Like a pair of lovebirds those two, always. Honored each other as man and wife in a way you won't find among many of our higher sort these days. Mark you, I'm not pointing an accusing finger at anyone. And if you think different, can't say I much care one way or the other. Because, either way, I intend to go on with my story.

Came a day though and Pini, that's to say, Paya's husband, that's how he was called, Pini, returned home and took to his bed for five days, and upon the sixth—Pini was no more! Gone. Just like that! Popped off. How? Why? You wouldn't believe! Had an infected carbuncle on his neck they were supposed to cut away and didn't. Why, you ask? Because Y is a crooked letter, is why! It's why we must have so many doctors about, isn't it? I'd brought a pair of them in to have a look at him, and instantly the two were at loggerheads: one said cut, the other said not to cut. Meantime the patient expired. Well, what do you expect? Oh, it's all very well, your praising doctors! But if I were to read you out just the short list of how many good folks these gentlemen have packed off to the next world, you'd be tearing your hair out! Poisoned my only sister! How do I mean, poisoned? Think they dosed her with poison? Well, I'm not so mad as to claim any such twaddle! By poisoned I mean they didn't give her what they ought to have given her. If they had at least thought to give her quinine, she might have lived. . . . Oh, don't worry, I haven't lost my place, so you can put your mind at rest! So, then. We'd finished off my friend Pini, hadn't we. Ah, me! How can I even describe what a terrible blow was the man's passing for me? Other, perhaps, than to say I shouldn't have wished a brother, nay, a father! to have grieved as I did then. Oh, Pini! Pini! It was as if they'd taken away part of my life. To say nothing of being overwhelmed by pity. What tragedy! What awful desolation was the poor widow's lot! Left with only a tiny babe in arms, Rosie. Dear, sweet Rosie, precious child! Our one consolation in all that wretched business. If it weren't for the child, I honestly doubt we should either of us have borne up. Neither she *nor* I. Now, I am no doting female nor a fond mother to be praising a child to the skies. So if I say to you the child was a rare child, you can believe I say the truth. The child was a perfect picture, a blend of two perfectly beautiful people. I hardly know which was the more beautiful, he or she? Pini was handsome, Paya lovely. The child had got her father's eyes; Pini had blue eyes. We both loved the child, though I hardly know which of us loved it more, she or I? But how is it possible, you ask? She is the mother; am I then the father? But that hasn't the least thing to do with it. You will have to look into the matter more deeply, sir. Consider what ties of affection bound me to that house —how I pitied the widow, how my heart had gone out to the orphaned babe; add to that the child's beauty and grace and the fact of myself being utterly alone as a tree is alone—now, take all of these things and put them together, and you end up with the one thing which you, sir, denominate psychology. Not buttered parsnips, mark you, but true, honest-to-goodness psychology. Or are you, perhaps, thinking it was because I loved the mother? Well, I don't deny it, I loved her very much.

Have you any idea how much? Completely! Head over heels! Had the devil to pay for it, what's more! But would I let her know? That, never! You know, I used to stay up nights on end, thinking how I should tell her. And the next morning I was always ready to go to her and say, "Listen, Paya, here is how matters stand, etcetera, etcetera; for the rest —you do as you think best." But once I had arrived—words failed! You will say I'm a coward? But what care I for what you may say! You see, you must try and look a little deeper into the situation. Pini was my very close friend, and I loved him more than a brother. Yes, but what of Paya? Now, that's the real question, isn't it! For hadn't you only just confessed to me, sir, that you were absolutely mad about the woman? Ah, but you see the answer to that is: Just so! It is because I love her, because I'm completely mad about her, because I'm dying for her, that I cannot do it! But I fear you will never understand me. You see, if I said *psychology* to you, ah, then you'd certainly understand. But only let a body tell you something from the heart, and you think it is whimsical. But why should that concern me anyway? You can think as you will! I shall do as *I* will and proceed with my narration. The child grew; but a radish may grow as well. There is a difference 'twixt growing and growing. For what a waiting there is till a child sit up, stand up, walk, run, talk! And when at last it does sit up, does stand up, does walk, run, talk—do you think you are done? Oh, it would be a fitting thing for me to do, I dare say, to be ticking off chicken pox, measles, baby teeth, and the rest for you as is a woman's wont. But I am no woman and have no intention of wasting your time with such foolishness. Nor shall I be telling you about the clever things the child had done and said. It grew, it matured, and finally it "blossomed as the tender rose"—or so should I have said had I wished just now to express myself in the style of your novelists, who know as much of roses as a Turk of Scripture. Quite a genius they have, your novelists, for sitting before a lighted fire and toasting their feet and writing you of nature and of green woods, of roaring seas and sandy dunes, of the snows of yesteryear, and of unseen suns of yestreen, of witches' broomsticks and cast-off besom stubs. I cannot bear to look at them, at those fool descriptions that are enough to give a body the dry gripes. Never read the stuff! And if I chance to pick up a book and find it full of sunbeams and moonshine and chattering birds, I cast the wretched thing down on the earth and trample it underfoot! You're laughing? Say I'm mad? Very well then, I am mad! And can you think of no worse things to be?

So, then! She grew up, that same Rose, and was brought up properly, to be sure, that's to say, in a manner that befitted a young lady from such a cultured home. Her mother oversaw her education, in part. As did I, in part. And in no small part, I assure you; you can even say I gave up all of my time to the child so the child might have the best tutors, might be enrolled in school on time, might play the piano, might go dancing. In short, I was everywhere. I alone. Who else? Even took charge of the family businesses. And if it weren't for myself, they'd surely have stripped the mother clean, borne away her very bones, if given half the chance! As it was, they made off with enough—trust our precious Jews when it comes to that! . . . Yes, I know it rankles you hearing me say "our precious Jews." How else would you have me call 'em? It's all on account of what they're like anyway. Oh, you can call me an anti-Semite, or whatever you choose. I shall keep to my opinions, notwithstanding. As for anti-Semites, I wish them nothing better than to live in misery for so long as they remain ignorant of what Jews are really like! . . . But if you want to know what Jews are really like, ask *me!* . . . Though, of course, personally I have very little to do with 'em. Well, you know. I have my houses and my shops, which bring me in a considerable income, and there's the end of it. But that doesn't mean I don't have my own peck of troubles every year when it comes to drawing up contracts, renovating, collecting the rents. So, I dare say, goyim aren't much better. Quite as bad, in fact, blast 'em! Still, you'd expect a Jew to stand a mite higher than the rest; after all, Chosen People and all that. You don't really imagine that by always harping away at them with that fool "Thou-hast-chosen-us" rigmarole, you're doing them any great favor? Doesn't even come near! What's that? You cannot tolerate such talk? Well, I'm not about to argue the point. Whatever you say, I'll allow that as well. After all, everybody has a right to his opinions. Myself, I couldn't care less what others think. I know what I know.

So, then. Where were we? "Our precious Jews." Well, of course, no sooner was my poor Pini dead and Paya left a widow than the horde of fine folk promptly came a-knocking at her door: do-gooders, men of good counsel, intent on reducing the family fortune in detail by hook or by crook, and they proceeded in good earnest then to euchre her out of her worldly goods. Well, I flew to the rescue: "Out, riffraff!" I said, and took immediate charge of all of her finances and in good time, too, I might add. And do you know she was even prepared to make me a partner in the family enterprises? But I told her, absolutely not! I wasn't about to sell my houses with all the headaches which that should entail.

So she said, why was there any need of selling my houses if I might as easily become her partner at no cost? Now, what answer do you suppose I made to her? I said that I'd thank her never to make me such an offer again because that sort of talk only made me angry. *He,* God rest him, I said, didn't deserve that I should demand payment of you, madam, I said, for my services, and as for my time, madam, I said, I've time enough, madam, I said, not to have to take money from you for it; time enough, madam, I said, to be running my head against a brick wall if I chose. . . . That's what I said to her, to the widow, and she held her peace. Cast her eyes down—and hush, not a word! Though if you know anything about the turmoils of the heart, sir, you will understand what I had meant. . . . But why, you ask, hadn't I spoken up directly then? Oh, never ask, sir! For plainly it did not come to pass. But I assure you it should have been as easy to do as smoking this cigarette now. For it wanted but one word from me—and the knot should have been tied! but then the thought entered my head, "Yes, but what of poor Pini? . . . No, it was unthinkable, not when we'd been such very close friends!" . . . Ah, but I know what you are about to say. You are about to say our passions must not have burnt so fearfully hot after all. Well, you are wrong! For I had told you earlier that I was head over heels in love with the woman; though about her own feelings toward me—well, I shall say nothing to you of that, lest you think. . . . But what care I for what you may think! In the meantime, you could do worse than ordering the tea brought because my throat's past being parched already.

So, then, mon cher prince, where had we left off, you recall? Ah, to be sure—the family enterprises. Family enterprises! Well, I suppose I shall have cause enough to remember that business for the rest of my life. Put upon is hardly the word: capped and belled! Now, now, you needn't be crowing over my downfall yet! It isn't myself that I was talking of anyway—but of her! Nobody plays *me* for a fool! And do you know why? Because I won't allow it! But what difference does willing or no make if you have to do with an unconscionable lot of sharpers and swindlers, with such a pack of villainous brigands and cheats as will ensnare even the grandest and most powerful in their toils? You know, but they really stretched themselves, bent over backwards, you might say, just so we might be deprived of every last penny. Well, of course, I'm not so easily persuaded as all that to part with money. So you can well imagine how I made them sweat for it, had that whole blasted lot wishing themselves in hell, sent them to the devil together with their fathers and their father's fathers, made them spit blood in plenty, you may be sure, before they were finally done with mulcting us, pumping us dry—and I suppose you'd like to know for how much? For as much as they could get! And a very good thing, too, I'd thought to look round in time and told my widow, "Enough! Make an end for weal or for woe!" Well, I tried cutting our losses as best I could; only they commenced carving up what little there remained of her fortune in dead earnest then. But how could I have let such a thing happen, you ask? Well, I should like to have seen how a man of your admitted superior wisdom, sir, may have loosed himself of the clutches of that gang of thugs! Though, perhaps, you'd have made a better job of it at that. I shan't dispute the point. The worst that may be said of me is that I am no businessman. And heaven help me for it! But rather that than a knave! And you think it didn't cost me a bundle, as well? Mark you, now, I'm not telling you this by way of a boast. I wish only for you to know how one thing had led to another, and all was tending then toward the widow remaining no longer a widow and myself being a bachelor no more. It wanted but a single word from me, a mere word from myself, sir—yet I never said it! Why didn't I speak? Ah, but you see, there you have struck the very spot beneath which the mother lode awaits discovery! Mark it well, sir. It is there that your true psychology begins! For a sequel to the tale began unfolding before me. A sequel named "Rose"! . . . Now, you'd be well advised to attend carefully to my every word next. Because what follows isn't just something from a made-up novel, but a living, breathing tale, wrung straight from the heart!

I don't know what it is, but there is some kind of force at work in every mother that the minute she perceives her daughter to have out-grown her girlish frocks she becomes determined at all costs to see the child engaged to be married. She experiences no keener delight than in observing young men to be prancing about her darling. And there is never a young man she won't regard with a glad eye as a son-in-law. And what though the fellow be a vain, bubbleheaded nullity of nought squared, a rakehell, a card player, a devil-knows-what-ne'er-do-well-else? Well, now, that's hardly any of her concern, is it! Oh, but rest assured that none of your featherbrained young humbugs, none of your dissolute womanizers ever stepped foot into our house because, first of all, Rose isn't your sort of young woman to be acquainted with every jackanapes fop who can cut a caper, twirl about on his toes, twist his hands into pothooks, and make a mincing leg and "kiss-your-hand" reverence to a lady for all the world like a proper officer and gentleman. So that's reason number one. Besides, where think you *I* was the while? You think I should ever allow anyone of that popinjay set of pipsqueaks to touch Rose, to approach even within three paces of her? I do believe I'd sooner have broken every bone in his body! Made mincemeat of him is what I'd have done! I once attended a ball with her, a Jewish ball, at the club, there hobnobbing with only purebred aristos, yes, quite the same class as you, sir, call the bourgeoisie. . . . Well, along comes your very pattern of a "swell young dandy," crooks an elbow in imitation of the bend in the tap over milady's washbowl, following with a mincing backward shuffle of a leg, and inclines a pretty head, oh, ever so daintily to one side, and, every feature awash then in honeyed smiles, it speaks up in a girl's squeaky treble, saying—Oh, deuce knows what the ass said! Asked if he might have the next dance, I suppose. Well, well, he had his dance, all right! I gave him such a dance as he was unlikely soon to forget. We afterward had us a mighty good laugh over that sissified sorry excuse for a lady's man. Thereafter, any young swains wishing to make Rose's acquaintance knew they had first to apply to me, pass my review, so to speak, before being let to proceed. Even took to calling me "Cerberus" on account of it, my being the watchdog barring their way to Paradise, you see. Much I cared! Know who was upset by it, though? The mother! "You're driving people away from the house!" she'd say. "Oh? What people?" I'd answer her. "Dogs would be nearer the mark, I should think!" And so it went, once, twice, three times—then catastrophe! You're not thinking we quarreled, maybe? Well, guess again! Because this time you have quite outsmarted yourself! But why guess, when you would do better to hear a body out to the end, for a change.

So, then. One day I had gone along to my widow and discovered that another caller had preceded me there. Young chap. Might have been, oh, twenty, say, thirty maybe. Know the type? Your manner of young fellow that, do your damndest, but you can never guess their age? I'll admit, though, the man was a charmer, your thoroughly amiable sort of a person that, once in a great while, manages to come your way, with a good, honest mug on him and a kindly look in his eye. Couldn't have found fault with the fellow even if I wanted. Took to him instantly, in fact, from the minute I clapped eyes on him. And why? Because I cannot abide a cloying, sweet-faced toady with a sugary smile. Turns my stomach, it does, the way that sort have of always grinning adoringly at your teeth, hanging on your every word, eager to agree that there is snowfall in midsummer, and should you venture perchance that fishes grow on cherry trees, why, that just suits 'em dandy, too. . . . Me, whenever I come upon one of that nauseous breed, I experience the greatest urge to cover him in honey and let the bees take their pleasure of him at will. . . . Ah! The young man's name, you ask? Fat lot of good it does to know! Say we call him Shapiro and be done. There! Happy now? So young Shapiro was a bookkeeper in a distillery. A bookkeeper, but more than a bookkeeper. For he was in a fair way to being the "boss" of the enterprise in his own right, having a better notion of the business, you might say, than his employer did, and an employer who won't put his trust in his own people has got no place being an employer, anyway. . . . Yes, well, you are quite welcome to take a different view of the matter if you wish —only as it happens, I'm not soliciting your opinion!

So, then, I ask you, here I am being introduced to a young man called Shapiro, who is a bookkeeper and the manager of a going concern and an honest fellow who plays an excellent game of chess, that's to say, quite as good as my own, better, if you want, for I already told you, I don't preen myself on being a chess player—so how in God's name was I to know that the stage was even then being set for romance, and no trifling attachment, either, but a most perilous, full-blown affair of the heart! And can I really have been such an ass as not to have realized it immediately on that first encounter? And mark you, I'd even taken a personal hand in stoking the fires of love myself, praising him to the skies as I did, making heaven knows what of him! Blast chess! And blast all chess players along with it! While I was playing chess with him, he had had his mind on something else. I took his queen, but he had taken away my Rose! I checkmated him in three moves, but he "mated" in four because upon the fourth move, that being his fourth visit to the house, my widow took me aside and, with a most deuced odd sparkle in her eye, I must say, announced that she had wonderful news to tell. It was all settled, she said, the wedding was on, and Rosie dearest was betrothed to the Shapiro chap and she herself was in seventh heaven and congratulations were in order, so God bless me and God bless her and God bless us both and amen forever!

As concerns the state I was put into when I finally was made privy to these glad tidings, I prefer not to speak of it to you. You will only say I am a monster, a lunatic, a madman. She herself told me no less. I mean, the widow. At first she laughed, then she scolded, and at last there followed a scene of hysterics and tears attended by an exchange of the most extravagant unpleasantnesses besides—in a word, a royal row! Matters between us, you see, had come to a head, and hard words were said on both sides, neither one of us showing an inclination to spare the other's feelings, and within the compass of half an hour we told each other as many home truths as both of us had not expressed in all the twenty years we had known each other! I told her bluntly she'd been the death of me, that she had murdered me just as surely as she would have done had she driven a dagger into my heart, that she had taken from me my one comfort in life, that she had ripped my soul from my breast, had taken away Rose and given her to another. She for her part countered that if anybody was the death of anybody, it was myself alone, and if anybody had ripped the soul from anybody, it was I who had ripped out her soul, not all at once, but slowly, inch by inch, over a span of more than eighteen years! . . . What she meant by this, I needn't explain; even a fool could tell you. And what answer I made her, I am under no obligation to relate. I shall only say that I did not conduct myself as a gentleman; I suppose you might even call my conduct coarse, very coarse! I snatched up my hat and slammed the door and rushed out into the street like one truly gone mad and promised myself I should never set foot in her house again for as long as I lived! . . . Well, what do you think? After all, you're by way of being a thinker, sir. So what says your psychology now? What shall I have done in the consequence? Gone and drowned myself? Bought a revolver? Hanged myself from a pear tree? Ah, but that I hadn't drowned myself nor shot myself nor hanged myself —that, please God, you can plainly see for yourself. Though, regarding what happened next—I must insist on putting it off for another time. I doubt you'll be much the worse for indulging me in this for a little while. I've got to be off to my widows. They are waiting dinner for me.

FINIS WIDOW NUMBER ONE

Widow Number Two

Why have I kept you waiting for so long? Because it suited me. Myself, sir, if I have a notion to tell anything, I tell it when it suits me, not when it suits *you*. . . . Though that it does suit you—well, now, that's plain enough to see; when it comes to stories, especially if there's a good yarn in prospect, then everybody will lend an ear gladly. For it's hardly any skin off my nose is it, if I happen to be sitting back in my chair at home, say, puffing on an after-dinner cigar, while you sweat away like a Trojan telling me a story? Ah, but that the tale happens also to be the cause of immeasurable grief to the teller—pray what concern may that be of yours? Anything to hear a good yarn! Oh, do simmer down, it wasn't you in particular I had in mind anyway! Best keep your mind on the story and let me get on with telling it. Which though granted is a separate thing entirely, having nothing to do with the previous story, I should, anyway, like for you to keep the earlier one in mind because there is, after all, something of a connection between them, indeed, a not inconsiderable connection! And in case you have forgotten any of it, I remind you of it now. Breeze you through only the highlights, a precis, as it were.

I had a friend, Pini, who had a wife, Paya, and they had a child, Rose. My friend, Pini, died, and Paya was left a young widow. I became one of the family to her and her constant visitor, a friend, a private secretary, a surrogate brother, and was absolutely mad about her. But I never could find the courage to tell her. And so our salad days went by. The daughter grew up; Rose had blossomed, and I lost complete possession of myself—mark you! lost it in the worst way. But then blasted mischance took a hand and brought along a nice enough young chap named Shapiro, who was a bookkeeper and a pretty fair hand at chess besides, and Rose lost her heart to him. Whereupon I let all my bitterness out on the mother; we quarreled, and I slammed the door shut swearing never to return! There, happy now?

Now, it strikes me that you are eager to know one thing. Did I keep my word or not? Well, you're the what-d'ye-call-it, psychologist? Well, go on, take a stab at telling me yourself if I kept my word or no. What, nothing to say? And do you know why? It's because you don't know! . . . Give ear now to what really happened.

The whole night I stalked the city like a madman in all but name; pacing off the length and breadth of every street three times over and arriving home only with coming of day, I proceeded to sort out all of my personal papers of which I tore up a great many—I hate old papers!—packed my gear and then wrote away to a couple of acquaintances, not having, God knows, any friends or kin otherwise, being as much alone in the world as a tree is alone, and finally I left a few instructions concerning my properties, and when all of this was done, I sat down on my bed cradling my head in my hands and thought and thought and thought—until daybreak. Then after taking pains with my toilet and dressing, I betook myself to my widow, rang the bell, entered, ordered coffee brought, and waited for madam to rise. My widow got up and perceiving me, remained standing awhile without moving. Pouches were showing under her eyes, and her face was pale. So, hadn't she slept the night then, either? . . . The first words I spoke to her were these three:

"Where is Rose?"

No sooner were the words out than, sure enough, Rose appeared: beautiful as the day, bright as the sun, and good as God is good. Catching sight of me, she flushed slightly, but then she came over to me and gently stroked my head, drawing her hand over it from the brow upward, as a little child might be stroked, looking me in the eye and burst out laughing. And what sort of laughter think you it was? Not a hint of malice in it, good Lord, no, but was rather so beguilingly infectious as to set yourself and everybody else and the very walls of the house a-ringing with laughter! Yes, mon cher prince darling, such is the power she has, this Rose of ours, even to this day. And for such a laugh of hers, I'd even now give away everything I have. The thing is, she no longer laughs these days; troubles, poor thing, troubles to spare, and little matter enough for laughing. No, but I quite hate taking things out of turn. Much prefer it if when you begin a thing, you proceed with it in the proper sequence. So, then, to proceed in proper sequence.

Every try marrying off a daughter, sir? No? Haven't had the pleasure? Then pray, sir, you never shall! Had a taste of the business myself once, quite a substantial taste, in fact, and notwithstanding the daughter wasn't even mine, I had still to go through with it. Oh, I dare say I'll remember it for a long, long time yet! But I ask you, what was I supposed to do if my widow, that's to say, Paya, is the kind of person who has been used always to having everything handed to her on a silver platter? And really whose fault is it but mine, anyway? After all, wasn't it myself who taught them, mother *and* daughter both, that if anything was wanted in the house, I need only be told, and though heaven and earth had to be moved, it was as good as theirs within the hour! Need money —come to me! Call for a doctor—me! Engage a cook—me! A dancing master—me! A dress, a shoe, a tailor, a butcher, a feather, a froufrou, a furbelow, a door latch—me, me, me, always me! Think I didn't say to them, "But what's to become of you? Lace hankies to dishrags, I suppose!" That's how I pleaded with them. But all they did was to laugh. Everything was a joke with them! Life itself all a great rollicking lark! There are such people in the world, you know. Not many, I grant you, but still there are. And who must it happen to?—Me! Who must fret over other people's children?—Me! Who lose sleep over other people's troubles?—Me! Who dance at other people's weddings?—Me! Who cry at strangers' funerals!—Me! Ah, say you, but who asked me to anyway? Though answer me this: Who asks you to rush headlong into a fire to save another's child? Who asks you to jump in the river to rescue another from drowning? Who asks you to wince because of another's pain? Ah, say you, but *I* don't go rushing headlong into fires nor jump into rivers, and I never wince. Then you, sir, are an animal! I am not an animal; I'm a man. Mark you, I make no pretense of being an idealist, just a simple, ordinary person, and a confirmed bachelor besides, even if your psychology affirms that all old bachelors are egoistical. Only suppose now the "self" too is egoistical? Can't abide speculation, you say? Can't stand philosophy? Nor can I, sir!

So, then, my widow's little girl was to be married, and I to play father of the bride. Well, if you've a more palatable title to offer, I'd be glad to hear it. Because I dare say you are a little acquainted with me and my tetchiness by now and know how much I may have relished the role. Father of the bride! Makes me sick just hearing the name! Call me dogsbody, call me menial, call me lackey, call me a horse and I'll ride it to the jakes—call me anything but father of the bride! She, on the other hand, that's to say, the widow, couldn't be more pleased by her own new moniker—mother of the bride! Puffed her up something grand, being called so. "Why, next, madam, they'll be calling you mother-in-law!" That's what I said to her. Well, didn't that just set her a-beaming though, and she said, "Please heaven and I see the day!" . . . Likely mother-in-law her! You should have seen her on the wedding day, standing together with the daughter under the wedding canopy. What a picture was there! What beauty! What youth! You'd never in all your living days have thought to say the pair were mother and daughter. Two sisters, rather! I tell you I fell to gazing at her standing there with that young bridal pair beneath the canopy, and I thought to myself then:

My God what an ass you are! Alone as a stone for all of these years! Here is your chance! . . . One word from you, one look, and presto! Alone no more! . . . Build your home now. . . . Plant your vineyard. . . . Step into your Garden of Eden. . . . Enjoy its fruits in peace and quiet amid your dear, faithful own. . . . Put Rose out of your mind. . . . Rose isn't for you. . . . Rose will do for a daughter. . . . Look at the mother! It's her you must speak to, you savage, to her and no other! Why this damned endless dawdling of yours still? Regard how she looks at you, can't you see the look in her eyes?

So spoke I to myself and met Paya's gaze, and my heart wrenched in my bosom—with pity, for her. . . . Hear that? Pity! Nothing left besides, but pity. . . . Once, I remember, there may have been another feeling, perhaps. . . . Now there remained only pity. . . . And if the talk is of pity, then am I not to be pitied as well? Perhaps pitied even more? Though who had she to blame but herself, anyway? Why hadn't she spoken up? And why keep silent still? Where does it say that I shall, and she shall not? . . . Modesty, you say? Convention? Way of the world? Well, I don't give *that* for the world! I acknowledge no distinction: "he" shall speak first, "she" shall speak first. People are people! If she will not speak, then neither shall I speak! You wish to call it obstinacy, ambition, madness? Call it what you will! I've already told you, it's all the same to me. . . . Myself, I've no other wish in baring my soul to you than to analyze, together with yourself, the reason why, to discover, if you will, the worm in the apple. Maybe it was because Paya and myself never really had two level minutes together alone? Always some other creature in our midst that occupied all of our time, our feelings, our troubles, our pleasures— everything always belonging to somebody else, never to ourselves. An idle minute, just the two of us together? Forfend! The deuce knows why! You'd have thought that both of us had been created solely for the sake of others. First, there had been Pini. Then, please God, little Rosie. And now, God thought to bring us fresh comfort to rejoice in, a son-in-law at the family board! Though, mark you! This was your genuine article in the son-in-law line. The kind of son-in-law any Jewish family might wish itself blest with having! You well enough know that I'm not your sort that is easily impressed and in the habit of praising a body to the rafters. So I shan't bend your ear with the usual humbug of vain puffery and extravagant praise. I'll merely say that to use the term angel from heaven in his regard would only be an affront to the fellow. Does that satisfy you? For if there is a heaven above and if there are angels flapping about in it and if this angelic host falls little short of Shapiro, then, I tell you, it would be worth dying and better to be with them than abide among the rest of the two-legged beasts that knock about idly underneath God's sky and defile the earth. You say I'm a misanthrope, that I despise the human race? But if you, sir, had received at the hands of one of the race what *we* received, then it isn't a misanthrope you'd have become, but a heartless murderer! You'd have stationed yourself in the middle of the street with a knife and begun slaughtering people like sheep! . . . Though what fashion of entertainment is this, allowing a body to talk away for hours on end without offering even a glass of water? Order tea!

So, then. Where were we? Ah! Our comfort and joy. Our son-in-law, Shapiro.

I think I told you last time that he was director of a distillery, that's to say, managed the whole works, and not only its director but by way also of being virtual "boss" of the place. All of it, lock, stock, and barrel, being then in his hands and registered in his name. Their confidence in him, you see, being nothing short of boundless, and loving him as they did like a son. So you can well understand that these loving employers of his, two partners, or crooks, rather—though begging both their pardons for saying so, as the pair of these gentlemen have long since passed on "to a better world," as we say, in other words, they absconded to America—that this pair of rogues, I say, should have attended the wedding in the capacity of the bridegroom's next of kin, not only thus fulfilling the charitable duty of giving the groom away but also presenting him with a box with silver as a wedding gift and conducting themselves in a fashion altogether so generous and a manner so mild as to give every appearance of being true philanthropists. Oh, I do so love a philanthropist, and most of all your type of employer-philanthropist, who, when he comes a-calling at your house on the occasion of a family celebration, makes such a gaudy show of his philanthropy as to compel everybody around to sit up and take notice that he, the employer, that is, knows how to appreciate what he's pleased to call his "man." . . . Ah, but that this "man" of his has peradventure made the employer his fortune? And that if it weren't for this "man" of his, the employer might never himself have become an employer and a philanthropist in the first place? . . . Oh, it is quite useless your grinning me that grin of yours! Mon cher prince, I make no pretense of being a Socialist. Only I do heartily despise an employer-philanthropist! Though what's it to me, anyway? What're my grounds? Hearken, then, to what shameless villainies your employer-philanthropist will stoop! It seems to me that if God sends and you are blessed in having a business that brings you in a very comfortable several thousand a year and you have a dependable, steady man running things for you, then you ought to be in the enviable position of sleeping the night through peacefully at home and of even going away on holiday abroad and of generally living the good life—now, don't you agree? Ah, but you've failed to include our precious Jews in the reckoning! Oh, I know you hate my bringing up the subject of "our precious Jews" again. But the world, you see, affords 'em so little scope! A Jewish gent is never happy but when he's at trade, always flying about, wheeling, dealing, forever getting cracking, being on the go, here, there, yonder, everywhere —so he may be seen! May be heard! Cut a long story short, my Shapiro's employers weren't satisfied with having but one daisy of a business in hand under so trustworthy a stewardship. No, they must be getting into fields and woods, into auctions and tax farming, into bran, wheat, and whatnot, and when the market in houses caught fire, the pair became so fired up by it, as also to want to give houses a go, but then the houses caught fire and burnt down, whereby the same pair got burnt themselves, so they went and dragged our Shapiro into it with promissory notes all signed by himself and grabbed what ready cash there was and departed then for America where (word is) they are doing "alright," as they say in the lingo of that country, but leaving him, Shapiro, that is, holding the bag, sunk up to his ears in debts and awash in signed promissory notes head to foot. Thereupon followed a great scandal, the upshot of which was that nobody cared either way if he was servant or master—he must anyway redeem the notes, and, as he hadn't what to redeem them with, he was ipso facto bankrupt, and, as neither could he prove that bankruptcy had resulted from natural disaster, he must be declared, as you may or may not be aware, sir, what we call in the trade a "fraudulent bankrupt," to wit: a low defaulting blackguardly cheat, and a low defaulting blackguardly cheat gets put away in the pokey, because there is nothing the world hates more than a low defaulting blackguardly cheat! Oh, you can be a defaulting blackguard ten times over and be getting away with the same old dodge ten times over, just as long as you manage the swindle roundly, brazenly, and in a high style, and then, cocking a fig (your pardon!) at the world, you pick out a house in another likely place and buy it for a song, that's to say "on credit," and soon enough you're playing the respectable gent again, brokering alliances between the best families, peddling influence, stepping on people's heads, and, having pushed your way in among the powers that be, the small clutch of select gentry who lead the town about by the nose, you preen yourself on being an altogether exceptional fellow and strut about puffing and sputtering like the cock of the walk and turn up your nose at everybody, thinking yourself entirely too clever a devil by half for Old Scratch to spoil the fun by coming untimely and fetching you away! . . . Please forgive me, I do hope you know I meant none of this personally, I wasn't talking to

you really, but to the wall. . . . Well, let it go! My dear boy, my Shapiro,
couldn't bear the disgrace, and in particular, by the way, did his heart
grieve for the poor widows and orphans (his employers not scrupling to
swindle even children, taking money wherever they could)—well, he
took poison!

I don't suppose you think it important how he poisoned himself or
where he procured the poison. And why poison especially? And what
kind of letter had he written to me? And what had he said? And what
was his manner of taking leave of Rose? Or of the mother, or of myself?
—None of it amounts to any more than the sentiments trafficked in by
novelists to wring a tear from a foolish reader. All I have to say, I can say
to you in a word: it wasn't himself the man had gone and poisoned—
he'd poisoned us all! So great was our calamity, so deep our pain, so
terrible our grief, that there wasn't a single tear to be found among the
three of us which we could have let drop! We turned to stone, congealed,
were utterly without life, had fallen face down on the earth, and should
have accounted ourselves infinitely blest if somebody had come along
and lopped off all our heads with a knife! . . . You know, you may say
what you will, but I cannot bear the sight of any of that stupid lot that
will drop in to console you whenever misfortune, preserve us, happens
to strike. What mournful faces they put on for you, in every one of which
you see plainly written, "Thank God it isn't me!" . . . Their wooden prat-
tle which you can't make head or tail of, their false praise, their slinking
away without so much as a civil handshake but a halfhearted mutter
under the nostrils by way of valediction. . . . Shall I tell you something
else? Even Job, whom it's the custom for every ignorant yahoo to look
into with scarcely any more notion than his backside has, makes me
heartily sick now. But what's this? Blasphemy, say you? Call *that* blasphemy? And what about hoodwinking an innocent person, telling him
to sign promissory notes, whereas you take yourself off to America with
money and leave your "man" to poison himself and the lives of three
other innocent people besides—so how do you call that, according to
your lights? Come, come, what label would you put to it? Not blasphemy? No? Aha! And say you also that from God there shall come no
evil? Because, after all, how can one speak ill of God? Well, let's just all
have a peek at what good old Job may say to that! The same pious old
Job it's the custom for us to look into with scarcely any more notion
than has our own backside. What? Nothing to say? Aha! Nor have I, sir.
Because you might talk till you have talked yourself blue in the face and

not be answered! You'd only be repeating the same old rigmarole, anyway: "The Lord giveth, and the Lord taketh away"—without becoming a whit the wiser for it. . . . So what say you to that, sir! Philosophizing, you say, is chawing on old straw? Aha! My sentiments exactly.

So, then. Getting back to my widow. . . . Did I say widow? Widows rather! Rose a widow, too! Ha ha ha! Sad, isn't it? An insult to nature so crude you cannot help laughing. Rose a widow! You should have seen her; a child of fifteen summers could not have looked younger. Rose a widow! Never mind, widow. Rose with child yet! Rose a mother! Three months on, following Shapiro's death, a little creature's voice made itself heard in the house, and the house became filled with the little creature. Birdy. That was the name they gave to it, and in that house Birdy was absolute sovereign. Everything done in the place was done only for Birdy's sake; wherever you happened to be sitting, or standing, or whatever else it was you happened to be doing, talk was always of Birdy and only of Birdy and of nothing but Birdy! If one were of a mind to be a religious man and believed in a "special providence," as you may call it, I should have said to you then that God expressly thought to compensate us for our great affliction by sending this child to console us. But as, however, you for a fact know that I am scarcely what you call your believing sort of person, and as I greatly doubt, too, that you . . . What's that? Oh, but surely you can't seriously mean to propose to me now that you *do* believe!—Well, suit yourself. I certainly shan't hold it against you, not so long as you are persuaded in good conscience that you are no pious humbug, sir, no religious hypocrite yourself. Because by God, sir, I hate hypocrites, hate 'em as a Jew hates pork! Be you as pious as you wish, for my part, just so you are in truth pious for yours. But if you are a deceitful rogue, sir, merely one of your posturing sanctimonious "amen-and-amener" poseurs, then you are of an alien kidney, sir, and I should have as much use for you as attending my own hanging. And there you have me all, sir, in a nutshell!

Right, so what's our recital for the day, again?—Birdy! Yes, well, from the minute Birdy came into the world, everything looked suddenly to have come alive again. The world at large and everybody in it took to going cheerily about and smiling. Faces beamed, and every eye sparkled and shone. With the child's coming we'd all of us been reborn. Shall I tell you something nice? Rose, you know, hadn't shown a smile on her face in a great while, and all at once she began again to laugh with the same peculiar laugh as she had had of yore that is so infectious you are com-

pelled to laugh yourself, even if tears better suited you then. Such was
the power Birdy showed when she opened up her little eyes and took to
regarding all three of us for the first time with a spark of understanding.
Never mind the first smile that formed itself on Birdy's little lips, which
positively drove both widows mad with wonderment and enthusiasm.
And when they next greeted me in such an all-fired, unlooked-for rush,
they scared me half out of my wits:

"Goodness, where on earth were you a minute ago?"

Such was the manner of the widows' sudden onslaught.

"Why, what is it? What's happened?" I asked in great dread and was
answered by both together:

"Gracious, it's Birdy! It couldn't have been above half a minute that
Birdy laughed! It's her first time!"

"Ah, is that all?" I answered dryly although inside I was really
pleased as Punch, of course, but not so much at Birdy's having laughed
as in observing what high spirits my two widows were put into by it.
Well, you can imagine the sensation brought on by baby's first tooth!
The first to perceive it, naturally, was the younger widow, the infant's
mother. She it was who called over the older widow, Paya, that is, and
together the widows proceeded probing away by the agency of a small
glass, and when a telltale ping! was heard, signifying a tooth's presence,
they raised such a confounded noise, I rushed in from the neighboring
room all of a panic and half dead with fright.

"God, what's going on?"

"It's a tooth!"

"There you go again, imagining things," I said, thinking to tease
them for a bit. Both widows, though, took hold of my finger and touched
it to a pointy nubbin in Birdy's warm little mouth that might have passed
for a tooth if you cared to stretch a point.

"Well?" they both asked and waited for me to bring them the good
word of baby's new tooth. But I wouldn't let on and remained pointedly
po-faced. I love teasing them. So I quizzed back,

"Well, what?"

"Well, it's a tooth, isn't it?"

"Tooth? Well, yes, what else did you expect?"

And it goes without saying, of course, if there's really a tooth, then
Birdy must be a prodigy whose equal shall not be found anywhere in the
whole world! And as Birdy is such an accomplished young lady she must
really be kissed for it and kissed so liberally and for so long that she must

at last be set to crying. Well, I finally snatched the child out of their hands and soothed it. For the child is never so quiet as she is with me, and Birdy loves nobody's hair so well as she loves my hair and nobody's nose gets pulled so often as her tiny adorable little fingers will pull my nose and feeling those tiny adorable little fingers upon oneself is simply Heaven, for couldn't you just smother each one of her tiny adorable soft, plump, white little fingers in a thousand adoring little kisses m'mmmmm? Ah, I can see you looking at me now, and you're thinking, "Now, here's a fellow with the soul of a woman; else why should he love little children so?" . . . Well, I've guessed right, haven't I? That's exactly what you were thinking. But truth is, I don't know what kind of soul I've got; but that I love children—that is a fact! And who else should I love if not little children? Would you really prefer I loved your big 'uns? Those same sleek brutish mugs with their protuberant stuffed little tums, whose entire life consists in partaking of pleasurable dinners topped off with a good cigar and a game of preference before retiring? Or is it your public-spirited fine gentry you'd rather I loved, the sort that empty the public purse by way of making a living while drumming up their own virtues and loudly proclaiming before the world that their only ambition is to serve the public good? . . . Or would you rather I loved those impudent young pups who want to reform the world and call me "boordjewahs vermin" and demand that I sell my houses and share out the proceeds among them in the name of expropriation? Or would you instead I loved your grandes dames of fashion, those fat overfed stupid cows whose only ideal in life is that of gorging themselves, wearing fine clothes and expensive jewelry, going to the theater, and being ogled by strange men? Or better to love your manly spinsters with the cropped hair, who once, in my youth, used to be called "Femino-nihilists" and today go by the names of "Ziono-socialites" or "Socio-revolutionettes" or "Constitutio-democrettes" and other such charming sobriquets in kind? . . . Ah, say you, it's because I'm an old bachelor that I'm malcontent and misan-thropic and I care for nobody? Well, say away—myself, sir, I care not a whit what you say! I do as I please, which is to tell my story. So, where was I? Yes, the child, Birdy, about how we loved her. We gladly gave up the whole of our lives to the child, all three of us, because the child sweetened our bitter portion in life, giving us renewed strength to carry the heavy burden of this tomfool, corrupt world. Though for myself, personally, the child also concealed within it a secret entire. One which you will understand if you would but recall what Rose was to me. The older the child grew, the more the hope was nourished in my heart that my solitude might come to an end, and I, too, should know at last what it meant to have a life in this world. . . . Nor was I alone in cherishing the notion—the same hope flourished in Paya's heart—and, though we never spoke of it aloud, still, to all three of us it was as clear as day that this must needs come to pass sometime. . . . You may perchance ask, but how is it possible for people to understand one another mutely? Well, that only shows that you know psychology, but not people. . . . Allow me to paint you a picture, by way of example, that you may understand how people are able to discourse with one another, catch one another's drift, as it were, without words almost. Here's your picture then.

A summer's night. The sky is awash in milky white streaks. I was about to say that the stars glitter, gleam, glow! But then I was reminded that I'd seen that before in a book somewhere, and I've no wish to rehash somebody else's words. I already said I hated their descriptions of nature, which bear as much resemblance to nature as I resemble a Turkish pasha. To proceed then: it was one of those rare warm, luminous, perfectly splendid nights, when even the driest person in the world will brim over with poetical sentiment and long himself to be yonder somewhere, far, far away, not knowing even where this somewhere is. And he is swept up on every side in a sudden strange rush of divine inspiration and sinking then into a serene sacred stillness, he loses himself in contemplation of the deep, blue Yarmulke which we call the sky, and he can sense the Heaven and the Earth conferring in whispered colloquy, quietly talking together of Eternity and of Infinity and of the thing that men call Divinity.

Well? What d'ye say to my description of nature? You don't like it? Why, I'm shown up then! Though stay! You're not done with me yet, you know. I forgot to tell about the bugs—big brown, odd-looking clumsy things that get aloft in the dark and spread their wings and go whirring and humming about, always smacking up against the walls and windows, and come tumbling down to the ground with their coattails half spread open and go all quiet then. You needn't worry yourself, though, because after creeping around on the ground for a bit, they'll spread their coattails and be aloft again and circling the light and whirring and humming about and smack into the window and come tumbling down again. . . . We're sitting out on the porch overlooking the garden, all four of us, that's to say, myself, and Paya, and Rose, and Birdy. Birdy's quite grown now; she'll be four years old come First of Elul and already talking as well as any grown-up. She talks and asks questions. A thousand questions! Why's sky, sky, and earth, earth? When's it day, and when's it night? Why's night, night, and day, day? Why's mama call grandmama "mama" and grandmama call mama "Rose"? Why was I her uncle—an uncle and not a papa? . . . Why's uncle look at grandmama, and grandmama look at mama, and why's mama look so red? . . . Well, as you can imagine, this sets all three of us to laughing. So Birdy asks why we're laughing, which only serves to increase our hilarity, the matter concluding then in all three of us exchanging looks, and all three of us understanding each other perfectly well about what that look signified. Words aren't needed anymore. Words are superfluous. Words were only created for prattlers, for women and lawyers. Or, as Bismarck expressed himself once, words were given to us in order to mask our thoughts. Consider how animals and birds and the rest of living things get along without words. Here you have a tree growing, here a flower blossoming, here a blade of grass shooting up, holding fast to the earth, exchanging kisses with the sunbeams—where, sir, is their speech? The eyes, mon cher prince, the eyes are the great thing in people! What a person's eyes can sometimes say to you in the space of a minute, the mouth could not express for you in a day! Our exchanging of looks that night with my two widows was a leaf, nay, a chapter, sir, taken out of all our several biographies, an entire poem, if you want, a song, the mournful song of three lost lives, of three crippled souls whom a variety of muddles and imbroglios had prevented from drinking at the spring which is called Happiness, from partaking of the fount which is called Love. . . . I let slip the word *love* in your presence only grudgingly just now. Believe me, sir, it nauseates me! And you know why? Because your writers, sir, have for too long been making free with it, turning this holy, exhalted word into merest common fare. The word *love* as pronounced in the language of your writers, sir, is a blasphemy. The word *love* should be poured out as sincerely and passionately, sir, as is a prayer addressed to God, or, as a sweet melody is sung without words, as is the song of poetry unalloyed, be it without rhymes: hurry-scurry, catch-snatch, breeze-sneeze, hooey-phooey, and suchlike poetasting jinglings as are contrived by your poets, that if I do read them occasionally, I am reminded of nothing so much as swallowing hot chickpeas by the handful and betweenwhiles taking bites out of the paper cone they come in by way of an appetizer. . . . Yes, well, just because my simile has failed to please, you've no call to be wrinkling up your nose at it. I've, anyway, nearly finished this history of my Widow

Number Two for you and shall be done in a trice, too, because I hate seeing anybody yawn. . . . Only, say, have you ever known the feeling of having such a blasted toothache you have to have the thing out, but you put it off for the next day, and then you put it off for the day after that until finally you pluck up courage and you go to the doctor; and you come up to the doctor's door and have a look at the nameplate and see: *Dr. So-and-So, D.D.S., rec. hrs. 8:00 A.M. to 1:00, and 1:00 P.M. to 8:00.* . . . So you promptly glance at your watch, and you say to yourself:

My, my, from 8:00 A.M. to 1:00, and from 1:00 P.M. to 8:00? So what's the rush then?

And you turn yourself right round and go home and go on nursing the same blasted toothache. . . . Well, it was the same thing with myself and Rose. . . . Each morning I'd be leaving the house definitely resolved that today should be the day, and there'd be no excuses this time! First, I should have a word with my Widow Number One, with the mother, that is, saying here was how matters stood, et cetera, et cetera. . . . Whereat she'd flush and then lower her eyes and say, "With all my heart, sir, but you shall have to persuade Rose!" . . . So I'd take my leave of Widow Number One and go and see Widow Number Two and say to her, "Listen, Rose, here is how matters stand, et cetera, et cetera." . . . So taking up my hat, I now go calling on both my widows, but then Birdy flies out to greet me and throws herself into my arms and clasps me round the neck and kisses my eyeglasses, pleading, "Oh, please, please, tell mama and grandmama, for they'll listen to you, it's just for today, I promise, only for today, oh, do tell them I shan't have to be taking my lessons, no playing the piano today, no dancing, but shall go with uncle to the Zoological Garden, 'cos they have just got in such monkeys there, such monkeys you wouldn't believe, everybody says so, such monkeys there you could just die laughing!" . . . Well, and you think you might be proof against that and *not* end up taking the child to the zoo to see the monkeys there you could just die laughing? . . .

"Gracious, but what will become of the child?" deplores Widow Number One.

"Why, he'll be the ruin of her!" chimes in Widow Number Two. But I pay neither widow a whit of mind and take the child along to the zoo and go with her to look at the monkeys there you could just die laughing —and so it goes, just as I have recounted to you, and each time there is a fresh excuse. And day follows day and month follows month and year follows year, and the child grows, comes to understand about the sort of things one cannot speak aloud, and it remains a settled thing among the three of us still, a shared expectation still unspoken, that, would but the child were grown a little older. For when Birdy came of age, had attained her years of discretion and chosen a husband, then our hands should be tied no longer, and we should reform our lives, order a new domestic arrangement for ourselves. And secretly each laid plans for how we should all live together then: the young couple, Birdy and her bride-groom; the old couple, myself and Rose; and widowed grandmama, Paya, who would rule the roost. Ah! What a life that should be! The only thing was, the waiting! God, to actually live to see the day that Birdy was all grown up, come of age, had chosen a husband! Yet all things come to those who wait. That, I believe, is what the proverb says. Y'know, I quite hate proverbs. Oh, you *do* like 'em? How very nice for you! But I forgive you, anyway. So, then, all things come to an end! You see, there, now, is where the proverbial worm lies hid! There, now, is where begins your true "psychology," as you call it. But you know? It's really quite unnecessary, your consulting your watch. Because I won't be telling any more today, anyway. I must really be going; otherwise my widows won't know what to think. Though I must insist on your coming to my place if you are partial still to hearing all about my Widow Number Three. If not? Well, please yourself then! For I certainly won't play the tout by dragging you in by the coattails. You'll come on your own. . . . Adieu!

FINIS WIDOW NUMBER TWO

Widow Number Three

Good thing you thought to visit when I'm at home. But, as a matter of fact, I am always at home, for myself, not for others. Everybody has got his own habits. Myself, for instance, when I dine, I am used to having my cat sitting opposite. Won't eat without the cat there. Puss-puss-puss! Well, what d'ye think of her? The cat. Oooo, there's a cwever cweeture —sharp as tacks, ain't we! Won't take up with you on her own, y'see, not if you stacked gold in front of her! Here, feel, ever see a coat like that? What? Y'don't like cats? Oh, piffle! Silly fancies picked up at the rebbe's knee! Fairy tales, we all know 'em! Oh, don't bother defending yourself! How d'ye take your tea? With milk? Or plain? Myself, I always prefer mine with milk. . . . Uh-oh! Whoa! Scaattt! Blast you! . . . Nothing she likes more than milk. Can set out all the butter you want in plain view, she won't touch it, but only put the milk out and next minute she's at it lapping.

Now, you know I don't hold with introductions, but I must give you one this time: Hate it when people smile! Laugh all you want, so long as you smile me no smiles. So, d'ye still remember all of it, everything? Because if you've forgotten—out with it! No point being coy, better heads than ours have been known to forget. Well, in that case, I'm afraid I'll have to go over it again with you, in brief, outline the plot for you, so to say, give you an abstract.

I had a friend, Pini, who had a wife, Paya, and they had a child, Rose. But my friend Pini died, and Paya was left a widow. I became one of the family to her, a constant visitor to her house. And I was quite fond of her as was she of me. But we never spoke of it. Locked it away. And so our salad days went by. Meanwhile, her daughter Rose grew up, and I was absolutely mad about her. When out of the blue came young Shapiro, who was a good bookkeeper and fine chess player besides, and Rose fell head over heels for him. So I quarreled with the mother and went away, resolving that I should never go back there again! But I did *not* keep to my resolution after all, and first thing next day I returned and went back to being the same homebody as before, this time playing father of the bride and arranging the nuptials of Rose and Shapiro, who was something of a "boss" over his principals' businesses, had signed his name to promissory notes on their behalf, and when they got in over their heads and departed for America, was left to himself to cover their debts. So he took his life, and Rose was left a widow. So, you've got two widows now. And just as her mother, Paya, or Widow Number One, was left after my friend Pini's death with an infant Rosie to take care of, so, too, was her daughter Rose, or Widow Number Two, left after Shapiro's death with the infant Birdy to take care of, who was born three months after Shapiro died. And the three of us loved the child with all our hearts, and the three of us, that's to say, myself and Paya and Rose, gave the whole of our lives to the child, having no time left for any thought of ourselves or of the romantic attachment between myself and Rose, which was put off during the interval until Birdy was grown up and had come of age. And when Birdy had grown up and come of age . . . see here, sir, I'll ask you not to be looking into a book while I'm in the middle of trying to tell you something; it's an ugly habit, sir, and besides, you'd do better anyway to attend to what I'm saying because this is the beginning of a new story.

Say what you will of me, but I am no fanatic, never been hidebound in my life. Always made a point of keeping squarely abreast with the times. Never let myself fall behind, sir, never hesitated about going forward, unlike others that complain about the younger generation and their new ideas.

I simply cannot bear your pompous variety of old sage with their eternal pretensions: What!? Shall the egg teach the hen? Who is older, sir, the egg or the hen? . . . Oh, what asses you all are, sirs! Just so: it is because your egg is younger that it is choicer! That it is abler! That it is cleverer! Ergo must we, sir, of the older generation, listen to what they, of the younger one, have to say to us? Because they are young, sir, they are fresh, sir, they study, they examine, they explore, they discover, they get things done. So what's your point then? That you have plumped your carcasses down on a pile of moldy old books and ancient volumes and shall not be moved? . . . Only thing that gets my goat, though, is your younger sorts, the new ones who would deny us altogether, reject us out of hand, turn us all into small change, say we don't come up to even the humble jackass in the brains' department—never mind your ordinary horse when it comes to plain common sense! We are nothing! We don't exist! We are not there! Phut, vanished, and there's an end! . . . Imagine the gang of 'em come barging in on us, that's to say, barging in on my two widows, nay, not my widows, sir, but our Birdy, the grandchild, no less, three swaggering, impudent young cocks, students by the look of 'em, but then again maybe not—though the devil only knows who sired that litter anyhow or what dam was brought to bed with the lot of 'em! All three of them done up in workingmen's black smocks, hair unshorn, tongues sharpened, and with Karl Marx for their God—not their Moses, mark you, but their almighty God! Well, now, if God it must be, then let it be God. After all, it's not something I'd be wanting to blow my brains out over anyway, seeing as how I'm not so very far from the socialist ideal myself, in my way of thinking, sir, knowing as fully as anybody about the meaning of capitalism, of the proletariat, of economic struggle, and of other such notions, and what is more, if the truth be told, I am myself also. . . . Now, now, you've no reason for crowing quite yet, sir, for I'm certainly no Bundist, which thank heaven for, though, come to that, sir, neither am I any of your hobble-along sort of botch tailor!

So, then. They took to dropping in every day, the three young personages I was telling you about: one being called Finkel, the other, Bottstein, and Gruzevich was the third. Made themselves quite at home, too, you may be sure, because my two widows, that's to say, mama and grand-mama both, are in the habit of absolutely falling over themselves trying to please visiting gentry, will wait hand and foot on 'em, most especially if the callers happen to be three such fine specimens of whom one was a candidate for Birdy's hand. Actually, all three were candidates for her hand, but Birdy couldn't very well have three husbands, so there had to be only one—though try and guess which one, if the subject was never even broached, oh, we couldn't have that, could we now! Nor could we ask on our own account—Who was there to ask? The mother? What was the mother to them?—a young woman with a pretty face, no more! The grandmother? What was the grandmother to them?—a taverness whose business was to set meat and drink before them whenever they happened to come along, nay, more, to set meat and drink enough for them to gorge on and guzzle to their heart's content. . . . To say nothing of myself, for what was *I* to them? Only an extra chair at the board, nothing else. You'd think in all that time they might have exchanged a word with me! Unless it was to ask to pass the salt, pass the sugar, or ask for a match sometimes—but even that without so much as a *bitte,* for form's sake, a polite by-your-leave, sir, a civil *s'il vous plaît*—a peremp-tory flutter of a hand at your waistcoat is all they managed, as if talking to a mute, or puckering a set of lips at you when you'd lighted up a cigar and got it drawing, and no other word besides! Sometimes it happened that they came in and found me alone, so they'd throw themselves down on the sofas with their feet up and loll about spitting. And never a word to me the while, if only for civility's sake. Nothing! As if I weren't even there! Well, now, of course, I'd never be the first to speak up, wasn't about to knuckle under to them like some others, giving out with a thousand simpering flatteries, toadying up with a nauseous unctious smile on my face. There is not a creature born that I will bow *my* head to, though, mark you, not because I'm given to inordinate pride. . . . Well, yes—say even I *am* proud, call it what you will, just so long as you keep your opinion to yourself! Quite hate it, though, people talking about themselves. I was telling about those three prattlers, describing for you the sort of savage creatures they were. Once, you know, I foolishly allowed myself to ask which of them played chess; well, you ought to have seen the face they made! Have heard their hilarity! Myself, I only reckon, so what if you *are* a Socialist, where's the sin in playing a game of chess, anyway? Karl Marx will forgive you, never fear! Only talk to them—No! But it wasn't them I cared about. I didn't give a tinker's dam about them! What rankled me was her, was our Birdy; Why should she laugh along with them? Why was every word *they* uttered accounted by her as sacrosanct, as holy writ, for all the world as if God had pronounced it on the top of Mount Sinai? What sort of idolatry is it with young people these days, what species of fanaticism, what new Orthodoxy, what latter-day Chasidism that has got Karl Marx for a rebbe and themselves as his disciples? And apart from Karl Marx, is there no one else? Is there nothing else? Is this the end-all, the be-all, and is there nothing in the world besides? Where's your Kant, then, where your Spinoza, where your Schopenhauer, and where are your Shakespeare, your Heine, your Goethe, your Schiller, your Spenser, to mention nothing of the hundreds of other great men who are known also to have said a clever thing or two on their own account, for pity's sake? Oh, not as clever as Karl Marx, certainly, but neither is what they said so irredeemably, so hopelessly foolish! Myself, sir, I have to tell you, I'm not the sort of man to let anybody spit in his porridge; I will not be trifled with, sir, and I won't let anybody put on airs, turn his nose up at me, which is why I enjoy being contrary sometimes. You'll say a thing is so, and I'll say it's the opposite, "just to show you." So you'll say, but, no, sir, it's as *I* say, so I'll say, au contaire, sir, like it or lump it, it's as *I* say! That sort of thing. So I overheard them talking of Count Tolstoy once, saying how the man was only a nobody. Now, I'm not among Count Tolstoy's claque of disciples that I should wish to deify the man along with his philosophy and his new docrine of Jesus Christ, whom he's only turned into something he never was, anyway, apropos; but I still rank the man no lower than Shakespeare as a literary artist. And if peradventure you shouldn't agree with me, sir, I shan't lose any sleep over it, either. After all, you know my nature, sir. . . . So "to show 'em," I brought over a book by Tolstoy and gave it to Birdy, so she'd have something to read. Well, now, you should have seen with what a scowl my Birdy pushed away Count Tolstoy! And why, pray? Because the Messers Finkel, Bottstein, and Gruzevich all don't approve of Tolstoy.

Now, *that*, I needn't tell you, absolutely sent me up the wall (I can be a pretty nasty customer myself, when need be!), and by the time I had got through with 'em, all three of their names were mud! I told them that Karl Marx was a theory, and theories change—today this theory, tomorrow that theory—whereas Count Tolstoy is a great artist, and art is for ever!

Well, well, well! Didn't tempers flare then! Had you taken a potshot at even the sacred person of the Tzaddik of Sadigur himself, you mightn't have sparked half such fury from any of his pious following!

I hardly need say that, but for my two widows having intervened just then, quite an ugly scene may have ensued between us in the consequence! I realized afterward, though, that I had been an ass because I had, anyway, to apologize to *them* in the end. And do you know why? Because my Birdy wished it so! And if Birdy wishes a thing to be so, then it must be so, and if she were to tell me right now, say, that I must move the house to another spot, do you think I should hesitate for even a minute and *not* do it?

The girl hadn't only bewitched me, she'd literally enslaved me, quite murdered my will, turned me into her bondsman, had made an automaton of me. . . . Not just myself, she'd led us all up the garden path over that "brilliant" match she made for herself. In a word, Gruzevich was her intended, third-year chemist, y'know, sort of fellow that—anyway, nothing to write home about, nobody special, really—but never mind! There are a lot worse! In the first place his people were what's called "respectable." That's important, you know. Say what you will, good stock counts for something in the world. Don't be alarmed, I'm not speaking here of pedigree. All I am saying is that there is value to the branch one has sprung from; if that's coarse, then be you as educated as God Almighty, you are bound anyway to remain a common lout yourself. Though of his remaining virtues I say nothing. These fellows, if truth be told, as long as they keep up appearances, they are honest and fine and noble enough, but only let 'em get out into the world on their own and become as it were "has-been" quality—then God help you! They are a thousand times worse than any ordinary mortal. Because your ordinary mortal, if he bamboozles you, will only run and hide, but if any of your "has-been" quality swindles you, he will proceed to prove to you on the basis of philosophical principle that it is you who are the swindler, not himself. . . . But why waste any more time with pointless philosophy. The fact remains our Birdy became Madame Gruzevich at seventeen years of age, and I'll not bore you with a long drawn-out account of the sort of wedding it was and who it was that arranged for the wedding and who had been put out of pocket on account of it and what exaltations there were at the house of the two widows. Mother Rose had finally lived to see the day she brought her darling under the wedding canopy, and Grandmama Paya the pleasure of taking pride in it. And I, fool, what reason had *I* to be so happy about? Giving my youngest away in marriage? . . . And what an enduring joy it turned out to be, too—all of Esther's fast to Purim night, as folk are wont say! Three days after the wedding, our Gruzevich was invited to take up lodging at the police lockup. Over a trifle, really; it seems only that a cache of bombs and dynamite had been uncovered, and, seeing as how our lad was a chemist, and quite a famous chemist at that, he'd fallen under suspicion, and, oh, by the way, this apart, a couple of letters of his happened to turn up besides, and so, well, what more do you need, for he was promptly put under arrest and led away.

Devil of a job I had then, too, always in a stew, running about, greasing palms, the headaches—though much good it did, anyway! Get caught up in something like that and, what is more, such an ugly business —well, go and write all the petitions you want, be my guest! To say nothing of watching the grief of that young sprig, a mere slip of a girl scarcely older than seventeen. And the suffering of the mother, Rose! And of the grandmother, Paya! Divine punishment, an outpouring of God's wrath that had overwhelmed the whole house! Mark you, neither were my affairs in the pink, the old pocket was beginning definitely to feel the pinch, I had begun cutting corners, to swindle, mortgaged my houses, took to dipping into the strongbox, and when the ready cash, too, finally gave out, I sold a couple of shops out of the remainder of my abundance. . . . But it isn't my shrewd dealings I want to talk about; I stand in no need of boasting to you! I only wish you to be aware of a trait that my three widows have. You'd think they might have shown even *that* much interest in what they lived on, whence came the where-withal that had put bread on their table, or from whence it might continue to flow. Nothing; none of it's ever their concern! Had always to see to everything myself. All of it always on my shoulders. Even made to crawl through hell for it! But who asked me to? Damned if I know who did! Why, sir, the thing asks itself! I should like to see yourself in my shoes in such a situation, among a set of folks that you can't tell who is the more dazzling! You know, you can never really be offended with 'em, never bear them any ill will, never nurse a grudge, and if perchance something happens that puts you into an evil humor, and you go home in a sulk, you need only come back and be greeted by a glance, hear the first word they utter, and it's all blown away in the wind, dissipated in an insubstantial smoke, and in the winking of an eye you've forgotten that you may ever have had something against them, and you're ready again to crawl through hell for 'em. That, sir, is the sort of creatures they are. Well, try dealing with that, won't you! And who's even talking of Birdy? The Lord's own sweet scourge, sir, that girl! Let her only level one look at you with those beautiful deep nearsighted eyes, and you're a goner—you are as good as dead, sir! Your pardon, I hadn't meant you, I meant myself, because she'd driven me absolutely mad, what with marrying the Gruzevich chap, Misha, that was his name. Why, the whole house became full of Misha! Let no one eat, let no one sleep, let no one live! And why? Misha! Always Misha! They have taken away Misha! They have put Misha in jail! They are putting Misha on trial! Save Misha! Well, try cupping a corpse! For pity's sake, they wouldn't even let you in to see the fellow, not myself, not her, not anybody! I knew it was over then; I could smell it! If he was lucky they might put him away for life; if not, it was the rope! . . . I see you're not very comfortable sitting over there. Why don't you come here, sit down next to the window? But I haven't got on your nerves, have I? Well, no harm done, it'll be over soon enough. You'll only hear out my tale—I'm finishing up, anyway, and you'll be on your way then. But I shall have to live with the thing for the rest of my life, like walking about with a blasted bomb tucked away in your bosom!

So where was I? Yes, the rope. . . . I suppose you have read on more than one occasion in the newspapers about two people being hanged somewhere today and that yesterday three others were hanged elsewhere (hanging human beings has become about as much news these days as slaughtering chickens). And what might you be doing then? You're either rocking in your chair, enjoying a nice Havana cigar, or having a good cup of coffee just then with fresh rolls and butter. Ah, but that somebody's hanging from the end of a rope out there, that the one writhing and kicking in the last seconds of his agony out there is someone you know, one of your own, whom you shared the same hearth with, whom you saw but a short time ago as full of life as you now are yourself? Ah, but that a warm body is lying out there whose soul was violently wrenched from him by hangmen? Ah, but that a human being is in torment, wanting only to die the more swiftly, but cannot because the hangman has made a botch of tying the noose about his neck, or the rope frayed and snapped between life and death, and he begs his executioners with pleading eyes to do right by him quickly? . . . What's that you say? You cannot bear hearing tell of such things? Squeamish, you say? Well, so am I squeamish. No less than yourself, sir. But would you believe that I followed every detail of it, knew the minute, aye, the very second, that he was executed, read the full account of it later in the newspapers, how one of the three—all three were hanged, you know— was very long in dying because he weighed a lot (that was Bottstein), so they had to hang him twice on account of it. . . . That was what they wrote in the papers afterward, and we read it, not all of us, that's to say, only Rose and myself read it; we had hid the pages from the grandmother and the granddaughter. And so the house had been made richer by another young widow, our Widow Number Three! . . . And a grief settled over the house, a still, dead sort of grief, a grief for which exists no color, no word; a grief which must never be described, for to describe it is to profane it; a grief which if any of your literary fraternity ever dared to touch, I should happily break all of his fingers in half for it! . . . A grief which should not, which ought not, which must not be spoken of! . . . All live in the past, live in recollections. Three widows—three lives. Not full lives, but half lives, nay, not so much as half, but fragments of life, lives merely begun. Each of the three lives had started out so well, so poetically, had shed its light for an instant—and vanished! . . . Of myself I say nothing. I am not there. That's to say, I go there every day, sit up with them for nights on end, talking of bygone, happy days, remembering all sorts of things and doings and stories of my beloved friend, Pini, of good, honest Shapiro, of the hero, Misha Gruzevich, about whom the newspapers afterward wrote that in his own field of chemistry he had been a genius. . . . And each time I leave, I go away heartbroken, aggrieved, and I ask myself why have I misplayed my life so stupidly? Where was my first mistake begun, and when shall be the last? For I love all three of them, hold all three of them dear, and each of the three might have been mine, perhaps may still be, even now. . . . And each of the three, severally, holds me dear, but redundant, as well, indispensable, but unwanted, too. Let a day pass without my coming, and there's the devil to pay; though let me overstay by half an hour, and they'll send me packing, show me the door outright. Won't move so much as an inch from here to there without asking me about it first. But let me raise the smallest objection, and they'll say I always liked sticking my nose where it's not wanted, so I grow angry and I rush out and I come home and shut myself in with the cat and I tell the maid that if anybody calls, she should tell them I'm out, that I've gone away, and then I sit down to my journal. Been keeping a journal these six-and-thirty years now, interesting book, of that you may be sure! Keep it for myself, nobody else. I'd see all your literature blasted clear to perdition first before thinking it worthy of such a book as my journal! You, sir, I might allow to look at it one day, but nobody else—not for any amount of money. . . . Cut a story short, not half an hour will pass, and there's a knock at my door: "Who is it?"—"It's the girl, sir, from the three widow ladies. Says you are to come straightaway, lunch is waiting. What shall I tell her?"—"Say I'll be along presently."

So. What d'ye say now, mon cher prince? And what's your psychology have to say for itself, eh? . . . Ah, ready to go? Come, sir, we'll leave together then. Have to be at my widows'. Just give me a minute, so I can leave instructions to feed the cat because sometimes I can stay on into the next morning. We play "jumble" whist together, preference, too, occasionally. Play for money, don't you know. Ought to see how everybody wants to win! And heaven help you if you play a wrong card! No respect for age or beauty then, sir, not I for them, nor they for me. Myself, I'm a devil if somebody plays me a wrong card, likely to make mincemeat out of 'em, chew 'em up and spit 'em out! But whatever might you mean by that smile you're smiling, I wonder? Oh, believe me, sir, I know exactly what you're thinking now. Read you like a book, sir, and I don't give *that* for your granny, either! You're saying to yourself, "Now, there's a bitter old bachelor."

FINIS ALL THREE WIDOWS

Talk about the Riviera

Talk about the Riviera?—Thanks but no thanks! Because I hope you
may know as little about the place as I ever knew, and I wish to God I
knew as little about it now. Want to know the kind of place the Riviera
is? Well, I can give it to you in three words. It's your stick 'em up, buster,
your money or your life kind of a place! Because the Riviera is the sort
of a place they've got over in Italy that doctors have thought up only to
squeeze money out of people. The sky is always blue there. Same old sky
as back home. Sun is the same too. Only the sea, that's the worst part!
Because all it does is heave and crash about and make a great thundering
nuisance of itself—and, by God, you never stop paying for it, either.
Why pay for it? Oh, no reason. No reason at all. Except maybe if you
are fool enough to get yourself talked into the Riviera, you can just as
well pay for it. Pay for it and how! Because just you try not paying for
it. Think maybe they go and kick up a fuss? Go to law? Don't count on
it! Fair means not foul, that's their way. Kill you with a kiss. One good
thing about the place, though—give credit where credit is due—it's warm
there. It's always warm there, the whole blasted year. Both summer and
winter. Yes, but what's the point? The point is the sun keeps you warm.
Well, yes, but what's the point? Keep a good fire going at home and you
won't be cold either. "Air——," they say. Well, yes, the air ain't too bad
as air goes. Don't smell too bad either. Got kind of a fragrance to it.
Only it's not the air that smells, it's the oranges that smell. Out there, they
grow oranges. But I don't know if that's reason enough to be traveling all
that way for it. Seems to me there is air all over. And you can buy oranges
at home, anyway. But doctors say some air is better than other air. Air
that smells, they say, has got healing virtues. That's what they say. What
the doctors say, that is. Only what *won't* doctors say? I mean, why do

149

they say the sea on the Riviera soaks up what ails you? Well, I can't say either way, if it ever soaked up what ails anybody yet. But speaking for myself, if there was ever a penny lodged anywhere about my person, it managed to soak it up pretty quick, that sea! Only not so much the sea as the doctors. Because, by God, was I ever put in the way of a doctor out there! I mean, what can I say? Real peach, that man! That's to say, as folks go, in only the ordinary way, he was quite likable even and Jewish, by the way, and not just Jewish, but real Jewish! Talked Jewish as good as you and me, and a treat it was to hear him, too, because he did it so sweet and delectable, you may as well have made a meal of him. Only talk about soaking, by God, could that man soak! Well, just let anybody try and soak me! Because if anybody thinks he can soak me, he has got another think coming. Because I am never one for letting myself get soaked. But then I thought better of it and let myself be strung along right up to the very last minute. Saw straight off who I had to do with, you see. Only I let on I didn't. Want to soak—be my guest. That sort of thing. Well, to begin with, it was your usual tap-tap, thump-thump, let's have a listen routine, and he says to come again tomorrow. So I ask him, "Craving your pardon, Herr Doktor, but I am unacquainted with your customs here; what do I owe for your services?" So he peers at me through his eyeglasses, keeps his hands in his pockets, and says, "Time enough for that later." So I think to myself, "Well I'm game, mister, if you are." . . . So next day I went along to him, and it's tap-tap, thump-thump, and let's have a listen again, plus come along tomorrow so I can have my injection. So I ask him, "Craving your pardon, Herr Doktor, but what do I owe?" So he says, "Later." Well I'm game if you're game. So next day I went along for the injection, and he says to come along tomorrow so I can have my massage. So I went along the next day for a massage, and he gave me my massage, that's to say, rubbed in yesterday's injection, or so I gathered, and he says to come again tomorrow. So I ask him, "So what do I owe?" So he says: "Later." Well I'm game if you're game. Day after day exact same dodge, ditto: injection one day, rub it in the next. Well, I was on to the swindle like a shot, and I can't say I cared for it. Want to fleece the same critter twice—be my guest. Only why be dragging it out so? Because who says you need a separate day for shots and then a whole other day for rubbing 'em in? I mean look, it only stands to reason: here, I've just given you your shot, right? So what's stopping me from rubbing it in then and there? I mean, what's the point? Etiquette? Which only begs the question. Want to soak me, mister? Well

I'm game if you're game. Only suppose it cannot be done? Suppose there's nothing to soak? You know who I am, mister? You know what I am? Got inside my britches pockets lately? Counted my loose change?

Sure enough, come end of the month, and his bill arrived in the post. Absolutely made me reel. For each shot the man was asking ten franks —they like soaking you in franks out there—and asked another five for every time he rubbed it in. Pretty fair reckoning, that! Make yourself a roomful in no time, offering cures like that. Well, I gave it some thought. Question was, what to do about it? Try and come to terms? Only I reckoned there was time enough for that, anyway. I mean, it wasn't as if the fool was clamoring for his money straight away, so why rush? So I went along to him in only the regular way for my shot and massage— shot one day, massage the next. Well, winter came and went, and, before I knew it, Purim had come and gone, as well. Time I gave some thought to going home. Particularly as I was feeling pretty fit by then, quite fit, in fact. Might even say I was fit as a fiddle—I mean, why should I deny it? —and God send I am never *worse*; for better is e'er meet, as folks like to say, because you can never have too much of a good thing. Well, as I said, the time had come to say good-bye to the artful doctor and take my departure. So I went along to him, and I said, "So you see, Herr Doktor, I am going home." So he said, "Then Godspeed, sir." So I said: "Yes, but what of the bill? Correct me if I am wrong, Herr Doktor, but haven't we some settling-up to do first?" . . . So he peers at me through his eye-glasses, keeps his hands in his pockets, and says, "Well, yes, so?" Much as if he had in mind to say, "Well, yes, so who is preventing that? So I said, "Craving your pardon, Herr Doktor, but before settling up, I hope you may allow me to tell you a story if you've the time?" . . . So he said, "Well, I haven't the time, but if the story isn't a long story, I'll hear it." So I sat down and told him the story.

"With me, sir, what you see is what you get," says I, "your unvar-nished sort of a Jewish gent, please God, without trimmings. Family man, too, sir, please God, with children, bless 'em. Five of 'em, sir. All sons. Now, four are very good boys that do their father proud, but one, preserve you, sir, well, now, he's the very devil, sir. Wouldn't study, sir— not a lick. A bad boy, sir. So I beat him, whupped that boy till he was fair fit to die, trying to knock the orneriness out of him—but spoilt or whupped, still he remained incorrigible. A bad boy, sir. Well, I was at my wits' end. Till one day the wife ups and says, "Teach the boy a trade." "A trade? Good God, woman, have you lost your reason?" "Why not?

Think he may improve with killing?" Well, I thought it over and saw she was right. So I went and gave him away to a workman, the best tailor I could find, and settled with him on three years at a price of three hundred rubles. "Here, take the scamp, sir, and make a workman out of him." . . . So we drew up the indentures, these expressly stipulating that in three years' time the tailor was obliged to turn the boy into a workman for which service I, for my part, should have to pay to him the sum of three hundred rubles. Come end of the first year—the tailor drops by, picks up his first hundred, and we exchange receipts. All well and good. Come the end of the next—the tailor drops by, picks up his second hundred, and we exchange receipts. All fine and dandy. Come end of the third year— no sight of the tailor. I wait a week. Two weeks—neither hide nor hair of the man. Well, that's odd! So I went round to see him myself: 'Master Tailor," says I, "why haven't you been by to pick up your last hundred?" "Ain't coming to me," says he. "But what sort of sense does that make?" says I. "Why, sir," says he, "it makes perfectly good sense. For our tailoring trade may be said to consist of three things: first thing," says he, "a tailor must know the art of tailoring. Second thing," says he, "a tailor must know enough to pick up the occasional 'tailor's scrap' when there is cloth left over. Call it thievery if you want, sir, call it what you will. Third thing" says he, "a tailor must know how to take his drink, that's to say, imbibe the occasional glass of spirits come the holiday. Now, about your son, sir," says he, "you have my word that on two of the scores he is the model of a tailor. For he is a tolerable thief, sir, and the match of any drunkard for being in his cups. But as to a workman, sir, you may rest assured he will never be one in all his living days. And such being the case, sir," says he, "how in all conscience shall I come to collect that last hundred?"

Well, the doctor heard my story out, and he says, "Now, what, sir, prompted you to tell me that story, I wonder?" "Well, sir," says I, "it's only that your own trade, sir, that's to say, doctoring, is said like all trades to consist of three things: first, sir, you must be a good doctor. Second, sir, you must be an honest person. Third, sir, a doctor must know how to make money. Now, which of the first two weighs more heavily with you—that, sir, is more than I can tell. But when it comes to *doctoring bills,* sir, I can only wish myself half your equal. And such being the case, sir," says I, "let us both get down to business—your goods, my money!"

Well, naturally, it was more than could be expected that I'd knock the fellow's price down by more than two-thirds. But believe me it wasn't worth even that, sir, because if only I'd have stayed home and not bothered, with any luck I'd probably get well just the same, anyway—so what use have I for your Riviera, eh?

Mister Grinn Gotta Job

As Told by Himself and Here Set Down in His Own Words

Havar you, Meester Sholem Aleichem! I donno if you know me, maybe?
. . . Because you might say we was related, how you say, kissin' cousins,
even. . . . Poddon, I didn't minn yourself especial, but your country
cousin, Tevye de milkmen, end his cousin, Menachem Mendel from Yehupetz, which you write about. . . . Aha! You interested, yeh? Stopping,
even? So how about you end me, we stop a minute here on de sidewock,
shoot de brizz a bissel, greb us a nice schmooze about good old America,
wot a Golden Country dis is? Only not so much America, as about
American business, how it is soch a privilege soffering in de lep of luxury
here end starving end den soddenly is God putting de right job your way
end when wid God's help you get de right job, den you got de hope
bime-by of woiking youself op gredual, become, how you say, good-off,
end grow op to be maybe a Jake Schiff or a Nate Straus or, at list, a
Hairy Fischel—in a woid, to be "alright." . . . About myself, poisonal,
for de time bean, I can't say I am so alright, but a job, praise God, I
already got, end wot is making dis job soch a lulu is I come op wid it all
by myself poisonal, using my noggin. . . . Podden, I notice how you simple dying to know who dis cherecter talking wid you is? But if I tole you
dis was Mr. Grinn talking, you'd only say: Grinn? Yaller? Blue?—Det's
as good as saying notting. Because over here I am called Grinn; over dere
I was called Grinnboig. Where from? Odessa?—Yeh, sure, from Odessa!
. . . Yehupetz?—Yeh, sure, from Yehupetz! . . . From Kasrilevke, Teplik,
Shpolya, Uman, Berdichev—in udder woids, from all de famous Jewish
places dey got over dere. . . . You name it, I been dere. Wot was my line
of business? Same as everybody else, dis, det, penny-ante middleman

stoff, mainly, but den de "good times" come along when we got run out of de country, end soprise, soprise! we toin op over here, in Columbus country, end we stotted eating end eating end eating till we ate op our lest shoit, so we try de kind of woik which you need a strong beck and a vick mind for—but it wasn't no good! So about det time, de Foist of Elul come rond. End when Foist of Elul come rond, I notice how in de papers dey stotted to advoitice cantors, shuls, minyans. End how in de stores dey got ot de prayer books end prayer shawls end shofars, end everybody stotted smiling, saying "chizz," end being extra polite to God, you know, cozying op to de Almighty because it's good business, so dis got me tinking, end I says to myself: "Mr. Grinn, how long you gonna go on acting like a grinnhorn? Because it is high time you greb a nosh of Foist-of-Elul gravy youself end kesh in on some of det High Holiday New-Yiss-to-Yom-Kippur trade!" . . . But it's izzy to say greb a nosh of gravy if you got de gravy. Only wot I got anyway to kesh in on? Pess myself off as a cantor?—If I was a barbershop I'd be singing four-pott hamony. . . . A kosher slaughterer maybe? If my fodder hed wheels I'd be a cabbie. . . . End I soitenly cannot be a shul Reverend because I am knowing Hibrew so ai-ai-ai. . . . So how about a strictly "glatt kosher" butcher?—Yeh, except I ain't got a horse tief for a brodder-in-law. . . . So, like your Tevye de milkmen is always saying, "Wid soch reflections veighink on mine mind I vent into de Lord's Holy Senctuary." . . . Foist of Elul, inside is everybody davening, saying *Ledovid oyri*. . . . So when dey finish op wid davening, somebody give a shot, "Okay, so who gonna give a blow?" So I says, "On de shofar? Live it to me!" . . . So I bet you asking how come I am knowing blowing? It's like dis. Beck home I wasn't no reggler shofarer, det's for sure. Nidder was my fodder. End my fodder's fodder wasn't idder. But boys will be boys, end come Foist of Elul, boys is gonna find de shofar no matter wot, end stott blowing end blowing till de shammes from shul run in wid a pail of water end chase dem ot. So det's de rizzon mainly I am soch a maven about shofar blowing, on account, how you say: dem det blows knows, end no two ways about it. . . . So to cut a long story short, when dey hend over de shofar, I give out wid a tekiye-shevorim-trueh, tru-Ah tru-Ah tru-Ah . . . tru-tru-tru-tru-tru . . . TRUA-aaaaaaaaaaaaaaa . . . end I finish op wid soch a tekiye gedoyle, TRUAAAAAAAAAAHHHHHHHHH . . . which, no kidding, you could hev hoid from here all de way to B'klyn Bvidge, izzy! So hearing soch a fency blowing, dey says, "Poddon, but where you coming from, young men?" So I says, "So who wants to know?" So den dey says,

"Maybe you like a job blowing shofar New-Yiss-to-Yom-Kippur by us in shul? Our reggler shofarer pess away." "If I can make a living from it, yeh, sure, why not?" . . . "Well," dey says, "making a living only from blowing shofar ain't so izzy, except maybe you get a extra job on de side." . . . "For instance, wot kind of job you got in mine?" I says, "like a driver? A gabbagemen, a stritt clinner?" So dey says, "No, de minute you a reggler shofarer by us, det's to say a *bal-tekeyeh,* you cannot be axed to do soch a low kind of woik. Only ting we can do for you," dey says, "is give you a chence to blow shofar in another shul rond here." . . . So de idea suit me foist-cless, end I'm tinking, if I got a chence to blow shofar in one more shul, why not in two more shuls? End if in two more shuls, why not three more? . . . So I went rond Dontown from shul to shul, from minyan to minyan, showing off my stoff wid de tekiye-shevorim-trueh business on de shofar, end I was a great soccess, how you say, a big hit, because when I am blowing shofar, everybody comes running from de udder shuls all over. Because I been hoid by jodges, congressmens, assemblymens, end dey all was saying: Simple Vonderful! Foist Cless! So netcheral you can figger youself de foist year I am heving only one shul wid two minyans. De second year—tree shuls wid fife minyans. Dis year, God willing, I figger I get op to tvelf minyans maybe, so det is making a even dozen minyans; in udder woids I stend to take home a nice couple dollars dis time, I figger. Ah, but how can one poison alone hendle all det business, you probably esking?—Don't esk; because dis is America, end in America is Gott helpink dose det's helpink themselfs. In vonn place I em blovink shoyfar a bissel oilier, in de udder a bissel later, end in a toid, ivven later. In udder voids, I em trying mine bast so de poblick should be setisfy, bicose Gott fobbid I em missink mine cue; den I em losink mine dzhab plus mine reputayshun. You probable vonderink, Meester Sholem Aleichem, how comes I em spicking Henglisch so poifec widdot I em usink almost no Chewisch voids?—It's all on account mine childern. By me are dey already honderd-procent Americans end dey don't vant to talk ivven a woid Jewish! You should see mine boyess, mister, because you couldn't never tell in a million yiss dey was yiddishe boyess. Myself, too, if you was to see me High Holiday New-Yiss-to-Yom-Kippur sizzon, you wouldn't hoddly reconnize me nidder. Because by me when it comes a short time before Foist of Elul, I trow off my soote end stott growing a beard; in udder woids I em pudding on de "heymish" Old Country look, end de minute High Holidays is over, I get a shafe end I am pudding my doiby beck on, end go back to bean a gentlemen again—because wot won't pipple do for business in America? . . . Poddon, I notice how you simple dying to do a "cherecter sketch" about me for de paper, mister, because I see you got your notebook ot already. Nevermine, be my guest! I'll even tenk you for it because by me is dis advoiticement. . . . Oh, no, de opposite, I insist! I'll even esk you put my address in: MR. GRINN (det's wid two ee's), CHERRY STRITT, NEW YAWK CITTEE, plizz. . . . End I hope we mitt again Optown soon sometime. In de minnwhile so long, end bye-bye!

A Business with a Greenhorn

How Mr. Tummler, a Business Broker, "Loined"
a Greenhorn Who Got Merry Wid a Goil
for Business.
Retold Here in His Own Words

You was saying how America was a lend of business? Never mine! Det's how it's suppose to be. But a fella getting merry wid a goil for business? Det, you'll poddon me, is mean end doity. Now, I ain't preaching no morality here, but I am telling you it's a fect; when nine-end-ninety procent of grinnhorns in dis country is getting merry for business, it is making me med! End if I am meeting op wid such a kind of grinnhorn, belive me he don't get off dry. You live it to me! Wanna hear a good one? Listen!

One day I am sitting rond in mine office mailing de post when a grinnhorn come in. Yong fella, just a boychick. Him wid his wife—end what a wife!—a doll, pitchers end crimm. So, coming in he says, "Hiye! You Mr. Tummler Business-Broker?" "Siddon! Yeh, so what's de good void?" So he put his cods on de table end stotted telling me so-end-so, abot how he was a new boy just ten yiss in de country, by trade a knee-pents maker, abot how he fall in loff wid a goil which she was a woiking goil which got a tousend dollar in kesh, so den he got merry wid de goil, so now he was looking for a business so dey can make a living widdout boddering woiking in a shop because he got de rheumatism bad like you don't wanna know, end so on. Minnwhile, I am giving de liddle woman de once-over, end I says to him, "So what business you got in mine, mister?" "Stationery!" he says, because det's de kind of business he got in mine. Den he come out wid how wid a stationery store *she* can

158

help out in de store. I minn, how you like det for a smotty-pents grinnhorn wid a noive? Because it ain't enough he got his hends on soch a poifec peach to make whoopee wid plus make hay wid her tousend dollar in kesh, but he wants she should woik so he can sid rond wid his pels all day playing pinochle, end so on—because, mister, I know my pipple! Tinks I: You want stationery? I give you stationery! Busted bladder widdout a pot is all de stationery you gonna get outta me, bub! Because I gonna fix it so you wish you was dead, mec. Because you gonna get a laundry, jeck. Wid me, you gonna be a laundrymen. End why a laundry? Because it so heppen I got a laundry on my hends to sell den. So I says to my grinnhorn: "What ye wanna bodder anyway wid a stationery store for," I says, "pudding in a eighteen-hour day, looking out in case some schoolboy run in end swipe a penny-candy off de counter, end so on? You live it to me—because I can let you have a nice business, a laundry op in de Bvonx, det way you gonna woik reggler hours, end live like a king!" So den I take out a pencil end figger it out for him—so much de rent, so much de shoit-ironer, de femmily-ironer, de delivery boy, de laundry bill, end so on, which live you in de bleck wid over toity bucks a vick, clear—so what you want more? "How much it gonna cost?" So I says: "A tousend, we got us a bargain, only live it to me—for you, I'll do it for eight honderd. All you gotta do," I says, "is hend over de jeck, pick up de key, end you gonna be alright, mec. You do it blind. Honest Injun! Minnwhile," I says, "so long, pel, end come beck in tree more days, on account I ain't got no more time now—so bye-bye!"

Me? I get myself over to my laundrymen right away end tell him mazel tov: because God just finish sending a pigeon my way, a grinnhorn, so seeing how he got a chence now of getting rid of de laundry at a good price, provided he was a mentsh he'd know what to do abot it, end so on. . . . So de gonnif take de hint okay, end he says: "You just make sure you bring de pigeon over, mister, end everything gonna be alright!" . . . Minnwhile, tree days later—my grinnhorn show op, pud down a deposit, den hubby end wife go to woik, figgering to give de laundry de usual vonn-vick trial, end you betcha my laundrymen make soiten de vonn-vick trial is alright, wid a bonus even, which is making it "end-how" alright wid room to spare—so den de business is settled. De grinnhorn is paying op de couple bucks what's owing, de laundrymen is hending over de books end keys, end y'rs truly is collecting his fee from *both* parties— because Mister Tummler Business-Broker knows his business—end, how you saying over in Rossia: *finita la commedia!* Oh, yeh? Says you, maybe.

By me is de comedy only stotting. Because after everything was sewed op neat all arond, den it really stotted getting to me abot de grinnhorn; because why did det momzer desoive getting soch a plum dropped in his lep anyway for, a pretty wife, a tousend in kesh, plus a ready-made business hended to him on a silver platter widdout no sweat? No, I gonna fix it so he gotta sell out at half price end give de laundry beck to de foist laundrymen. Except you asking how? So det's de rizzon why I am Mister Tummler Business-Broker because dere's notting I cannot do if I wanna. So I went across de stritt opposite from de laundry end rent a nice room on de corner dere from de agent, which after slipping him ten bucks advence on de rent, I put op a sign in de vinder:

LAUNDRY OPENING HERE SOON!!!

Well you betcha a day don't pess end my grinnhorn come rond again, looking like he just lost all his mobbles: Gevalt! He's a dead men! "Yeh, so what's de beef, pel?" So he stotted telling me de bad news abot how some momzer just now rented a store across de stritt from him end was opening op a laundry! "So what d'ye want from me, Grinnhorn?" So he says he wants me to find a buyer for him for de laundry, which he'll make it woit my while if I do end remember me in his prayers for de rest of his life, end so on. So I calm him down, saying it ain't so izzy now finding a buyer. Only live it me, I am trying mine bast. Minnwhile, so long, pel, see you in tree more days, on account I am op to here in woik right now—so bye-bye!

Me? I sent for my old laundrymen right away end tell him so-end-so: he got de chence now of buying beck his laundry for only a song, at half price, end so on. So he says, "So how you gonna do it, mec?" So I says, "So what's it to you, jeck?" So he says, "Alright." So I says, "I'm gonna get a commission out of it, yeh?" So he says, "Alright." So I says, "It's gonna cost you a honderd, yeh?" So he says, "Alright." End so on. Minnwhile, tree days later, my grinnhorn show op wid de liddle woman, which I notice she was looking considerable paler but odderwise still beautiful like a rose. "So you got any news?" "News?" I says. "Well it took some doing, but I finally found you a buyer. Except you gonna have to take a loss." "Yeh, so how much?" "Don't esk how much you loosing, better esk how much you winning. Because anything you get is gonna be like hitting de jeckpot. Tink you can play games wid American competition? Because you do, end dey gonna drive you into soch expenses you gonna end op taking a moonlight powder wid only de shoit on your beck!" . . . Well whatcha tink, but by de time I finish, I put soch a scare into hubby end wife dey was gled to take beck half de money dey put in, plus dey paid me my commission, because I ain't obliged to give away my soivices for free, end so on, end det's det—no more laundry! . . . But hang onto your hat, mister, dere's more to come yet. Because if you been kipping count, you remember I popped de agent a tenner advence on de store, which I henged op a sign abot a laundry? So I esks mysef, why should I trow ten smeckers out for widdout getting my money's woit outta it foist? Whatsa madder, Mister Tummler Business-Broker, soddenly don't know de value of a dollar? So det's vonn rizzon. Besides which I was still plenty boined op yet abot de grinnhorn, end it was eating me op: because de momzer still got a couple of honderd simoleons steshed away in his pocket, not to mention de sweet little dish he got for himself—soch a poifec peach! So why should he have it so good, anyhow? Because here you got Mister Tummler Biggest Business Broker on de East Side, which he is stuck wid a old lady det's got a face on her which you'll podden me will stop a clock, end all she do is neg, neg, neg —while God is giving de grinnhorn soch a pretty baby doll, you know, a reggler knockout—well, I gonna see him choke on it foist. So I don't sid rond just twiddling my tumbs, but I write him on a postel cod he should come see me by appointment on soch end soch a time because I got a business proposition for him. So de fella don't wait to be esked twice end showed op on de dot, as per appointment, plus he brung *her* along, det's to say, de liddle woman. So I am pudding ot de red carpet, telling dem plizz to be sitted, make youselfs at home, end so on, end den hending dem a line, saying so-end-so: "You simple got no idea abot American bloffers! You wouldn't belive what kinda trick det gonnif de old laundrymen played on yez—it make ye hair coil!" . . . "Yeh, how's det?" "How's det?" I says, "Because it was him all along what rent de store across de stritt den henged op a sign abot a laundry to scare yez into selling out so's he'd get his old laundry beck for half de price." Hearing soch a story, de hubby end wife look each other over, end dey was positive steaming, especial de liddle woman. Her eyes was boining like hot coals. "So it only be fair," I says, "if you was to get even wid de gonnif in soch a way he got something to remember yez by!" "Yeh, only how we suppose to get even wid him?" "Live it to me," I says, "because I'm gonna settle det smott aleck's hash for good," I says, "so he gonna wish his mudder never had him—end youse two," I says, "you gonna come op smelling like roses; because," I says, "yez gonna get a business outta it better den before!" By now my pair of pigeons was looking at me like somebody is saying, "From your mouth into God's ears, long may you prosper, end so on!" So I laid de gig out for dem: Why buy somebody else's business if you gonna pay through de nose for it anyhow? But say I was to go down to de same landlord end rent de same store off of him which de old laundrymen wanted to rent, end for abot three, maybe four honderd dollars I fixed op a laundry right opposite his laundry, end den I stotted giving him competition, no matter what he was charging, I am charging less, well, I betcha I get him outta dere in three vicks' time—or my name ain't Mister Tummler! Well, whatcha tink, but by de time I finish, hubby end wife was simple delirious; de grinnhorn looked fit to kiss me on both my cheeks, end his pretty wife was blushing so she looked even prettier den usual. So de same day I rented de store for dem, end I got a laundry fitted out in no time, de whole kit end caboodle, wid a sign, tables, de woiks, end my hubby end wife rolled op dere sleeves end got down to it. So pretty soon my couple end de old laundrymen was having a bang-up time undercutting each other. If he was asking twenty-four cents a dozen "flat," dey went right down to eighteen cents a dozen plus a free "spread"; if he knocked down shoits to only eight cents per, dey dropped to a penny end a half a shoit-collar, so netcherly he had to come down to a penny a collar, end so on. So de clincher is—dey plugged away for so long at cutting end slashing prices till de grinnhorn was shook loose of his last dollar, cleaned out widdout a red cent to even pay rent wid. So he closed down de laundry end left wid his pockets toined out because like it says in Provoibs Chapter Whosit Verse Whatsit: EASY COME, EASY GO. Right now he's sidding rond on his keister taking it easy in Ludlow Street Jail—det's my doing because I fixed de liddle woman op wid a lawyer, which he is putting de squeeze on him, on de grinnhorn det is, in his wife's name for three things: (1) her money, which it's her tousend dollar dowry; (2) a divorce; end (3) until such time as maybe she finally get a divorce out of him, he gotta sopport her according to de laws of de country—so det'll loin him, goddam grinnhorn!

Glossary

Selected Bibliography

Glossary

Curious Terms and Abstruse Names Found in This Volume
Prepared on the Author's Behalf by His Editors
Adapted and Arranged by Ted Gorelick

Yinglish terms follow U.S. preferred spelling. Yiddish terms follow YIVO transliteration.

Ahad ha-Amism: named for Ahad ha-Am (Hebrew, One of the people), pseudonym of Asher Ginzburg (1856–1927), exponent of Cultural Zionism, calling for a spiritual rebirth of the Jews to precede political rebirth in the Land of Israel.

ai-ai-ai: Yinglish (from Yiddish) equivalent of "my-my-my," usually said of something wonderful; when phrased negatively, "not so ai-ai-ai."

alright, to be: Yinglish, then informal U.S. Yiddish *zayn olrayt,* to do all right, live on easy street, have it made. Cf. **alrightnik.**

alrightnik: (from Yiddish epithet *olraytnik*) coined by Abe Cahan, editor of the *Jewish Daily Forward,* for parvenus of Mr. Tummler's kidney or aspirants thereto of the stamp of Mr. Grinn.

Ashkenazic: of or relating to the Jews of central and Eastern Europe.

bal-tekeyeh: Yiddish (from Hebrew *ba'al-toke'a,* master trumpeter), person who blows the shofar in the synagogue. Cf. **shofar.**

bar mitzvah: 1. said of a Jewish boy reaching the age of thirteen and assuming full religious responsibility; 2. celebration of the event.

Berdichev: city in west Ukraine, center of both Chasidism and secular Jewish culture.

bime-by: U.S. mid-nineteenth- to early twentieth-century dialect for "by-and-by," in the fullness of time, eventually.

bissel, a: Yinglish (from Yiddish *a bisl*), a bit, somewhat.

165

B'klyn Bvidge: Brooklynese, the oldest bridge over the East River.

bloffer, bluffer: Yidlish/Yinglish, then standard Yiddish *blofer*. 1. swaggerer; 2. sharper, con man.

Bobruisk: town in Belorussia (Belarus); struck by a disastrous fire in 1902, three years before "Advice" was written.

boychick: Yidlish/Yinglish, unfledged male person of any age.

Brody: small but historically significant Galician town bordering on Austria; center of Chasidism and modern Jewish secularism.

Brooklynese (properly, **New Yorkese**): misnomer for lower-class and lower-middle-class vernacular spoken in New York City and east New Jersey in the early twentieth century.

Bundist: member of the Bund (Yiddish, union), or General Jewish Workers' Union of Lithuania, Poland, and Russia; Jewish socialist party and labor union founded in 1897, reaching the height of its influence in 1904–5. The largest working-class movement in Eastern Europe at the time.

Bunimoviches, the: 1. Jewish banking family of Vilna whose name was a byword for wealth; 2. in the singular, Vilna epithet for anyone thought to be rich or otherwise well endowed; "Madame Bunimovich," a woman with large breasts.

business broker: Yinglish for Yiddish *mekler* (from Slavic *makler,* broker, agent), professional middleman who brokers business transactions in exchange for a fee from the principals.

business with, a: Yinglish (from Yiddish, *a mayse mit*), a fuss or commotion (over).

Butchers' Row: (from Yiddish *di yatkeve gas;* Slavic *ulitsa Yatkova*), street in the Old Jewish Quarter of Vilna and site of the *yatkeve shul,* or Butcher's Synagogue. Cf. **Glaziers' Shul.**

Bvonx, op in de: 1. Optown; 2. Brooklynese, northernmost borough of New York City.

casino: four-handed card game in which players pair cards from their hand with others exposed on the table.

Chaliapin, Feodor: (1873–1938), renowned Russian operatic bass during the "golden age" of opera; regarded by many as the greatest bass of all time.

challah, hallah: white bread usually in the form of a plaited loaf eaten by Jews on the Sabbath and other holidays.

Chandrikowa, Khandrikova: small suburban town situated a few miles outside of metropolitan Vilna. Cf. **Wilejka.**

Chanukah, Hanukkah: eight-day Jewish festival beginning on 25 Kislev (November/December); commemorates the rededication of the Temple of Jerusalem in 164 CE after the successful revolt of the Maccabees against Syrian rule.

Chasidism, Hasidism: influential religious movement in Eastern Europe founded by Israel Baal Shem Tov in the eighteenth century and stressing the primacy of spiritual zeal and prayer over learning and study.

cheder, heder: a private Jewish elementary school originating in Eastern Europe where children are taught to read the Penateuch, the Prayer Book, and other sacred texts in Hebrew. Cf. **Talmud Torah,** definition 2.

cock a fig (at): (from Yiddish *shteln a fayg,* to show the fico), rude gesture made by inserting the thumb between the forefinger and middle finger.

Consitutio-democrettes: parodic feminization of Constitutional Democrats ("Cadets"), political party founded in 1905 by Russian liberals.

Count Tolstoy: (1818–1910), Lev (Leo) Tolstoy, Russian writer and thinker, celebrated for his novels *War and Peace* and *Anna Karenina.*

crown rabbi: in Czarist Russia from 1859, an "official" rabbi who was a graduate of a state rabbinical school and discharged civil functions, as opposed to "ecclesiastic" rabbis ordained by traditional rabbinical academies and responsible for the religious affairs of a community.

cupping a corpse: (from Yiddish phrase *helfn vi a toytn bankes,* "as useful as cupping a corpse"; figuratively "to no avail"); cupping here refers to the obsolete medical practice of bleeding a patient with cupping glasses.

davening: Yinglish (from Yiddish *davenen*), recital of Jewish prayers.

Deborah-Esther, Dvoyre-Ester: (1817–1907), Vilna benefactress who devoted her fortune to the support of charitable works and Jewish learning.

derda: Russian card game.

donno, dunno: Brooklynese, incognizant (of).

Dontown: 1. opposite of **Optown;** 2. Brooklynese, Lower Manhattan. Cf. **Bvonx, op in de.**

dry, to get off: Yinglish (from Yiddish *aroys trukn*), to escape uninjured.

Duma: Russian parliament before and after Soviet period. See also **Third or "Black" Duma.**

Eleeyohoo Hanovee: 1. Ashkenazic pronunciation of the Hebrew Name of Elijah the Prophet (*Eliyahu Hanavi* in modern Hebrew); 2. name of a popular Sabbath hymn.

Elul: sixth month of Hebrew calendar (August/September), the period of penitential prayer in anticipation of the Jewish High Holidays. Cf. **New-Yiss-to-Yom-Kippur.**

end: Yinglish, along with, in addition to; "boys end goils."

Esther's Fast: a short fast on the eve of Purim. The Yiddish phrase translated as "Esther's fast to Purim night" denotes a very short time, something that is over before it begins. Cf. **Purim.**

Femino-nihilists: Ironic feminization of Nihilists. The term Nihilism refers to a number of revolutionary doctrines in late Czarist Russia upholding terrorism; the word obtained currency in Russia from Turgenev's novel *Otsi i deti* (Fathers and children), 1862.

femmily-ironer: former U.S. term for laundry specialist who irons family washing. Cf. **shoit-ironer.**

finita la commedia: Italian, the comedy is ended; ironic colloquial usage in Yiddish and Russian, it's all over; said of an ordeal or death. Literary origin, Lermontov's novel *Geroi nashego vremeni* (A hero of our times), 1840.

Fischel, Harry: (1865–1948), Russian-born New York City property developer and philanthropist who gave his employees both Saturday and Sunday as a paid weekend holiday when the standard workweek in the U.S. was six days.

flat: former U.S. term for laundry "whites," undyed domestic washing.

Friedman, N. M.: one of two Jewish deputies who, in the **Third Duma,** continued to work in defense of Jewish civil rights into the period of the First World War. Cf. **Nuselovich.**

from your mouth to God's ears: Yinglish piety, now in general use in English (from Yiddish *fun ayer moyl in gots oyern*), expressing hope that a well-wisher's assertion of better times to come will be fulfilled.

Gemara: main body of the Talmud and primary source of Jewish law.

gevalt!: Yinglish interjection (from Yiddish *gvald, gevald,* violence). 1. expression of shock, consternation, alarm; 2. often used as a cry for help.

Gitke Toyba's Alley: (from Yiddish *Gitke Toybes zavuleg*), name of a famous street in the Old Jewish Quarter of Vilna. The street was officially named for St. Nicholas.

glatt kosher: (from Yiddish *glat kosher,* strictly kosher), often seen on signs in U.S. kosher butcher shops to assure patrons of strict adherence to Jewish dietary law.

Glaziers' Shul, the: (from Yiddish *di glezershe shul*), synagogue attended by glaziers in the Old Jewish Quarter of Vilna; one of a number of Jewish prayer houses in the city reserved for use by worshipers in a given trade. Cf. **Butchers' Row.**

Goethe, Johann Wolfgang von: (1749–1832), German poet, dramatist, novelist, scientist, and towering figure of German letters.

Golden Country: (from Yiddish *di goldene medine,* the golden land), Jewish equivalent of El Dorado; popular epithet for the United States.

gonnif: Yinglish (from Yiddish *ganef;* Hebrew *ganav,* thief). 1. thief, dishonest person; 2. clever rascal, slyboots. Cf. **momzer.**

goyim (plural of **goy**): (via Yiddish from Hebrew *goy, goyim,* nation), Gentiles; sometimes used pejoratively.

grinnhorn, greenhorn: Yinglish/Yidlish, then standard Yiddish. 1. recent immigrant; 2. any immigrant so named by one who arrived earlier.

Hairy Fischel: see **Fischel, Harry.**

havar you: Yinglish equivalent of Yiddish **sholem aleichem,** definition 1.

Herzl, Theodor: (1860–1904), journalist, author, and founder of the Zionist Movement. See **Zionism.**

heymish: Yinglish (from Yiddish *heymish,* domestic, cozy, snug); said of people, places, things, or practices that are "down-home," especially if Jewish; "a heymish meal."

High Holiday: see **New-Yiss-to-Yom-Kippur.**

hiye: perfunctory slovening of **havar you.**

honest Injun (Indian): U. S. mid-nineteenth to twentieth century, avowal of truthfulness.

Jake Schiff: see **Schiff, Jacob Henry.**

Jewish; talk Jewish: U.S. early twentieth century, for Yiddish and speaking Yiddish.

Jews' Street: (from Yiddish *di yidishe gas;* Slavic *ulitsa Zhidovska,* the Jewish street) major thoroughfare in the Old Jewish Quarter of Vilna.

"jumble" whist: (from Russian *yeralash,* jumble) four-handed card game similar to whist; popular in Russia before the Soviet period.

Kamenets, Kamieniec: historically prominent town in Podolia region of the southwestern Ukraine bordering on Bessarabia.

Kasrilevke: fictitious town invented and populated by Sholem Aleichem to satirize small-town Jewish life in the Ukraine; associated with Voronkov, where Sholem Aleichem lived as a child.

Kharkov: administrative center of the Ukraine during Czarist and Soviet periods; outside the **Pale of Settlement.**

Kishenev: town in Moldavia with a large Jewish population that suffered two successive pogroms. The first was in 1903 and aroused an international outcry; 49 Jews were killed, 500 injured, and the Jewish quarter was demolished. Cf. **pogrom.**

Klausnerism: named for Joseph Klausner (1874–1958), early advocate of militant Zionism as well as leading Hebrew literary scholar and Jewish historian in Russia and later in Israel.

knee pents (pants): U.S. early twentieth century, boys' knee-length trousers.

kosher: (via Yiddish from Hebrew *kasher*), proper, fitting. Cf. **glatt kosher.**

kosher meat tax: in the Czarist period, a Jewish communal tax whose revenues were earmarked for charity; the income was in fact appropriated by the government. Collectors of the tax were hated figures in the Jewish community. **Lechoh Dodi:** initial words of the prayer welcoming the Sabbath pronounced in **Ashkenazic** Hebrew (Come, my friend, to meet the bride).

Ledovid oyri: initial words of Psalm 27 pronounced in **Ashkenazic** Hebrew ([A Psalm] of David / [The Lord] is my light); name of a prayer in the Jewish liturgy.

live it to me: Yinglish, I'll attend to it.

loin (somebody), to: Brooklynese, to chastise.

Lubavitcher: of or referring to a Chasidic sect founded by Schneour Zalman of Lyady in the late eighteenth century. Today the largest Chasidic community. Cf. **Chasidism.**

luftmentsh: (from Yiddish *luftmentsh,* "air man") an idler or small-time operator the likes of Mr. Grinn.

making whoopee: U.S. early twentieth century, having a good time, lovemaking.

matzo, matsoh: (from Hebrew, *matza, matzah*) unleavened bread eaten at Passover.

maven: Yinglish (from Yiddish *meyvn;* Hebrew *mevin,* one who understands), an expert or connoisseur, anyone with a knack or flair.

mazel tov: Yinglish (from Yiddish *mazl-tov;* Hebrew *mazal tov,* good luck), felicitations.

Menachem Mendel: eponymous hero of Sholem Aleichem's epistolary novel in which the provincial small-time operator with no fixed occupation is satirized. Cf. **luftmentsh.**

mentsh: Yinglish (from Yiddish *mentsh,* human being or decent person), someone worthy, as distinguished from lowlife.

merry (wid), to get: Yinglish, to wed.

mine: Yinglish alternative (but not inevitable) form of the pronoun my (from Yiddish *mayn,* my).

minyan: (from Hebrew *minyan*), the minimum quorum of ten adult males required by Jewish law for certain religious services.

Mizmoyr-Shir-Leyoym-Shabbos: title of Psalm 92 pronounced in **Ashkenazic** Hebrew (A psalm [or] song of the sabbath day); part of the liturgy inaugurating the Sabbath.

momzer, mamzer: Yinglish (from Yiddish; Hebrew *mamzer,* bastard); synonymous with **gonnif,** definitions 1, 2.

Nate Straus: see **Straus, Nathan S.**

nevermine, never mine: Yinglish, think nothing of it, makes no difference.

New-Yiss-to-Yom-Kippur: the Jewish High Holiday season, consisting of the Ten Days of Penitence from the Jewish New Year (Rosh Hashana) to the Day of Atonement (Yom Kippur) during the first ten days of the Hebrew month of Tishri. Cf. **Yom Kippur.**

nine-end-ninety procent: Yinglish (from Yiddish *nayn un nayntsik protsent*), 99 percent.

nosh: Yinglish (from Yiddish *nash,* nibble); said of sweets and savories.

Nuselovich (properly, Nisselovich): one of two Jewish deputies in the **Third Duma;** in 1910 succeeded in obtaining signatures of 166 deputies for a legal draft abrogating the **Pale of Settlement.** Cf. **Friedman.**

Odessa: Ukrainian port city on the Black Sea, leading center of secular Yiddish and Hebrew culture in the late nineteenth and early twentieth century.

okka: Russian card game resembling poker.

Old Country, de: general term used by European immigrants in the United States for the mother country.

Old Shul, the: (from Yiddish *di alte shul,* also known as *di alte kloyz,* or *kloyz yoshn*), historic synagogue in the Old Jewish Quarter of Vilna.

Optown: opposite of **Dontown;** Brooklynese, Upper Manhattan and the Bronx. Cf. **Bvonx, op in de.**

Pale of Settlement: during the Czarist period, territories in Russia to which Jewish residence was restricted by policy and law. Cf. **right of residence.**

Pargament: Duma deputy from Odessa for the Constitutional Democratic ("Cadet") party. Cf. **Constitutio-democrettes.**

Pasch: (pronounced *pask*), another word for Easter.

Passover: seven-day Jewish festival beginning on 15 Nisan (March/April); commemorates the liberation of the Hebrews from Egyptian bondage.

Pesach, Pesah: Hebrew for Passover.

pitchers end crimm: fair complexioned; said of female persons.

pogrom: (via Yiddish from Russian *pogrom,* destruction), organized massacre, especially of Jews in Russia from the 1880s onward.

pomeshchik: Russian landowner, usually of noble rank.

prayer shawl: (Hebrew *talit,* cover, cloak), a white shawl with fringed corners worn by Jewish males during certain religious services.

preference: popular Russian card game.

Purim: Jewish holiday on 14 Adar (February/March) commemorating deliverance of the Jews of the Persian Empire from a planned massacre, as recounted in the Book of Esther.

Purishkevich, V. M.: (1870–1920), head of the anti-Semitic faction in the Duma and founder of the notorious "Black Hundreds," organized gangs of thugs carrying out pogroms in Jewish neighborhoods throughout Russia from 1905 onward, most notably in Kiev and Odessa.

Reb: Yiddish honorific title corresponding to Mr.

rebbe: (from Yiddish *rebe),* orthodox rabbi in the chasidic tradition; as distinguished from a *rov,* a non-chasidic rabbi.

Reverend: clerical title formerly appropriated by some U.S. Jews for rabbi.

right of residence: in the Czarist period, official permit allowing individual Jews to live and work outside the **Pale of Settlement.**

scape hen: (from Yiddish *kapore;* Hebrew *kapara,* atonement), a cock or hen ritually sacrificed for one's sins on the eve of **Yom Kippur.**

Schiff, Jacob Henry: (1847–1920), U.S. financier and philanthropist to Jewish and Zionist causes.

Schiller, Friedrich von: (1759–1805), German dramatist, poet, and historian, second only to **Goethe** in his position as the great figure of German literature.

schmooze, greb a: Yinglish (from Yiddish *khapn a shmues,* to have a chat on the spur of the moment), shoot the breeze, chew the fat.

shammes: Yinglish (from Yiddish *shames;* Hebrew *shamash*), caretaker; usually the beadle of a synagogue.

Shmargon: Vilna Yiddish pronunciation for *Smorgon,* a nearby townlet and local byword for provinciality.

shofar, shophar: Hebrew, the ram's horn blown in the synagogue during the month of Elul and the ensuing Ten Days of Penitence. Cf. **Elul; New-Yiss-to-Yom-Kippur.**

shoit-ironer: former U.S. term for a laundry specialist who irons shirts. Cf. **femmily-ironer.**

sholem aleichem: 1. standard Yiddish for **havar you;** 2. (sometimes) capitalized, name of a famous Yiddish author.

shop: Yidlish/Yinglish, then standard Yiddish, small garment factory, dressmaker's workshop.

shtetl: Yiddish diminutive of *shtot,* city, town; in sense 2. now standard English. 1. literally, a small city or town; 2. colloquially, a small-to-medium-sized city in Eastern Europe with a majority or large minority of Jews.

shul: Yiddish, synagogue.

Simchas Torah, Simhat Torah: Jewish festival immediately following **Tabernacles** on 23 Tishri (in Israel on 22 Tishri); celebrates completion and recommencement of the annual cycle of Torah readings.

Sirota (Yiddish **Sirote**): cantor of the late nineteenth and early twentieth century in Vilna; once a household name among Russian Jews.

sixty-six: Russian card game resembling pinochle.

skaz: oral-style narration, as discussed by the Russian Formalist critics.

Socio-revolutionettes: parodic feminization of Socialist Revolutionaries, Russian populist party founded in 1901 that carried out political assassinations with the aim of ending Czarist rule and establishing a classless society.

so-end-so: Yinglish (from Yiddish *azoy un azoy*), as follows.

spread: bedspread.

Straus, Nathan S.: (1848–1941), New York City parks commissioner (1889–93), public health advocate, and contributor to public health causes in pre-state Israel, where the northern town Netanya was named after him.

Tabernacles (Hebrew *Sukkoth, Sukkot*): seven-day Jewish harvest festival beginning on 15 Tishri (September/October); commemorates the temporary shelters used by Jews during their wandering in the wilderness. Celebrated by building a hut (Hebrew *sukkah*) with a roof of branches under which meals are eaten for the duration of the festival.

Talmud Torah: 1. Jewish religious elementary school; 2. formerly in Eastern Europe, a Jewish school supported by the community for the education of poor boys.

tekiye-shevorim-trueh, tekiye gedoyle: Hebrew terms (as pronounced in Yiddish) for the sequence of four blasts sounded on the **shofar,** "long-broken-loud," and "extra long."

Territorialism: non-Zionist movement founded in 1905 to establish an autonomous Jewish community in any suitable territory in expectation of the failure of Zionism to achieve the same, in the Land of Israel.

Tevye the milkman: eponymous hero of *Tevye der milkhiker,* Sholem Aleichem's best-known work and the source of *Fiddler on the Roof.*

Third or "Black" Duma: Russian Duma convoked on 1 November 1907; infamous for its anti-Jewish legislation and the virulence of the anti-Semitic rhetoric of its deputies. Cf. **Purishkevich.**

Torah: 1. the Pentateuch; 2. the scroll used in Synagogue services; 3. the whole body of Jewish religious teaching.

tummler: Yinglish (from Yiddish *tumler*, noisy person), loudmouth.

Tzaddik of Sadigur: Tsaddik (Zaddik) is the title of the spiritual leader of a Chasidic group; here of Sadigur Chassidim, a community founded in 1841 by Rabbi Israel of Ruzhin in the town of Sadogora, Bukovina.

Uman: small town in central Ukraine; Bratslaver Chasidic center.

Vilna: Russian name of Vilnius, capital of Lithuania. Known in Jewish history as "Jerusalem of Lithuania" in recognition of its role as the center of Jewish civilization in Eastern Europe.

Wilejka, Vileika: small suburban town situated a few miles outside of metropolitan Vilna. Cf. **Chandrikowa.**

"X-squeeze-doory" courtyard: garbling of Vilna Yiddish usage *eksvidorske hoyf,* inherited property consisting of a block of flats around an inner courtyard owned in common by a group of legatees.

yarmulka, yarmulke, yarmelke: (from Yiddish/Slavic), skullcap, usually black, worn by orthodox Jewish males.

Yehupetz: Sholem Aleichem's fictitious name for Ukrainian capital, Kiev, but independently, a proverbial Yiddish term for "back of beyond," a remote backwater.

yez, youse: Brooklynese, plural form of you.

Yiddish: the language of **Ashkenazic** Jews in Eastern Europe since approximately the year 1000.

yiddishe, yiddisher: Yinglish adjective (from Yiddish, *yidish -er, -es, -e*), used for Jewish persons or things.

Yidlish: Yiddish dialect in Anglophone countries.

Yinglish: English dialect of Yiddish speakers in New York City and later of their descendants in the United States.

yiss: Yinglish pronunciation of years (filched from Leonard Q. Ross [a.k.a. Leo Rosten] H*Y*M*A*N K*A*P*L*A*N books).

YIVO: Yiddish acronym for the Institute for Jewish Research.

Yom Kippur: usually pronounced 'yom kipper' (via Yiddish *yom-kiper* from Hebrew *yom-kipur*), Day of Atonement, annual fast and most solemn day in the Jewish religious calendar. Cf. **New-Yiss-to-Yom-Kippur.**

Zionism: Movement for Jewish national revival by the establishment of a Jewish homeland in Palestine. Cf. **Herzl, Theodor.**

Ziono-socialites: parodic feminization of Socialist Zionists, whose ideology informed that of the Labor Zionist movement and ultimately of the Labor Party in modern Israel.

Zschokke, Heinrich: (1771–1848), minor German author of historical potboilers written in imitation of Sir Walter Scott.

Selected Bibliography in English

Sholem Aleichem's Writings

The Adventures of Menahem-Mendl. Translated by Tamara Kahana. New York: Paragon, 1979.

The Adventures of Mottel: The Cantor's Son. Translated by Tamara Kahana. New York: Collier, 1961.

The Best of Sholem Aleichem. Edited by Irving Howe and Ruth R. Wisse. Washington, D.C.: New Republic Books, 1979.

The Bewitched Tailor. Translated by Bernard Isaacs. Moscow: Foreign Languages Publishing House, 1958.

Collected Stories of Sholem Aleichem. Translated by Julius and Frances Butwin. Vols. 1–2. New York: Crown, 1965.

Favorite Tales of Sholem Aleichem. Translated by Julius Butwin and Frances Butwin. New York: Avenel, 1983.

From the Fair: The Autobiography of Sholem Aleichem. Translated by Curt Leviant. New York: Viking, 1985.

The Great Fair: Scenes from My Childhood. Translated by Tamara Kahana. New York: Collier, 1970.

Inside Kasrilevke. Translated by Isidore Goldstick. New York: Schocken, 1965.

The Jackpot. Translated by Kobi Weitzner and Barnett Zumoff. New York: Workmen's Circle Education Department, 1989.

Jewish Children. Translated by Hannah Berman. New York: Bloch, 1937.

"Joseph." Translated and edited by Golda Werman. *Fiction* 11 (1992): 137–48.

The Nightingale: Or, The Saga of Yosele Solovey the Cantor. Translated by Aliza Shevrin. New York: New American Library, 1987.

The Old Country. Translated by Julius Butwin and Frances Butwin. New York: Crown, 1946.

Old Country Tales. Translated by Curt Leviant. New York: G. P. Putnam's Sons, 1966.

Selected Stories of Sholem Aleichem. Translated by Julius Butwin and Frances Butwin, Isaac Rosenfeld, and Shlomo Katz. New York: Modern Library, 1956.

Sholem Aleichem Panorama. Edited by M. W. Grafstein. London, Ontario: Jewish Observer, 1948.

Some Laughter, Some Tears: Tales from the Old World and the New. Translated by Curt Leviant. New York: Paragon, 1979.

Stempeniu: A Jewish Romance. Translated by Joachim Neugroschel. In *The Shtetl,* 287–375. Woodstock, N.Y.: Overlook Press, 1989.

Stories and Satires. Translated by Curt Leviant. New York: Thomas Yoseloff, 1959.

The Tevye Stories and Others. Translated by Julius Butwin and Frances Butwin. New York: Pocket Books, 1965.

Tevye the Dairyman and Other Stories. Translated by Miriam Katz. Moscow: Raduga, 1988.

Tevye the Dairyman and the Railroad Stories. Translated by Hillel Halkin. New York: Schocken Books, 1987.

Tevye's Daughters. Translated by Frances Butwin. New York: Crown, 1949.

The Three Great Classic Writers of Modern Yiddish Literature. Vol. 2: *Selected Works of Sholem-Aleykhem.* Edited by Marvin Zuckerman and Marion Herbst. Malibu, Calif.: Joseph Simon/Pangloss Press, 1994.

A Treasury of Yiddish Stories. Edited by Irving Howe and Eliezer Greenberg, 151–68. 2d ed. New York: Penguin, 1990.

Wandering Stars. Translated by Frances Butwin. New York: Crown, 1952.

Why Do the Jews Need a Land of Their Own? Translated by Joseph Leftwich and Mordecai S. Chertoff. New York: Cornwall Books, 1984.

Secondary Literature on Sholem Aleichem

Erlich, Victor. "A Note on the Monologue as a Literary Form: Sholem Aleichem's 'Monologn'—A Test Case." In *For Max Weinreich on His Seventieth Birthday,* 44–50. The Hague: Mouton, 1964.

Frieden, Ken. "A Century in the Life of Sholem Aleichem's *Tevye.*" B. G. Rudolph *Lectures in Judaic Studies.* New Series, 1. Syracuse, N.Y.: Syracuse Univ. Press, 1997.

———. *Classic Yiddish Fiction: Abramovitsh, Sholem Aleichem, and Peretz.* Albany: State Univ. of New York Press, 1995.

Miron, Dan. "Sholem Aleykhem: Person, Persona, Presence." New York: YIVO Institute for Jewish Research, 1972.

———. *A Traveler Disguised: The Rise of Modern Yiddish Fiction in the Nineteenth Century.* Syracuse, N.Y.: Syracuse Univ. Press, 1996.

Norich, Anita. "Portraits of the Artist in Three Novels by Sholem Aleichem." *Prooftexts* 4 (1984): 237–51.

Ozick, Cynthia. "A Critic at Large: Sholem Aleichem's Revolution," *New Yorker,* 28 Mar. 1988, 99–108.

Roskies, David. "Sholem Aleichem: Mythologist of the Mundane." *AJS Review: The Journal of the Association for Jewish Studies* 13 (1988): 27–46.

Sholem Aleichem: The Critical Tradition. Prooftexts 6 (Special issue) (Jan. 1986).

Voices from the Yiddish: Essays, Memoirs, Diaries. Edited by Irving Howe and Eliezer Greenberg. New York: Schocken, 1975.

Waife-Goldberg, Marie. *My Father, Sholem Aleichem.* New York: Schocken Books, 1971.

Weitzner, Jacob. *Sholem Aleichem in the Theater.* Madison, N.J.: Fairleigh Dickinson Univ. Press, 1994.

Wirth-Nesher, Hana. "Voices of Ambivalence in Sholem Aleichem's Monologues." *Prooftexts* 1 (1981): 158–71.

Wisse, Ruth R. "Sholem Aleichem and the Art of Communication." *The B. G. Rudolph Lectures in Judaic Studies.* Syracuse, N.Y.: Syracuse Univ., 1980.

Wolitz, Seth. "The Americanization of Tevye or Boarding the Jewish *Mayflower.*" *American Quarterly* 40 (1988): 514–36.

Judaic Traditions in Literature, Music, and Art
Ken Frieden and Harold Bloom, *Series Editors*